Beautiful Lies
Painful Tr

Volume II

An Anthology of Short Fiction
Contemplating the Complex Relationship
Between Life and Death

Edited by Karen T. Newman

Copyright © 2018 Left Hand Publishers, LLC
9716 Rea Road, Suite B-501
Charlotte, NC 28277
All rights reserved.
ISBN: 978-0-9996839-4-1

https://LeftHandPublishers.com
Twitter.com/LeftHandPublish
Facebook.com/LeftHandPublishers
editor@LeftHandPublishers.com
Cover design by Paul K. Metheney

Beautiful Lies, Painful Truths Vol. I
Amazon - http://amzn.to/2reSyIe
YouTube - https://youtu.be/4m1BR6BIBTM
The Reviews on YouTube - https://youtu.be/tTtdf0LQC7Q
LHP's Web Site - http://bit.ly/2FHXzw9
The Reviews on LHP's Web Site - http://bit.ly/2FHhMlN

Realities Perceived
Amazon- http://amzn.to/2Dbe1ny
YouTube - https://youtu.be/3SLjzDd9o3Y
LHP's Web Site - http://bit.ly/2Do87SE

Beautiful Lies, Painful Truths Vol. II
YouTube - https://youtu.be/i8dAMSAbkAM
LHP's Web Site - http://bit.ly/2Dxu9n8

Other Left Hand Publishers' Videos
Intro Video on YouTube - https://youtu.be/7lTG-5ednmU

Other Left Hand Publishers' Books
The Demon's Angel by Maya Shah on YouTube -
https://youtu.be/FZuvbiGjMcU

"Life asked Death,
'Why do people love me, but hate you?'

Death responded, 'Because you are a beautiful lie,
and I am a painful truth.'"

~Anonymous

Reviews: Beautiful Lies, Painful Truths Vol. II

"You have to love an anthology that can give you well-written stories no matter what the genre is and it looks at important issues in addition to death such as love, religion, and redemption.
Don't let the idea that this anthology is about death keep you from reading it, there are some great stories here that will really make you think."

David Watson, Book Reviewer

***

"Wonderfully and amazingly intense
This is the second volume of an anthology that brings life and death in a new light. I read the first volume and was more than excited to read a new collection. First, I must say that I enjoyed each story that was within this collection, and all of the authors should be commended for their work. I can imagine the thought that it took to put these stories together in one collection. Life and death is not just black and white, but all the in-betweens, and as the title alludes, both are beautiful, but also full of lies and truths. I usually can pick one or two of my favorites of the book, but I enjoyed each one immensely. I've even reread all of the stories to make sure I didn't miss something. Bonds are broken and bonds are reunited on the sides of life and death."

Amy Shannon, Author. Writer. Poet. Storyteller. Blogger. Book Reviewer.
Review Blog: http://bit.ly/2iPVV4x
Amazon Author Page: http://amzn.to/2ynn2qM

***

"This collection is a recipe for a lost weekend as I found myself wanting to read 'just one more' until by nearly midnight I had finished all sixteen, and yes, I went back to reread my favorites. Edited by Karen T. Newman, this banquet of wonderful stories draws you to course after course of excellent writing, fantastic ironies, amazing insights and delectable nuggets of human nature wound together by the complex flavors of life and death and what is in between—perfectly reflecting the 'Beautiful Lies, Painful Truths' promised by the title. Anthologies are often a reflection of the curator as much as the writers included in them and the quality of writing and choice of stories add up to a book I will recommend to my friends and fellow bibliophiles without reservation."

Natalia Corres, Book Reviewer

***

CONTENTS

ACKNOWLEDGMENTS

Special thanks go out to Karen T. Newman, and her company, Newmanuscripts.net, for her tireless efforts in editing, formatting, and compilation. Many kudos to Paul K. Metheney, one of the authors included, and his company, Metheney Consulting, for invaluable assistance with our cover design and marketing.

Recognition should also go out to our friends and families who tolerated our working hours during the creation of this publication. None of this could have been possible without the creative imaginations and perseverance of the wonderful writers who submitted works to this anthology.

To the readers who purchased this volume, thank you.

The Unchosen
by Trece Angulo

U.S.: A new fantasy revealing the deadly lies behind The Choosing.

The Mother Draephlix was dying.

They heard her clear across town, broadcasting her agony in a series of strained ululations and drawn-out, unlovely screeches. They knew it would continue for days. None of them were old enough to remember the last time a Mother Draephlix had passed, but they had heard stories from their parents and the elders of the town. They all knew what it meant. Death, fire, then dozens of pearl-like eggs left to incubate in the warm soft sand ... mounts for a new generation of warriors to keep Eliira safe.

"She could die more quietly, don't you think?" Geelson said, leaning carefully over the basin to set his toy boat in the water.

Maevig gave her boat a gentle nudge to follow his, pushing back her braids. At the center of the fountain, a magnificent metalwork draephlix took to the air. No reins were needed for its human rider: the two shared a bond of mind, lifelong companions and trusted friends. "Look at it this way," she said. "She suffers so her children can live."

"True," Geelson said. He was a heavyset boy, slightly awkward, beginning to notice the girls but not yet ready to slot them from playmate to sweetheart. "After all, we don't have wars like they do in other lands. The riders protect us."

Wasli, his other friend, shot him a dark look. Geelson's father was a draephlix rider, and it accorded him a higher status, even though his father was bound to the aerie and only visited his family a few days each month.

Another loud screech split the air, carried with awful clarity from the nesting field in the hills. Even Maevig winced and put her hands over her ears.

"You will be attending the Choosing?" Wasli asked.

"Of course," Geelson answered. "And you?"

Wasli frowned and dipped his head. He was dressed poorly compared to the other children, in a stained tunic and drab, baggy leggings, his hair lank and unwashed. But the Choosing was open to all boys of a certain age, no matter what their parentage or heritage. Most looked forward to it. With tales of the rider's heroism told at cradles and sung at the temple, how could they not? They had been drenched in it from birth. Even seeing the noble creatures crossing the skies stirred their hearts.

Yet, Wasli hesitated to speak the dream Geelson knew he had, keeping it close like a precious object that might be snatched. "I don't know."

"You don't know?" Maevig cried. "I see you watching the riders every day, noting what time they leave, what time they return."

Wasli flushed. He thought he could keep secret his study of the faint, sinuous shapes in the sky, which was all the non-riders could see of them. The actual creatures were sacred, not to be profaned by common eyes.

"And I saw you hang the Wish flag on the temple," Geelson said. "Wasli, we need not be rivals. Who's to say we won't end up comrades, a draephlix for you, and one for me?" He spoke what Wasli dared not. "Besides, it's not always a given a rider's son gets to follow in his path. Sons of tradesmen and farmers get Chosen as well. I've no more advantage than you."

"What about me?" Maevig said with determination, brushing back her dozens of braids. "I intend to go to the Choosing too."

Geelson frowned. "That's impossible. Girls aren't allowed."

Maevig planted her fists on her hips and stuck her chin out. "What about Queen Amonet?"

"She was taking the place of her husband the King. If he'd been alive, she wouldn't have ridden."

"But, she saved Eliira from the mountain raiders. So you can't say girls cannot ride."

"It's in the Holy Scriptures." Geelson returned her stubborn look. "They say a woman's honor is to wed a rider and take care of him and bear the rider's children. Besides, there aren't any kings and queens anymore. The priests rule us."

"I'll disguise myself as a boy when the Choosing ceremony comes," she said archly.

"It wouldn't matter. The baby draephlix would know. It wouldn't bond to you. You might fool the priests, but not the draephlix."

"How do you know? Have you ever been to one of these ceremonies before?" Maevig's mocking laugh suggested she knew well he hadn't. Angered, Geelson splashed her. She squealed as water dripped from her dress's draephlix-scale collar, ruining their luster. "Oh, now you've done it! The scales will dull."

Geelson stuck out his lip. Draephlix riders kept codes of conduct for their offspring and gentility was one of them, though Wasli often told him it included a certain arrogance. He frowned after Maevig, as she hitched up her skirt and ran, her sandaled feet sending up puffs of dust from the square.

"Watch your temper," Wasli warned, ever his watchdog.

"I'm sorry. I'll make it up to her," Geelson said, shamefaced. The three had been friends since their toddling years, meeting in the temple square to splash and play. "I don't know why I became so angered."

Whatever the reason, it was catching.

The following day, all the townspeople were on edge. Elders chewed the fat in the temple square, discussing the intensity of the Mother's cries and if they were louder, or less loud, than those they had heard decades before. Tales passed around of riders long gone and the names of their mounts. Mothers spoke in whispers, wondering if they would lose their sons.

Geelson studied with his tutor the art of keeping of records for trade. "You are restless," his tutor, an old merchant in threadbare robes, said. "I sense your mind is not in your work."

"It's the Mother Draephlix," Geelson said.

"You only imagine you hear her. These walls are thick."

"It's not that. It's that ... I fear she's in pain." His words were a lie. What he really feared was the loss of Wasli and their friendship, Maevig and her smiles.

"It's to be expected. She's dying," his tutor said archly. He had once been wealthy but foolish with money, so he had been forced to seek other ways of making a living. He nudged Geelson's waxed tablet and draephlix-quill stylus. "Back to your studies."

"Yes, Maestro." Geelson scraped his chair closer to the desk for his practice calculations. He wished he could ask his father about the Choosing ceremony. But his father was at the aerie, making preparations for the inevitable. He had often thought his father was as absent as Wasli's dead mother.

A stone plinked at the window. The tutor turned, but Geelson knew who it was. When the maestro's bald head dipped to make a correction, Geelson gestured outside: *Later, I'm busy now.* He saw Wasli's shoulders slump.

"Have you ever participated in a Choosing, Maestro?" Geelson asked.

"No," his tutor said quietly. "That event comes only once a generation. If a boy is too old, or too young at that time, he misses it. You are fortunate you are the right age. Not a child, yet not a man. The priests look at boys' faces, and only the smooth ones, without the coarse hair of maturity, are accepted." The contours of his own face saddened. "I matured early for my age. I was turned away."

"What does age have to do with being Chosen?" Geelson said.

"The priests look for purity and tractability. As a youth matures, he loses these."

Another pebble plinked on the window.

"Who is throwing these stones?" the tutor said in annoyance.

Geelson shrugged, but he wanted to see his friend very badly. Wasli's home life was difficult. Often he visited just to get some food, or even study in the light from the kitchen window when the sun went down. Geelson shared his lessons with him then, both of them crouching in the dirt with scrolls and tablets.

A servant girl poked her head though the door. "Maestro Hvulsa, you're wanted at the merchants' guild house. A meeting I was told."

The tutor sighed and packed up his things. "It's about the Mother Draephlix no doubt."

"I was not told," the maid said. But the way her eyes darted toward across the square and to the western hills, Geelson guessed she thought it too.

When the tutor departed, Geelson ran out of the house to see Wasli. His mouth fell open when he saw his friend's face. "You have a bruise!"

"It's nothing." Wasli said, with a swipe at his face as if trying to scrub the dark smear away. "May I sleep at your house tonight?"

Geelson glanced toward the wall that hid his family's courtyard. A clump of bamboo in the southern corner screened a space just large enough for a youth of Wasli's size. He could be gone before sunrise, before the servant girl and cook arrived. "Yes, but be careful." Behind Wasli was a bundle of burlap sacks, his bedding, as if he knew Geelson wouldn't say no.

"Thank you." Wasli's unkempt head cocked, as if hearing ... or trying to hear ... the screams that had kept the town company for two days. "Have you noticed, Geely? The Mother's gone quiet."

Geelson held his breath, not making a sound. Wasli was right. Then a new sound came from the hills, a muffled thump, more a vibration than noise. Baffled, they stood listening. There came a louder thump, and another. The dull sound seemed faint, powerless; yet if they had been standing closer to it, it would have split their eardrums.

"She's digging her grave," Geelson said. His stomach clenched with anxiety.

"Let's see," Wasli said, no less anxious, but also curious.

They climbed up the wall, finding footholds in the rough volcanic stone, and from there scrambled to the side of the house where a metal trellis ran up the side. Two stories, then three, they climbed, gaining a view of the town and its bowl-shaped valley. From the direction of the aerie, a column of dust was rising, timed with the thumps. Wasli swore in surprise. Then they looked to the temple. In the yard, a sculpture took shape, a creature in the form of a springing fox with the wings of an eagle, the scales of a snake. Foreigners often called it a dragon, which was untrue. A draephlix was its own being.

Geelson crawled closer to the roof's edge, forgetting danger in his fascination. The priests were sparing no effort to create the procession effigy, using animal pelts laid over a frame of wire and wood. Colored foil served for scales and from its shoulders four wings took shape, trailing silk feathers longer and gaudier than any pheasant's. Strands of dyed wool were glued into position for the tufts on its pointed ears and a priest with a pot of gold paint gilded the creature's claws. Another inserted two eyes of dark glass.

"It's beautiful," Wasli said with awe. "What do you think it's like to touch a real one? Sit on it?"

"I bet it's soft," Geelson said. "All that fur, it must feel like clouds." It sparked a yearning in him, as if all his life had led him to this point and become a part of him as much as his heart and lungs were.

"What does your father say about it?"

"He doesn't talk about the draephlix. It's a vow the riders take after they are Chosen. The priests tell us what we should know about them," Geelson said. Wasli looked at him questioningly, a hank of hair falling across his forehead. Geelson cleared his throat. "A rider's job is important. He can't be bothered with questions like that."

Yet Geelson wished very badly that his father would, even once, talk of what it was like to fly and care for such huge creatures. But all he spoke of was whether the enemy had been routed and how many merchants' wagons had been saved. He preferred to spend his days away from the aerie relaxing with his family. Geelson was grateful for it, of course, but that was what commoner's fathers did after a day at the stone yard or on the fishing boat. His father was special, and he deserved to hear of that specialness.

A group of youths on the ground peered likewise at the priests' construction, hooting and boasting amongst themselves. Geelson wished Wasli was older, or younger, than himself. If so they would not be pitted against each other, and the boys below, for a draephlix egg. He sent a fervent prayer to Vashti. *Please, let the hatchlings pick us both!*

Above them, in the westering sun, dozens of long, snakelike shapes cleaved the sky, fore and aft wings beating the air. The dying Mother had called her children home. Occasionally a bright scale fell to the town below, an omen of good fortune to whoever found it.

"Geelson?" his mother called from below. "Your dinner is ready."

"Can Wasli eat too, Mother?"

"I suppose so. I'll make up a basket for him." Class being what it was, the sons of riders and the sons of tanners did not dine together. But Geelson's mother was kindhearted and gave Wasli a hot meal to take home whenever he came to visit. "Come down, please. Your father is here, and he wishes to speak to you after dinner."

Geelson had assumed his father was staying at the aerie making preparations for the Mother's death. That he had chosen now to visit filled him with both joy, and suspicion. "See you tomorrow?" he said, and Wasli nodded. He clambered down the trellis to make his bed in the garden.

"You shouldn't have been climbing on the roof," his mother scolded when Geelson came in.

"The boy's curious, is all," Geelson's father said, taking a seat at the table. He cut into the roast.

His mother spoke of how the townspeople were reacting to the impending Choosing. His father said little, but Geelson could tell he was listening, digesting her talk as he was his food. When dinner was over, he rose, tall and straight in his riding uniform, and gestured Geelson to the parlor. He closed the doors.

"You have your heart set on being a draephlix rider, is that right?"

Geelson stood dazzled by his close attention, so wanted, yet so rare. "Yes, Father."

The lamps burned their oil, casting shadows in his father's face. He was a stern man and did not express himself freely, but the warm light betrayed a softness there. His throat moved like he was holding something back, like Wasli's did at the times he was afraid ... though his father was a man and beyond a boy's fears. "You are indeed my son, and my father's son. He was also a rider. I do not fault you or your desire. But you must see something first."

Geelson waited. He felt like he was being initiated into something unknown. His father lifted his tunic, exposing a taut, muscled abdomen covered with scars. "This is what being a draephlix rider does to you," he said, giving Geelson a level look. "Do you still wish it?"

Geelson stared at the puckered pink dots. He wanted to ask "How?" but his father would think less of him for questioning their origin. Draephlix riders were warriors. Everybody knew that. "Yes, Father. I do."

His father nodded, expressionless. He had brought a cup of wine with him into the parlor and commenced to take a sip. Geelson felt disappointment. Why wasn't his father pleased by his ambition? Why wasn't he taking Geelson in his arms now, laughing, congratulating him?

"The scars I bear are the least of the pain this rider's uniform has cost me," he said. "You are an intelligent boy, Geelson. That's why I pay to have the merchants school you, so you may have a life other than mine. If you wish to continue your studies, I will not fault you. If you refuse this Choosing, I will not mind. Your mother and I will support you in whatever you do."

Geelson fidgeted. Why was his father speaking so strangely? Warmth flushed his body, not from joy, but from fear. Still he said, "Father, I truly wish to be a draephlix rider."

His father nodded like Geelson had passed some test. He drained his wine. "Get some rest, then. The eggs will hatch soon, and you will need stamina and fortitude for the Choosing."

Geelson touched his brow as he left the parlor and found it beaded with sweat. He trembled. *I will go to the Choosing, and be made a rider,* he thought. *I won't let strange words stop me.*

He went upstairs to ready himself for bed, glancing towards the aerie one last time. The hills there were burning, the red glow an echo of sunset. The Mother Draephlix had immolated herself, leaving her eggs to incubate in the ashes.

From his parents' room, he heard his father speaking, and his mother wept.

*

Wasli watched the hills until the flames died down, then arranged his bedding. The sacks had held buckwheat for the baker and the scent reminded him of his mother and her cooking. A pang of loss, still sharp, tore through him. He knew he should be lucky to still have a father; many street urchins lacked both parents. But it was hard to feel grateful for his father's bad temper or penchant for drink.

He shifted, making himself comfortable, and tucked his arms behind his head. The stars burned like draephlix eyes. How often had he dreamed of one that would sweep him away, far from his father and the tannery's stink of curing skins? Even now he could imagine the soft, fur-caped shoulders pressed against his clenching body, the graceful dipping of the wings. Clouds would part between them as they flew in graceful rhythm, one set of pinions rising, the other falling. In his imagination the draephlix would turn its foxlike head to look at him with knowing comfort. *You are not alone. You are with me. We share a bond, you and I.*

Geelson was his friend, of course, and Maevig, but they were different. No matter what kind words they spoke, they did not truly understand him or the circumstances of his sorry life. Only a creature to whom he could open up his heart entirely could do that.

His father would not care if he left. Perhaps, he even looked forward to it. Wasli was just a burden on him.

A shooting star with a greenish white trail shot across the sky, blazing. Wasli knew it to be the soul of a draephlix and its rider, visiting Eliira to make sure all was well. Reverently, he made his wish. *Powers that be, Nameless Rider, choose me to claim a hatchling's egg! I have suffered too much, gone too long without.* He knew he would be competing with hundreds of other boys from the town and the small villages beyond, all drawn by the glory and excitement. But he, Wasli, was the only one who mattered. His life so far had shown him he was no one special; perhaps a reversal was in order. Surely he deserved it, through the karmic balance that the priests spoke of.

He was obliged to work with his father at the tannery the next day, but day after that he walked all morning to the nesting field. The aerie leaders had blocked it off with a long fence, but the boys, and there were many, peered through the slats at the cooling eggs. They would incubate quickly, in a matter of days. *Choose me,* Wasli thought, hoping the breeze would carry his desire.

"They are beautiful," Wasli told Geelson when he saw him again. "Like giant pearls." He stretched out his arms, making a circle with them, to indicate the size. "The shells glisten with all the colors of the rainbow. The priests walk among them with their rakes, spreading sweet hay to keep them warm."

Geelson brightened at the image Wasli painted, but the pull of his lips was tight, and his smile went away too quickly. They were sitting on the lip of the fountain as housewives scrubbed their laundry in the basin, the metal draephlix manifesting a kingly lack of concern. Maevig was absent. Wasli knew her sisters sang in the temple girls' choir. Perhaps she was practicing for that.

"How many?"

"I counted thirty," Wasli said. "What's the matter, Geely?"

"My father visited last night. He told me some things."

"Was it about the draephlix?" The notion came to Wasli that his friend was going to selfishly keep his secrets to himself, for some advantage at the Choosing ceremony. He grew angry. "Geely, I thought we were friends! Whatever it is, I should know too."

"Being a rider has risks," Geelson said. "My father bears scars. He showed them to me." His mouth compressed again.

"And my father can hit me," Wasli said. "So what?"

"And my mother ..." Geelson began. "My mother, when she knew for sure I was going to the Choosing, she started to cry. Wasli, she never cries!"

"Her eldest may be leaving her. That is why she cries," Wasli said. But the story made him uneasy.

Days passed in summer heat and dust. The sun became a dull red plate by evening, setting behind clouds the color of marigold and mango. Wasli tried to avoid his father's attention. His nights were spent in yearning dreams of cloud and sky.

Then, one dawn, the temple gongs began to sound and a stentorian-voiced caller set off through the town. "The draephlix eggs are ready to hatch! Hark! The eggs!"

Wasli leaped from his cot, nearly tripping over the sprawled, snoring body of his father. The procession would start soon, heading from the temple to the nesting field, the Choosing initiates following behind. He splashed his face and wet a comb to rake his hair. Frowning at the length, he tied it back with a piece of string, knowing all the other boys would be looking their best, and pulled on the cleanest and finest of his shirts. His mother had embroidered it with red thread for him to wear on temple holidays. To his chagrin, he found he had grown since the last time he had worn it, the sleeves stopping well short of his wrists. Stifling a curse, he rolled them up and dashed out of the hovel.

Around him, everyone was running to the temple square, where horns were blasting in deep, mournful tones. Venders assembled along the central boulevard, hawking fried cakes, shaved fruit, and boiled eggs wrapped in strips of smoked fish. Wasli waited before them, bouncing eagerly on the balls of his feet. More and more boys arrived dressed in fine silks and dyed cottons, wearing garlands of flowers made by their female relatives. Some sported henna tattoos on their faces for luck. Emboldened by their numbers, they crowded before the temple gates, only to be shooed back by the waiting priests.

This is it, Wasli thought. *Choosing Day. Nameless Rider, do not fail me.*

The sun rose over the bulk of the temple. The priests pushed the surging crowd back as the gilded gates swung open.

First to emerge were nine priests walking abreast, blowing with vigor the great mountain horns that stretched a horse's length before them. Behind them walked another row of priests beating timpani attached at their waists, and a third with brass cymbals. Temple clowns threw candy and played tricks on the crowd to alleviate the somberness. After them came the girls' choir singing in high, sweet voices, wearing scarlet and blue ribbons in their braided hair. Maevig was not among them. Neither could Wasli see Geelson in the crowd. Whatever happened now, he would be alone in it.

After the choir, came the draephlix riders, as many as could be spared from the aerie. They did not march, for this was not a military parade. Gravely, they waved to the spectators, but there was merriment in their eyes. The boys cheered, seeing their future.

Then came more priests swinging censers of incense, after which murmurs of awe rippled through the crowd. Four snow-white oxen plodded down the street, pulling a cart on which the draephlix effigy reared ferociously. Though smaller than the actual creature, it was still large and detailed enough to make the spectators gasp. To either side, and far above, stretched its quartet of wings, spring-wired to bobble at each turn of the wheels as its hooked beak clacked open and shut. The smaller children began to cry in fear, supposing it to be truly alive. Incense smoke swirled, heightening the illusion, while the priests' horns bellowed. All about him, Wasli heard the mutter of prayers, the soft click of Wish beads.

Slowly, the parade moved from the square. Now came the great march to the nesting field, all the Choosing candidates joining in. There were hundreds of them now, their families sending them off with hugs and kisses. Wasli ignored the displays and found his own place in the moving queue. His determination hardened to stone under the barrage of tossed flower petals and shouted cries for success.

Through the town, then out, they went, past Eliira's fields and farms. More boys joined them from the outlying hamlets they passed. They had rough, sunburnt skin and the look of gawking yokels. Knowing the number of eggs, Wasli kept a rough track of the odds in his head, and to his dismay, they kept going down. One in thirty might bond with a hatchling; now one in forty. He told himself the odds didn't matter.

All morning the parade climbed into the hills, stopping at the nesting field in early afternoon. Farmwives waiting there, replenished the boys with water and food. A boy in a red tunic flashed him a knowing grin, biting with enthusiasm into a piece of fruit. That was no boy — it was Maevig!

"What are you doing here?" Wasli said, sidling up to her. Her hair had been cut short and her tunic and leggings padded for girth.

"The same thing as you," she said unconcernedly.

"They will discover you! Then what happens?" The priests were walking among the boys now, rejecting those that looked too old, or too young, and sending them home. An entirely personal and arbitrary decision, Wasli thought with disgust. But he also knew, being the right age, he had nothing to fear from them.

"See old Sabir over there? My father told me he has cataracts and can't see too well. I'll go up to him for my inspection." She tossed aside the core. "Well, good luck!"

Wasli scratched his head. How could she be so blithe about such a blasphemy? But he did see her waved ahead, then it was his turn, and he was passed as well.

Now the initiates were waiting by the fence. Their number had not diminished by much. The high priest in his purple cape came to address them. "Listen, all of you," he said. "This Choosing of Tan Falan Gunga will commence. You may walk among the eggs in the field as you wish. Each one you may circle three times, touching if you want, then move to the next. When your circuit is complete, you may do so again. If a crack appears in the egg as you touch it, stay in your place. The boy the newborn draephlix first touches with its beak is the one it chooses as its companion and rider. Remain with the egg then and we will come to finish the rite. There is to be no pushing, shoving, fighting, or bullying among you. Remember, the draephlix choose only those with the purest hearts, the best intentions. Do you all understand?"

The boys called assent. A few of them were already maneuvering closer to the opening in the fence. In the field, the eggs trembled in the hay, emitting a soft thrumming noise.

The hierophant spread his hands and spoke a soft prayer. "The Choosing begins. May Vashti bless you all."

The priests had been standing in a human chain before the boys, holding them back, their scarlet hoods fallen. But now the youth burst through, shoving them aside, to scatter over the field. Some went directly to the nearest eggs, others to the largest ones. Wasli arrowed towards one in the far side of the field where not too many boys had congregated yet and projected his thoughts: *I'm here, I'm here!* A guardian priest stood watching as he stretched out his arm to touch the shell's pearly surface and walked slowly around it three times. But the shell remained intact. The priest shook his head, telling him he had to move on. Five boys shoved in after him to take his place.

Wasli felt disappointment, but he really hadn't expected to be Chosen right away. He dashed off to another egg buried under a charred tree. Brushing away the hay, he stretched out both arms this time, whispering and walking around again, three times: nothing. The priest stationed there shook his head also.

The last of the stragglers had now entered the field. At the next egg, Wasli had to wriggle through the crush, angling for a space. Fights broke out behind him despite the priest's orders. One boy rolled around on top of another, punching his face. This time, the draephlix riders themselves broke it up. They ejected both boys, one wailing, the other bleeding. *Don't think about them. Concentrate on the egg.* But there were too many pushing behind him, and he only had time to touch it with two outstretched fingers before he was squeezed out.

Chaos now reigned in the field. He saw larger boys pushing smaller ones out of the way, and smaller boys taking up sticks to hit the larger ones. Before him, a boy was torn away from an egg by the back of his shirt, the aggressor raising a stone to crack a hole in the shell himself. The priest noted the heresy and brought his staff down on the boy's skull. Wasli winced. The Choosing was far from the stately ceremony he had imagined it to be. But he also had the advantage of a hard life at the tannery, and was no stranger to brawls himself. Despite that, he only managed to touch and circle two more eggs, again with no success.

Then an egg hatched. Excited cries came from the center of the field as the priests erected a set of screens. Behind them a boy shouted in triumph while the priests chanted. Draephlix riders ordered the remaining boys, some protesting, back. Wasli looked around in desperation. Now another egg was hatching, with the same screens, the same chanting. Lungs burning, Wasli ran for an egg he was sure he hadn't touched before. Maybe this one would be his. But a stitch caught in his side and he fell in the Mother's ashes. By the time he reached the egg, the gaggle of boys was packed too tightly for him to enter.

The cries and shouts increased. Now all the eggs were hatching. Priests ran back and forth with their screens, hiding them from view. Wasli was pressed back with the others by the temple guards, pushed to the edge of the field past the barricades. To his far right, he saw Maevig being ejected in her stolen boy's clothes by her shoulders and rump. No! This couldn't be happening! Where was his hatchling?

Weeping bitterly, he stumbled out the gate.

*

Maevig ran down the empty country road, her heart pounding. When she could go on no further, she stopped, rested, drank a little from the water gourd at her waist, and ran again. How could the priests permit that travesty? Boys broken and bleeding, crying in fear.

It wasn't worth it. The creature's beauty did not excuse the cruelty. Tears made themselves known at the corners of her eyes. Not only for her own aborted dream, but for the dreams of all the others.

When the shadows lengthened she slowed to a walk. She realized her parents must long know how she'd slipped out of the girls' choir. What sort of punishment might that call for? Her throat tightened.

Maybe she should have stayed one of Vashti's precious flowers, warbling his praises in song.

Her sisters saw nothing wrong with being little dolls waiting for a draephlix rider to wed, but that had never been her. Maevig loved them, yet she was cut from different cloth. Long had she studied birds in their flight, imagining how it felt to swoop like a swallow, dive like an eagle. In her dreams, she soared high above the town on

15

draephlix wings, letting them carry her to the glaciers in the west. When the priests told her it wasn't possible for her, that made them all the more vivid.

Now, for wanting that, she had found out the truth of it.

It was a disaster beyond disasters.

She reached the town. Her boys' clothes hung loosely, for she had long ago shed their padding which she had torn from old quilts. Workers swept up the remains of the ceremony, a few spangles, a half-eaten sausage. In an abandoned shed near her house, she had secreted a pack containing extra clothes, dried food, and the coins she had saved. Naive as she'd been about the ceremony, she still understood her decision carried consequences, and had planned for them. It was better to disappear than risk her parents' wrath, or the priests'.

From her pack, Maevig retrieved a wool cap, which she placed over her shorn head. With melancholy, she adjusted the tassels. *So it begins,* she thought. She squeezed her eyes shut, halting the tears. She had no time for them. Perhaps later, when the shock of her departure had worn off, she might send a letter to her family telling them of the choice she had made, and why.

She pattered down the empty street, but stopped when she heard a strange cough. Peering into the alley's mouth, she blinked, then straightened in surprise. "Wasli? Is that you?"

Wasli rose from the pile of skins where he'd been sitting. In the fading light, his eyes looked red. The linen shirt he wore was ripped up the side and dirtied by the nesting field. They stared at each other, two rejects.

"I'm sorry," Maevig said. She knew how much Wasli had wanted an egg.

Wasli shrugged like it didn't matter. "I know. It isn't your fault. It's just ... fate."

"I guess that's all it came down to, then. Fate. Not purity of heart like the priests told us." Maevig shouldered her pack. "Listen, I'm leaving. The desert nomads have a camp by the river, a little way past the canyon. They need tutors for their children in letters and math. They said they would have me." She gestured. "Wasli, come with me.

There's nothing for you here. Your father is a drunk and he's given you no prospects. I know Geelson shared his tutor's lessons with you. Maybe you can work with the nomads too. They are an honorable and ambitious people."

"It's a reckless plan," Wasli dismissed. "What if you wind up a body-seller?"

"I won't," Maevig said, insulted. "Come on, Wasli. What do you have here to stay for? Come with me to say goodbye to Geelson, at least."

"He's been Chosen," Wasli spat. "I saw the riders at his house. Why would he want anything to do with us?"

"Why would he not want to see us?"

Wasli opened his mouth, but he couldn't find an answer. His shoulders slumped as he followed her.

Evening lay on the town now. They passed the crafters' district and then the temple, coming to the block where the elite kept their homes. Horses were tied outside Geelson's portico, their trappings bearing the symbol of the aerie. Light blazed from downstairs and they heard men talking. "Let's leave," Wasli said. "They wouldn't want us to intrude."

"Shhh." Maevig motioned him to the side of the house. In the room that she knew to be Geelson's, a single lamp burned. The branches of a cherry tree supplied easy access. She couldn't have climbed up in a dress, but in boys' leggings she slung herself up easily.

"How can you do this?" Wasli protested. "He stole your dream!"

"It's not my dream anymore, and he's my friend, and I want to say goodbye. You should too. Come on!"

Grumbling, Wasli climbed after her. They stood on the roof of the mantrap below the window and popped their heads inside. Geelson sat on the edge of his bed folding some clothes and putting them in a canvas bag. His face looked drawn, not happy like they had expected. He wore a new silk shirt, but underneath it they could see his neck was bandaged. A red spot marred the white gauze. Seeing it moved Wasli to speak. "Geely?"

Geelson turned, saw them at the window, and smiled. "Wasli? Mae?"

"We came to say goodbye," Maevig said. "And ... congratulations."

Geelson sighed and his expression darkened. The cloth he held bunched in his hands.

"What is it?" she pressed.

"Being made a draephlix rider is not what you think it is," Geelson said. "If I could change things, I would not have gone to the Choosing."

Maevig shared a look with Wasli. Whatever violence they had experienced at the Choosing, Geelson had suffered worse. "We were all wild animals," she said. "All of us."

Wasli's throat moved as he spoke and his voice came out clogged. "Still. Your hatchling? Is it well?" Geelson stared blankly, and Maevig felt a chill. "I've always wondered what they were like," Wasli continued. "Is it soft, like a kitten? Does it mew, does it speak to you with its mind?"

A terrible look came over Geelson's face. Blood rushed to his skin, darkening it. "There is no hatchling," he said.

Maevig shrank back as he stalked to the window. "It's a lie," Geelson said. "There are no draephlix. There are eggs, yes, and a creature. But it is not what you think. It looks like a white worm or a big fat slug. It has five red eyes on little stalks and a sharp black beak that opens in five parts. Out of it comes a tongue, a long tongue tipped with barbs that hit me right here." He jerked down the bandage on his neck where a small, round sore festered. It looked like a puncture, but also a burn. "The slugs do that to all they Choose, to claim them." He shuddered. "As for a mind, it has none. There is no friendship there. Only hunger."

"Oh, Geely ..." Maevig gasped.

"The slug grows fur and scales, in time, but the growths are like those found on spiders, on moths. The hair is rough and it irritates. As for the wings, they are featherless, like huge paddles filled with gas. Bring a fire too close to them and the creature explodes!" He rubbed his arms through his new shirt. "The aeries are cold and unwelcoming. Fire is not permitted there."

Wasli shook his head. "That's not true. It can't be true! You're lying. You worry about upsetting us with your fortune, so you're trying to make it sound worse. Tell us that's not so. That's all it is, isn't it, a lie told for comfort?"

Maevig couldn't stop staring at Geelson's wound. That was why the priests screened the eggs when they hatched. Why the shouts of triumph were really shouts of pain. "It drank your blood?" she whispered.

"Yes. It must drink from a wound like this every day, or it dies. Later, it requires flesh. The aerie keeps herds of livestock to feed them. When the slaves disobey, the slugs eat them, too." Geelson smiled bitterly. "You didn't know the aerie keeps slaves? Oh, they have many riches there. Everything but warmth! The riders don't protect Eliira, they raid for Eliira. Cloth, grain, silver, jewels. They are no better than thieves!" His fists trembled.

Wasli went very quiet, realizing, as she did, that Geelson spoke the truth. "Why did they lie?" he whispered. "Why?"

"Who wants to ride a bloodsucking slug? And moreover, who wants to be a hypocrite to everything they've been taught? That is the real horror. Not the slugs!"

Maevig closed her eyes. All her life, she'd been lied to. How true was the tale of Queen Amonet, even? Or the priest's tales of how Vashti sent the first draephlix to Eliira in an egg that fell from the sky? Her world had been turned upside down, inside out. She clutched at the things she did know were true: her sister's love, her friends.

"Geely, come with us," she said. "I'm leaving Eliira and joining the nomads. Wasli is coming too." She squeezed Wasli's hand, under the ledge, as he opened his mouth to protest. "Three can make their way more easily than two."

Geelson thought on it, and shook his head. "I can't. What of my father's honor? What of my grandfather's honor?"

"They honored falsely, it seems," she said.

"Geelson?" A man's voice called from inside the house. "You're needed downstairs. The priest has some more things to say to you."

"Please go," Geelson said, coloring again. "They expect me to keep silent about this, they won't like it if they see us talking."

"They will punish you for leaving?" Wasli asked. Geelson's face hardened. "Geely, tell us!"

"No punishment is needed, because none dare to walk away," Geelson said. "For being Chosen is an honor. We have been taught that all our lives. Enough to kill for it. You know that, Wasli, and you too, Mae. I saw you there." Maevig flushed. "And if any of us did leave, and we did talk about the slugs, who would believe us? Who believes the truth, next to a pretty lie? Who wants to be known as a failure and not God's warrior?"

Maevig watched in surprise as Wasli leaned over the window ledge to catch Geelson in an embrace. Wasli had never embraced anyone that she had seen, his body too used to abuse to make itself so vulnerable.

"Look, we've all had our dreams broken," Wasli said. "But think on this. They were broken even before we had them. Come with us, Geely. You said they won't keep you. Whatever we do next, at least it will be our story, our lives."

"I don't know ..." Geelson whispered. His body shook.

Maevig embraced him as well. "Please, think on it. We'll be waiting for you outside the canyon in the stand of poplar trees."

They slipped from the sill and off the mantrap to run away into the night, stopping at Wasli's hovel so he could take what meager belongings he had. He came out with a small bundle of clothing and a wooden box that rattled. "We'll need these more than my father's liquor-seller," he said. His voice still sounded unsteady. He looked back one last time, then began to hurry through the darkened town.

"Don't walk too fast," Maevig said. "Give him time to catch up to us."

"How do you know he's coming?"

"Who wants a falsehood, when he can have what is real?" Maevig said. "That is us, Wasli. That is us."

***

Grace, Regardless
by Kevin Henry

U.S.: A futuristic gunslinger faces gangsters and self-delusion in this urban fantasy.

Reclining in his library, surrounded by ancient biblical texts, hand-annotated and rigorously studied, Johnny jammed the business end of a cigar into the aged skin of his left forearm. The odor of burning hair and searing flesh assailed his nostrils. He was surprised at the pain: not the amount of it, which was negligible, but that it hurt at all.

Sometimes he felt that he wasn't a real person, that he was detached from the world and everything around him, like a ghost, too stubborn to move on. He always felt that he belonged to another time, another place ... or maybe to nowhere at all. Now he focused on the pain, let it ground him in the here and now. The pain was the only thing that was real and feeling it proved that *he* was real as well.

The distant whir and hum of a Personal Automated Smooth-Ride System caught his attention. He cringed a little, thinking of the way the damned things hovered over the ground like a rich man refusing to shake a mechanic's hand for fear of getting dirty. He got up slowly from his chair, ambled to the window, and peered out at the incoming and unexpected guest. Expecting a young glory-hound, come to dethrone the king slinger, he almost fetched a firearm. But he hadn't encountered one of their ilk in several years. The younger generation had all but forgotten him and his accomplishments. *Just as well*, he thought. *I'd forget it all myself if I could.*

When he saw the woman who emerged from the hovering vehicle in his dusty driveway, a shock went through him and his breath caught in his chest. He thought his feelings for her had disappeared beneath the stains of time, but he didn't realize how wrong he'd been until he saw her standing there looking up at his house. Even so, he didn't want her here now, didn't want her to see him like this, a shell of who he'd been. He rolled the sleeves of his shirt down to cover the evidence of his self-mutilation.

June climbed the steps to the front porch. The door opened before she could knock. Johnny stood there in the doorway, drinking her in. She was as beautiful as he remembered. Her fiery red hair wasn't quite so fiery anymore and her face bore the marks of time, but with a grace and dignity that put most women her age to shame. He stared into her eyes, but couldn't hold her gaze for long. When he felt water seeping into his own, he looked away.

"June," he said in his deep, baritone voice. That was all he could manage. There was too much to say ... too much to apologize for. It all got caught up in his mind like too many people trying to squeeze through a door at the same time.

"Johnny Blaze," she said. "My god, you look like shit."

He smiled. There was the honesty he expected from her. She was the only person he could count on to tell it like it is, to call him on his bullshit, to tell him the truths that hurt. "Come in," he said, moving out of her way.

She stepped inside, her sharp eyes darting around. The house looked like something from a museum, with all of the old-time touches like wooden floors, clear glass windows instead of vidscreens, and real wallpaper instead of on-demand color changing fiber optics. "I hear it's one of the few homes left with real grass," she said.

"You know me, Junie. Real or nothing."

She nodded. "It was never like you to keep up with the times."

"Time left me behind long ago." He offered her a cup of joe.

She accepted the cup, sat down at the kitchen table. "If only other things could have left *you* behind," she said sadly.

He knew what she meant and the words were a knife in his gut. He sat, reaching for his own steaming cup with trembling hands. "Been straight for four months now," he said. There was no sense of pride or accomplishment in the comment. He'd quit too many times for her to be truly impressed by such a meager milestone.

"Good," she said, neither praising nor judging, but simply acknowledging. "Looks like you've done well for yourself. I'm glad for you." She had never approved of how he made his money, but it hadn't been any of her business for a long time.

He didn't want to voice the words that came out of his mouth next, but they came tumbling out before he could stop them. "I'd give it all away, this empire of dirt, for one more day with you, Junie. Like the old times." He hated the desperation that he heard in his own voice. He sounded weak, pathetic.

June was visibly disturbed. She sat her cup down on the table and adjusted her top, flattening out the wrinkles and creases. "This wasn't meant to be a trip down memory lane, Johnny."

"Why *are* you here? I haven't seen you in years and one day you show up out of the blue to bump gums?"

"I need your help." The words came out of her mouth like bitter things dripping off her tongue.

"You need dough? That's about all I can manage these days."

She stared flatly into his blue eyes. "We both know that's not true. I'm sure you remember how to use the tools of your trade."

He seemed surprised. "I haven't been that person in a long time. I retired from that life."

"That was the one thing you were good at. Besides slowly killing yourself, that is."

"I told you, I've been straight for months." There was resentment in his voice now, although he knew she was right about him. She was always right. "I'm not a slinger anymore. If you need someone blipped off I can recommend—"

"I need you to be a father." There it was. It wasn't as difficult to say as she had imagined. Anger helped push the words out.

"A father?" he asked.

"Yes," she replied sharply. "You *are* a father. You remember *that*, don't you? Or has the juice taken that much of you away?"

He was quiet for a moment, gazing down at his hands gathered in his lap. When he spoke, she could hear all of the years of sorrow and pain in his voice. "It's taken all of me, June. Can't you see that? It's been taking me away slowly, all these years, bit by bit. That's why you left me. Everyone I know goes away in the end because they can't stand watching me kill myself."

"You haven't been straight for four months, have you?"

He shook his head like a child who's been scolded. "I'm a liar, June, just like I've always been. A liar and a junkie and a killer. That's why I never deserved you and I never deserved to be a father. Grace is better off without me."

"All of that is true," she said, leaning forward as she spoke, tears running down her cheeks. She slapped her hand on the table hard enough to spill her coffee. It got his attention and he looked into her face as she spoke. "You're a lying, junkie, bastard, but you're also a right guy. Even though you do wrong and you hurt the ones you love, you have a good heart. I've always believed that."

"I've wanted a lot of things, but never anything as much as I wanted you." He held up his hands to stop her when she opened her mouth to speak. "I know that window is closed. You're a different person and here I am, still the same. I've never changed. That's why you need to leave here and never come back. I don't want to hurt you again."

"I wouldn't be here now if I didn't need you, Johnny. If Grace didn't need you."

"What's wrong?" His brow furrowed in concern. He knew that to bring June around after all the time that had passed and all of the things that had happened between them, something must be very wrong, indeed.

"You've heard the name, Diesel?"

"Yes." He knew Diesel was a drug dealer and a dangerous man. He wasn't someone you crossed if you wanted to go on breathing. "How's she mixed up with *him*?"

June sat back. She was trying to maintain her composure. "He has her, Johnny. You know what he does to girls, what he makes them do."

"She's so young."

"She's twenty now. Even if she was half that, he'd have her turning tricks."

"How'd she get mixed up with Diesel?" he asked again.

"Her boyfriend. It doesn't really matter, does it?" She waived the question away testily. "This bad man has our little girl and you need to get her back."

She saw something in his eyes then that she had never seen in all the time she had known him: fear.

"I can't do this. I'll let you down." His voice was a deep rasp.

"You always have, but I know you won't let your daughter down."

He nodded, his gaze unseeing. He knew what she was asking and he knew that she was aware as well. There was no need to say anymore. He owed June and Grace this. He owed them everything.

After working out the details, Johnny saw his guest out onto the porch. There was still so much he wanted to say to her, the love of his life, but the time for that had passed long ago.

She started for the steps, then stopped and turned around. She looked up at the tall man before her. "We had some good times, Johnny. It wasn't all bad. I just want you to know that."

"The needle took so much of me," he said grimly. "If I could start again a million miles away, I would. I'd keep myself this time ... for you and Grace. I'd find a way."

She reached up and gently touched his cheek. "That's the thing you never understood. It doesn't w that way. It doesn't matter how much you love me or Grace. You can't kick it for us. It has to be for you and I think you've always hated yourself too much to quit."

"What have I become, my sweetest friend?" There was a desolate sorrow in that question that hurt her heart more than she wanted to admit.

She turned again and swiftly retreated down the stairs. In seconds, she was back inside her PASS, the electric motor humming. She left without looking back.

*

Johnny went to his bedroom. He opened a secret compartment built into the floor and removed the wooden box that lay there. Inside were the "tools of the trade" that June had mentioned. They were like old drinking buddies who had shown up to talk him into tossing back some liquor and getting into trouble, just like the good old days. Except those days weren't so good, and he was the one who had gotten old.

He had long ago retired his gats, The Twins, as he called them. Now, like him, they had been recruited back into service. One final job and then they could rest in peace for good. They deserved it because, unlike him, they had always been faithful and true.

*

Johnny climbed into his boiler, a relic from the previous century. They were banned from roadways now because of the illegal and highly flammable mixture of liquid hydrocarbons that fueled them and the resultant environmental danger it posed. Johnny got a special historical dispensation for his, which had cost a pretty penny. He loved the feel of wheels on the road and the visceral experience of steering three thousand pounds of flammable steel himself instead of relying on an automated system. He rolled down the windows and anticipating the exhilaration of wind in his hair, dropped the hammer and burned rubber.

He paid a visit to his peddler, Itchy. There were supplies he would need to accomplish the job at hand. Itchy was none too happy about the visit or his requests. Not trusting him to lay dormy until the job was done, Johnny tied him up and promised that someone would come to release him when it was safe. Now there was only one stop left. The one that mattered most.

*

There weren't many places in the city for darkness to linger, even at night. The ever-growing urban sprawl was lit with neon and animated, digital billboards until very few shadowed corners remained. Diesel had found one of those corners for the creep joint from which he dealt in drugs, sex, and worse.

Johnny parked his bucket a full block away from that place. He sat in the dark, contemplating what he must do next with reluctant resignation. He pulled out the needle he had prepared earlier at Itchy's. His hands trembled as he stared at it.

He had tried to put the curse of addiction behind him many times before, but every time, it came back. He had tried to kill it all away, each contract he fulfilled being a stand-in for the monkey on his back. That monkey would never let him forget the way it made him feel, the things he'd done to get it, and the relationships it had destroyed. No matter how hard he tried, he needed it just the same and that realization made him hate himself. Or maybe June was right. Maybe he didn't hate himself because of the drugs, but needed them because he hated himself. The distinction didn't matter now.

He reminded himself that this was part of the plan. Grace needed him and he wouldn't let her down again. He needed just a little juice to achieve the right effect.

The needle tore a hole. He felt the old familiar sting. Warmth flowed through him and the colors of the night exploded inside his head.

*

Johnny strolled down the street wearing a long, black coat and a wide-brimmed hat pulled low to provide cover in case he ran into anyone who might make him from the old days. He carried a heavy satchel in his right hand.

As he neared the rear entrance of the joint, an old man approached from a pile of trash in the alley. He recognized the lonely fellow as a former soldier who used to travel in the same circles as himself, looking for work to support his family. Now the work was gone, and the family with it. He had sacrificed much and gotten little in return.

Johnny stopped and opened the satchel. What he handed the man was more than generous and he hoped the old fellow would use it to better his life. He realized the man would probably waste it on booze and drugs, but he had to believe in a man's ability to better himself. Surely someone, somewhere, must be capable of it even if he wasn't.

When he reached the thick, steel door in the alley, he kicked it with one heavy boot and waited. He spotted the camera that watched him and kept his head bowed, his face in shadows. After a beat, he kicked again. The door opened and a broad, bald man stepped out into the alley, pushing Johnny backwards.

"Go climb up yer thumb, pal," the doorman said, looking like a junkyard dog protecting his territory. "Whatever yer lookin' for, it ain't here."

"Got some sugar for the high pillow," Johnny said. "From Itchy."

"Why ain't Itchy bringin' it himself?" the doorman growled suspiciously, chest thrust out to accentuate the heater clipped into his shoulder rig.

"Don't know the man's business," Johnny said. "Just doing what I'm told." He saw the man's right eye light up, bright yellow in the dark. It wasn't a hallucination brought on by the drugs. The eye was equipped with an x-ray, and the bruiser was checking Johnny for weapons. When he was satisfied that Johnny wasn't carrying, he nodded.

"I'll take that," the doorman said, holding out a hand for the satchel.

"Sorry," Johnny said. "I deliver it myself or not at all."

The doorman reached out and swatted the lid from the older man's head. Looking up at Johnny Blaze, he didn't see a former slinger come to burn powder, but a white-haired boob with a satchel full of money. "All right, cat," the doorman said at last. "But don't try anything stupid or you'll get the bum's rush. If you're lucky. Savvy?"

"Never been particularly lucky," Johnny said, trying to appear small and frail, "but I'm not looking for trouble. It's eggs in the coffee." He left the hat laying in the alley. It probably smelled like piss now, like everything else there.

The man motioned for Johnny to follow him as he stepped inside the club. Another man was in place to watch the door, while the first bruiser led Johnny through the backstage area where the girls got themselves ready for their turns in front of the leering crowd out front. Johnny craned his neck, checking out the dolls as they powdered their noses and oiled their gams, looking for Grace. He didn't see her.

One of the chicks punched Johnny on the shoulder as he passed by. "Hey, pal," she said fearlessly. "Got your conk on a swivel, do ya'? If you're not payin', you're not lookin', got it?"

"Excuse me, ma'am," Johnny said with his rascal's grin, tipping an imaginary hat. "Just passing through. I apologize for the inconvenience."

"Ya' better," she spat at his back, not sounding quite as angry as before.

He turned back to the broad. "Say," he said quietly, so the doorman couldn't hear, "do you know Grace? Is she here?"

At first she thought he was some kind of pervert chasing after one of the girls, but she didn't know anyone named Grace. She noticed the look in the tall man's eyes and recognized the anguish of a father worried for his little girl. She wished she had a father, or anyone, who cared enough to worry about *her* that way. She shook her head slowly.

Johnny leaned in close, his voice going lower and deeper. "Think about getting a new job, honey. What would your momma think about this?" There was no judgment in his tone, only concern, and it resonated with the young woman more than she would have imagined.

"Don't mess with the skirts; they're crazier 'n jailhouse rats," the doorman said, grabbing Johnny by the arm and pulling him along through another door.

The dope was in full force now, but something was wrong. He must have taken too much. He wasn't supposed to be flying this high. His face was gaunt, his eyes were blurred, his shirt all soaked with sweat.

He finally found himself in a room where Diesel sat in a big chair, behind a big desk, like a king holding court. There was a flimsy door in the western wall which Johnny assumed led to a bathroom.

Mounted in the eastern wall was another of those heavy, steel doors, this one secured with an iron bar inserted through steel rings.

Diesel, a black man with a mane of shoulder-length dreadlocks, looked to Johnny like an ebony lion. There were two men wearing bowler hats, their bodies roughly pear-shaped, one a head taller than the other. Johnny saw them as mismatched bowling pins. The doorman, who had led him to Diesel, now looked every bit like a door: broad and flat.

Standing near Diesel was a scrawny, scruffy man whose voice sounded like the buzzing of a gnat. And in one corner, sat a man with the shifty eyes and general demeanor of a coyote. On his lap sat Grace, one arm draped around the coyote's shoulders.

Even though it had been years since he'd seen her, Johnny would always be able to recognize his daughter. She was tall and thin, like him, with long black hair, and a smile that drew the corners of her mouth down instead of pulling them up. She was his little girl, all right. Now all he had to do was get her out of there.

"Look at his eyes, boss," Gnat was saying. "Old timer's trippin' balls!"

"Of course he is," Diesel growled regally. "Don't anyone recognize who we got in our midst?" When no one replied, he answered for them. "This here is Johnny Blaze, slinger extraordinaire."

"I've heard that name," Coyote said. "He was some kind of badass back in the day."

"Not *some kind* of badass," Diesel said. "He was *the* badass."

"Don't look so tough now," Gnat said. "He's just an old, used-up junkie. I don't think he even knows where he's at."

Gnat and the Bowling Pins laughed.

"I brought this for you," Johnny said, stepping toward Diesel's desk with the satchel.

"Whoa," the doorman said, moving to intercept Johnny, his hand on the rod in his shoulder holster.

"You checked him? What's in the bag?" Diesel asked.

The doorman nodded. "He's clean. Nothin' in the bag but cabbage. Said it's from Itchy."

Diesel motioned for Johnny to step forward and place the satchel down in front of him on the desk. "Why you deliverin' for that wretch?" He wanted to know.

Johnny sat the bag down as he was directed. "Said he's leaving town for a spell. Wanted you to have this before he left."

"Itchy don't have a drop for a couple days," Diesel said thoughtfully. "I've known that weasel to be a lot of things, but I never knew him to be early." He scrutinized Johnny with suspicious eyes. "And why you? I heard you was lousy with Jack, up in that old-timey place outside o' town. What happened? You puttin' all that shit in your veins?"

Johnny reached toward the satchel.

"Far enough," Coyote said, standing up, knocking Grace unceremoniously onto the floor in the process. Johnny didn't like that. Coyote drew a pea-shooter and held it on the former slinger. Johnny put his hands in the air.

"You said you checked it?" Diesel asked the doorman.

"Nothin' gets past me, boss," the doorman said proudly, pointing to his artificial right eye.

"Let's buzz Itchy and clear this up," Diesel said. He touched his left wrist and a display lit up on his forearm. He touched a couple of icons and a ringer could be heard. No one answered. Diesel flicked his wrist and the display disappeared. "He ain't answerin'. Why you think that is, old man?"

Johnny shrugged.

"Maybe he croaked Itchy," Coyote suggested.

Gnat shook his head. "Nope. That sounds hinky to me. If he popped Itchy, why would he come here? Why not just scram out?"

"I need to give you something," Johnny said, slurring his words as if he'd had a stroke, reaching for the satchel again. Tension ran through everyone in the room like an electric current.

Diesel motioned for Johnny to do whatever it was he was going to do. There was no danger. Coyote and the doorman both held their pieces on the old man like they were hunting bears with forks. Bowling Pins seemed ready to draw if need be. That was more than enough firepower to take out one old, unarmed, former slinger, even if he happened to be Johnny-freakin'-Blaze.

Johnny unzipped the satchel.

"You know somethin' 'bout those x-ray eyeballs, boss?" Gnat said.

Johnny reached into the satchel and began removing stacks of cash, dumping them onto the table. Diesel watched with bemused curiosity.

"They're really not that reliable when it comes to anything but soft tissue," Gnat went on.

Johnny closed his hands around his Twins, which had been buried in the middle of the satchel of cash and thus unrecognizable to any but the strongest of x-rays. The doorman's eye wasn't that strong.

Diesel realized what was happening a fraction of a second too late.

Most gangsters carried the new battery or gas-powered weapons. Johnny felt that their velocity rates were underwhelming. He preferred his weapons, as he did most things, to be vintage. His Twins were stainless steel .45 caliber Winchester Magnum revolvers with ten-inch ventilated rib barrels, checkered walnut grips and adjustable rear sights.

Johnny tore his guns out of the satchel, cash flying into the air like a paper smoke screen. He didn't so much aim the pistols. He pointed them in the general direction of his targets and let instinct take over. He fired one round from each weapon, simultaneously. The first shot caught the doorman in the head and reduced everything above his shoulders to a fine, red mist. The second shot struck Coyote in the chest, tossing him backwards over the chair on which he had so recently been sitting. Grace screamed in terror.

Bowling Pins drew their weapons as they ran, squirting metal on the move. Most of their shells went wild, one even striking Gnat in the throat. They did, however, manage to nail Johnny in his left thigh, his left side, and right shoulder.

Gnat didn't have the decency to go down easy, but stood there holding his throat, eyes bulging as blood poured out of the wound.

Johnny took pity on the little guy and finished him off with a round to his pump.

Another shot from one of the Bowling Pins struck Johnny's right hand and the gun he'd held went flying.

That was when Diesel flipped his desk over with a mighty effort and crouched down behind it. It was lined underneath with sheets of steel for just this sort of situation. Johnny knew the big man wasn't sleeping back there. He was readying a weapon.

More shots were coming from the Bowling Pins, who were behind Johnny. He slipped in Gnat's blood and found himself tumbling to the floor in front of the desk. He put his back against the smooth-polished wood and found the Bowling Pins. They were reloading. He fired and knocked them both down. He couldn't decide if it was a strike or a spare, since he had fired multiple times.

Johnny could hear Grace crying where she lay on the floor, beside the body of the dead Coyote. He called out to Diesel, "Let me have the girl and I'll dust out."

"This 'bout a ho?" Diesel called from behind his wood and steel barrier, only feet away from his opponent. "What you want that skank for? Don't matter anyway. We way past you dustin' out. Only place you goin' now is into a wooden kimono."

Johnny was hurting from the wounds he'd taken, but managed to clamber to his feet, despite Gnat's quickly pooling blood which threatened to undermine his balance and send him back to the floor.

Diesel came over the desk like the black lion that he appeared to be in Johnny's current state, teeth bared, extravagant mane flying, eyes dangerous and wild. He gave Johnny a Harlem sunset with an enormous knife. Johnny, however, was never one to go down easy. He was too stubborn for that.

Johnny clutched his wounded right mitt to his stomach to hold his guts in while slamming his remaining pistol against Diesel's head and pulling the trigger. CLICK ... CLICK, CLICK, CLICK. Empty.

Diesel grinned a very feline sort of grin, like the one he uses when he's cornered a mouse and is about to pounce for the kill. Johnny struck the man-lion in the left temple with the barrel of his heater. When that didn't take him down, Johnny struck him twice more. Diesel crumpled to the floor finally, covered in Gnat's blood, dazed and moaning incoherently.

Johnny had no interest in finishing Diesel. He had no beef with the man except for the fact that he was currently holding his daughter against her will. He aimed to rectify that now. He limped to where the girl lay staring at the carnage around her. She seemed to be in shock. He held out his good hand. "Come on, honey. I'm taking you out of here."

She looked up at him as if she'd never seen him before. Her ears were still ringing from the Chicago lightning, so she wasn't sure she'd heard him correctly. "What?" she asked.

"Come on, Gracie. There's bound to be a chopper squad on their way. We have to go." He offered the hand again.

"I don't ... I can't ..." she stammered, obviously still confused.

He reached down and grabbed her under her arms. He hoisted her to her feet, pain shooting through his abdomen. At least the pain was dulled by the drugs or he would have been on the ground beside the Coyote.

He pulled Grace by her wrist. He went to the big metal door, pulled back the bar that held it shut, and pushed it open. He nearly swooned from the pain and loss of blood. Tossing a curse out to the night, he heard men entering the room behind them. He heard Diesel, still conscious, directing his boys to "fill the old man full o' daylight and bring back the ho."

Once he and Grace were clear of the door and standing in the alley, Johnny slammed the door shut. He put his strong back against a dumpster and shoved it in front of the door with a Herculean effort. He knew it wouldn't hold for long, but it would buy them some time. Immediately, they heard fists and feet pounding furiously on the other side of the door.

Johnny had led Grace only a few feet toward the opposite end of the alley when he collapsed.

"You all right, mister?" she asked.

"Don't treat me like a stranger, Grace," Johnny said, his voice thick and raspy. "I know I did wrong by you and your mom, but I'm trying to make up for that now."

"You got the wrong girl. I'm not Grace. She's not here anymore."

The pounding on the door intensified when Diesel screamed at his men to "gank that fucker" or forfeit their own miserable lives. The dumpster was moving back an inch at a time under their efforts.

"Don't act like this, Grace," Johnny implored. His breath was coming in rapid, shallow gasps. Blood trickled from his nose.

The girl pulled off the black wig, revealing the ratty, blonde hair beneath it. Johnny saw now that what he took for his daughter's upside down smile was actually a frown. He saw the bruises and the needle tracks. He knew at last that this was not his little girl, but she was someone's girl and she had been mistreated.

"Where ..." he asked, "... where is she?"

The young woman knelt down beside Johnny, putting a hand on his shoulder. "I knew a girl named Grace. She was beautiful. Diesel sold her to some freak in Croatia." She saw the disappointment in the old man's eyes. "I'm sorry," she said. "She's lucky to have a dad like you."

Ever the pragmatist, Johnny refused to believe he'd made the trip for biscuits. "Go to the end of the alley," he said, his voice naught but a whisper. "I have a friend waiting there. She'll help you make a clean sneak."

"I can't. Diesel owns me. I'll be in such a jam—"

"Don't think this life is anything but a long, slow death." He was staring directly into her eyes, his still strong hands gripping her arms. "I lived it myself and I've been dying for a long time."

The dumpster moved farther. Arms appeared through the breach between the metal door and the brick wall. Angry voices were shouting.

"Go on now," Johnny said in a fatherly tone that was hard to resist. "My friend will make sure those trouble boys never find you."

"But I'm not your daughter. I don't know your friend."

"Grace's mother is the greatest person I ever met. She'll help you. Go to her."

"What about you?" she asked worriedly.

"It's time to take the fall for all the wrong things I've done."

He laid his head down on the cold pavement. He could hear the blood pounding in his ears, but it sounded like the rhythm of a train, and not one of those modern Maglev abominations, but an old style steam engine.

"Rattler's coming to get me," he said, his eyes staring longingly into the distance.

"What?" the girl asked.

"People used to think a ferryman took them to the Other side in a boat. I always knew a train would take me. I hear it. It's slowing down. Must be almost here now."

The girl looked around, but saw or heard no train. The dumpster moved again and the door came open farther. A skinny man could force his way through the opening. She had to decide what to do. She hated the life she had been forced into. Maybe she could get away and disappear. Maybe she could have a regular life with a husband and kids. They wouldn't have to know the things she'd done. But things like that didn't happen for people like her. She was a screw up.

She looked down at the old man again. He was fading quickly. The men who would take her back into slavery were nearly through the door. She stared down the alley. She saw a PASS hovering there in the shadows. Two worlds were calling to her.

The old man coughed up blood, sputtered, and spoke one final time. He sang actually, fragments of a song that the girl recalled having heard long ago in her youth. The words said something about a man going around, taking names. This man would set some free and place blame on others. She got the feeling that the old man bleeding out on the ground in front of her was the person in the lyrics. There was no way he could be, of course. Still, chills ran down her arms and the short hairs on the back of her neck stood on end.

She clambered to her feet and pumped her getaway sticks for all they were worth. She ran for the PASS awaiting her at the end of the alley as if her life depended on reaching it before the bad men on the other side of the door got to her. And, of course, it did.

The door burst open behind her and loud men rushed out. Shots were fired, but the girl slipped away unharmed.

Johnny heard the train slow down and finally stop. He could see it there in the alley beside him. The conductor, dressed all in white, stepped out and stared at Johnny, lying still on the pavement. "Come along, sir," the conductor said. "We have more stops to make. Can't wait here all night."

"You're here for me?" Johnny asked hopefully.

"Don't you think you've hurt enough, sir?"

Johnny felt the hurt falling away as he stood. He felt the weight of his sins sloughing off like the old skin that a reptile has outgrown. "But I don't have a ticket."

The conductor held up a golden ticket and grinned. "I've been holding this for you, sir. For a long while, I wasn't sure if I'd be able to give it to you. You have to earn it, you know."

"Have I earned it, then?" Johnny asked humbly.

"Yes, sir. You certainly have. Come aboard now. We're on a tight schedule."

Johnny boarded the train eagerly. The door swung shut behind him and he heard familiar, friendly voices in the car just ahead.

***

The Truth in the Dark
(What Lies in the Dark)
by Paul K. Metheney

U.S.: Two modern tales combine the supernatural, serial killings, and a hidden truth.

His Prey struts into the mouth of the darkened alley. It's almost cliché. He awaits in the back entrance of a closed restaurant, past the reeking dumpsters.

Shadows drape across his still form as he watches her.

The staccato of the spiked heels punctuating her shapely legs; the swish of her black miniskirt paired with a snug leather bodice. Short, fiery auburn hair tops her slender neck. Of all of her features, her neck fascinates him the most. Her attire does not interest him. After all, one doesn't concern themselves with the packaging of their food.

Earlier, he had taken the precaution of breaking the bug-speckled light bulb in the metal fixture above the doorway. After years of a nocturnal existence, he requires very little light to see. The neon from the club a block away provides his Prey enough light to navigate the alley. He watches her consider retracing her steps. The darkness and stench of rotting lettuce and seafood wafting from the dumpster may be making her skittish. He smiles in the dark as she sees the lights

THE TRUTH IN THE DARK

from the club at the far end of the alley and pushes on. It would be a shame to lose a prey due to rotten shrimp.

Covered from neck to toe by a long black coat, black T-shirt, slacks, and gloves, his pale face seems to float in the shadows. His features, mostly obscured by the collar of his coat and the brim of an old-fashioned fedora, display a preternatural calm. Beneath the hat, his blackened hair slicks back from the slight widow's peak at the center of his boyish face. Had anyone been able to see him clearly, his youthful features place him between late teens and early thirties. Damien is definitely older than he appears.

*

It is not even ten p.m., and the Prey is on her way to a nearby club that caters to the local wannabes and pretenders.

Damien himself visited this particular establishment just last weekend, slicing through the dancing throng the way a shark circles through a school of cod. He noted the number of unescorted females among the prey, how early they arrived, and what time they departed. The female prey dressed as harlots, showing not only ankle but knee and thighs nearly to their privates. The males, while more conservatively dressed, wore as much makeup, or even more, than their inappropriately dressed counterparts. All of the posers were fair-skinned, ruby-lipped, garbed in black, with nails polished deep obsidian. Piercings and tattoos, displayed proudly, were more common than watches.

While lacking in body art, Damien, too, wore black exclusively, not to be trendy or Goth, but to better stalk the night, in what he considers his personal game preserve. He glided through the crowd, as untouched by the bone-shaking thump of the bass subwoofers, as he was unseen by the clientele. When Damien found a darkened corner from which to observe, he paused his shark-like drifting. He occasionally sipped from a glass of wine. Stronger spirits burn his throat and wither his control, unleashing a more unpleasant side to his personality. Even if someone noticed him, what would they actually see? One more black-clad, faceless drone among a sea of white-faced, eye-lined imposters. Damien estimated many of the dancers were of college age.

He was all but invisible. The mere thought of any comparison to prey irritated him more than the strobing lights and the pulsing beat ever could. Looking around, he mused at how many of these self-deluded cattle consider themselves dangerous or even predators. He watched, and he hungered.

*

Tonight's Prey looks as healthy as she does haughty. Her bare arms are free of any visible needle marks. He will not risk contamination. Her hair conveys a healthy sheen. While not slender, she will never be considered obese. She is perfect for his needs.

He selected her specifically in advance, knowing this is one of the few shortcuts from the free public parking to the club. Besides the minimal lighting, he chose this particular pathway to the night spot to avoid traffic light cameras or ATM video cameras. Damien isn't terribly concerned about himself appearing on videotape, but it wouldn't do for his Prey to disappear on video.

To further confound the authorities, he never hunts in the same town where he rests during the day. This hunting ground is distant enough to divert suspicion and large enough to host a number of the clubs he uses as bait. Besides, in a city this size, no one will concern themselves over a few missing prey amongst a population of hundreds of thousands.

*

Distance becomes more critical as The Need wracking Damien grips him more often than it did in his younger years. When he Became, just before leaving university, what seems an eternity ago, he needed to feed but every few months. Now, The Need has grown, threatening to consume him, drive him mad if he does not satisfy it. Through experimentation, he learned to preserve and stock refrigerated supplies, but even they dwindle faster than in years past.

He thinks back to the days when he first Became the creature he is now. His father couldn't understand the transformation in his son and sent him to numerous doctors and sanatoriums. None of them had been able to *cure* him of his *affliction*.

Damien refuses the pollution of television or a cellular phone in his abode, but he does partake in the riches of the Internet. Using a laptop to avail himself of a wi-fi signal near his lair, Damien keeps current on the latest techniques in modern criminology. Well aware fingerprinting has been used since the mid-1800s, gloves are mandatory. After all these years, the authorities may have his prints on file, but he learned long ago to never underestimate an opponent. Even a being such as himself must learn to adapt over time in order to elude his pursuers.

His online research includes news. The authorities discovered the bodies of several women in the region. Each cadaver displayed discolored neck wounds, suction so intense no human mouth could produce it. Puncture wounds located on the throat, the exact same distance and size every time. The media dubs them "The Dracula Killings."

*

Damien fades deeper into the shadows as his Prey passes by, unaware of his presence. He reaches out to silently render her unconscious. She struggles for a moment, and he lowers her tenderly to the rough pavement of the alley. His senses drink in the aroma of her shampoo, her perfume, her soap. He looks down on her smooth face and for a moment contemplates what it would be like to take a mate, to allow someone to truly see him, in all his dark glory. Would a beauty with skin like this ever forsake the sun? No. A mortal woman could never acknowledge the reality of his existence, let alone accept his appetites. Even if they could, sooner or later, they will age and die, or he will need to make them prey. He looks away from her face, his eyes welling with unspoken fury at the inequity of his fate.

He must carry her to his vehicle where he will transport her to his lair. Once there, he will exsanguinate her and drink his fill. The old, white van is as modest as it is unassuming. No one would give it a second glance. Even though he inherited his family's fortune, he needs to make it last for what he imagines will be a very long lifetime. A predator such as he should never have to sully himself with manual labor, so he lives as frugal a lifestyle as possible. As unmemorable as the van may be, Damien takes the precaution of cross-swapping the license plates with several white vans whose registration stickers indicate they will not renew for months. Long before the rightful owners notice the switched tags, he will swap them out several times more.

He reaches to pick up his Prey.

*

Damien's face smashes into the brick of the alley wall like a speeding car. An iron-hard hand holds him by the back of the neck, lifting him off his feet, scraping his face along the rough wall. The spent hypodermic syringe and fedora fall to the ground.

"Do you know how much trouble you are causing, boy?" a deep voice rumbles from behind him. Damien's only thoughts are the indescribable pain in his face and neck. With his face pressed sideways into the wall, he is unable to see the figure behind him.

"You have no idea what you are playing. I have been watching you. If even *that* comes to light, it will draw more attention my way than I care for. I have spent decades crafting this persona, and frankly, I have no wish to change at this point. I am quite comfortable now. The thought of uprooting my life because some petulant youth feels the need to cosplay irritates me. You are not going to enjoy seeing me 'irritated.'"

Through the pain, and still pinned to the wall, Damien kicks backward, like a child in a temper tantrum. His kicks land solidly against his attacker's shins. Too solidly. There is no effect. The iron grip around the back of his neck doesn't waiver. The pressure holding him to the wall is machine-like in its power. No human could so effortlessly pin a full-sized adult off the ground with one hand like this.

"Even if no one discovers my personal interest, you are drawing too much attention to the truth. 'The Dracula Killings'? Could you be more obtuse? The only aspect of this whole episode that vexes me more than having to locate and deal with you is the fact a self-deluded, little brat such as yourself considers themselves a predator. You wouldn't know a predator if one bit you, which, unfortunately, I am not going to do."

Even through the pain and pressure, Damien could not withhold his shock. "You're going to let me live?"

"Do not be ridiculous. Even had you not drawn so much attention so closely to the truth, I could not possibly suffer an insult such as this charade."

Effortlessly, his attacker spins him around and slams his back into the wall, knocking the breath from his lungs. Shocked and gasping, Damien looks down in time to see a ghostly white hand stab him multiple times in the chest with a small knife. Unbearable pain rips through his frame as he drops to the ground like an empty sack. The last thing he sees is the dark form planting the knife in the Prey's hand and retrieving a can of pepper spray from her small purse.

"A shame to waste all of this warm blood really, but finding your drained corpses would fuel the media fires and incite the police all that much more. As worthless as you were in life, your death will, at least, provide a nice misdirection. As you fade away, even a pretender such as yourself can appreciate that truth."

*

What Lies in the Dark

Death is waiting on them. Detectives Grapewin and Esteban smile at each other as they approach the crime scene. Dr. Death is not only the best in the field but a perfectionist. It is a common perception among the homicide investigators, Grapewin and Esteban are his favorites.

His real name, of course, is not Dr. Death, but Dr. Samuel Chefliu, senior medical examiner and CSU lead. He has been a medical examiner in Mecklenburg County for so long no one else even remembers his predecessor. His appearance on a scene means someone has passed beyond the mortal coil by means other than accidental. Dr. Death does not *do* accidents. His lackeys handle those. Chefliu may not be the actual personification of murder, but he is at least its personal assistant. The man knows more about inflicting death on a human body than anyone alive. A reputation Chefliu does not discourage from others perpetuating. It tends to keep subordinates quietly in line.

*

The crime scene officer logs the detectives in and hands them blue rubber gloves and booties. An anonymous call came in at 11:23 p.m. saying someone is struggling in the alley. Uniformed officers arrive at 11:45 to investigate and find two dead bodies.

*

"Yo, Senior Muerte, the tan looks good on you. I take it the Bahamas was a fun trip?" Esteban asked. Dr. Death has taken his first vacation in years.

"That's *Muerte del Médico* to you, Esteban. And I can honestly say I find my new coloration interesting. I haven't sported a tan in a very long time. I think it suits me. My time off was both rewarding and relaxing. Much of the pressure I felt prior to my sabbatical seems eased. Speaking of which, may we begin?"

"No blue gloves, Doc?" Grapewin asks.

Without looking at his white latex covered hands, Chefliu replies, "No. Sometimes, I prefer the old ways. The modern blue ones, I find unnatural."

"Hey, who doesn't like Smurf hands?" Esteban quips.

"Doc, would you do the honors?" Grapewin, ignoring Esteban and passing Chefliu the hand scanner.

Dr. Death himself had lobbied tirelessly with the procedural boards to ensure detectives not touch dead bodies at any crime scenes. It isn't that he doesn't trust detectives, but wants to ensure the integrity of the chain of evidence. The fewer the number of hands touching the body, the less chance of a jury's perception of mishandling, and a higher conviction rate. One of many procedural and technical changes Dr. Death had made over the years to increase the city's homicide closure rate.

He found funding, donations, and corporate sponsors to provide the homicide divisions with portable hand scanners which scan someone's fingerprints in the field, link data to VICAP and numerous other police and federal databases, and in just moments, have the identity and background of the scanned individuals. The data ports instantly to a laptop, or in this case, an iPad, carried by the investigating team.

"The young lady's name was Cynthia Durban. No wants or warrants. Student at UNCC. Led a relatively clean life. Despite her goth appearance, a good girl. Pretty rare these days," Esteban summarizes.

"Ah. Here we go. It looks as if our other DB, Mr. Damien Johnson, was a person of interest for stalking while in college. The vic, Lisa Bannister, reported it and the detectives in charge brought him in for questioning. There are hints in the report about the possibility of other stalking victims, but no one came forward. Seems the problem went away when Daddy Johnson's checkbook showed up." Esteban's scanning through the electronic report.

"Many a youth's troubles can be traced directly to overindulgent parents." Doc Chefliu comments.

"You sound like you have some firsthand knowledge, Doc?" Grapewin asks.

"Yes, I guess you could say I come from a family of some means and my parents not only indulged my excesses but encouraged them. Many a time, my family's social position enabled my somewhat petulant early life. It took me years to realize I need to live *in* this world and not above it. From that moment, I realized I needed to contribute to society, not be a drain on it. What about you, Detective Grapewin, is your badge recompense for a misspent youth?"

"Just the opposite. Kansas farm boy goes military to see the world. A hitch at Fort Bragg and a few college courses later and I am serving and protecting here in Charlotte. A few years from now, I'm eligible for my 'twenty and out.' Pretty boring stuff. Christ. I think I just depressed myself."

"Good, because you depress the rest of us all the time," his junior partner, Esteban, jibes.

*

Grapewin watches as his younger partner wanders off to see what he can find. Jorge (pronounced "George") Esteban is perhaps one of the ugliest people Grapewin has ever met. A gap in his front teeth does not complement the pushed-in face. Esteban explains it as one too many fist fights in his youth. Grapewin met the Latino's mother and knows genetics is at play. Squat and muscular, Esteban is a just a few years from getting a paunch that will slow him down. One too many churros. Esteban spent most of his youth denying his Hispanic roots, but flipped his position in the past decade, and has become a zealot about embracing his heritage. Despite his sometimes inappropriate humor, Grapewin considers Esteban one of the finest investigative minds in town.

*

"What's your take on this, Doc?" Grapewin asks, knowing damn well Dr. Death would never offer an incorrect initial assessment. It would tarnish his reputation.

After some thought, Chefliu stands and gestures to the bodies.

"Mind you, this assessment is at first glance, and when we get them to the lab, we might come up with completely different findings." As if. "It looks to be much as it appears. Ms. Durban was injected with a syringe containing an unknown chemical agent. You can see the puncture mark here on her neck. The syringe lays there. Trace evidence in the ampule will tell us exactly what to look for in her tox screen.

"Mr. Johnson received an ample dose of pepper spray, as evidenced by the irritation and redness around his eyes and face, and, more obviously, the empty can of spray here. Stabbed several times to the torso with the knife laying there, Mr. Johnson's COD, obviously, is the numerous puncture wounds to his chest. We will compare the stab wounds with the blade, but there is no doubt in my mind, that is the weapon that killed Mr. Johnson. Her cause of death will likely be the injected chemical, the ensuing struggle, or both. Time of death is not really an issue. They were still fresh when we arrived on the scene. The evidence in this scene is so blatant it is nearly a waste of my time."

"So, your take is Johnson attacks her with a syringe to kill or snatch her, she fights him off with pepper spray and a knife, and they both end up cold?" Grapewin asks.

"Not at all what I said," Dr. Chefliu says coolly. "I merely present facts, it is your job to make deductions from the evidence."

*

"Esteban, what have you got?" Grapewin asks.

"Not much. I started the uni's canvassing the neighborhood, talking to everyone, looking for anything out of the usual. We are interviewing people at the club down the alley. Standard stuff. What about you?"

Grapewin summarized Chefliu's initial thoughts.

"There are a couple of pieces of physical evidence that fit his theory. Someone broke that light bulb recently. You can tell by the size of the fragments. If it had been broken a while back, the pieces would be trampled smaller. Johnson probably did it to make the alley darker," Grapewin says.

"Probably didn't want anyone to see him in that dumbass hat. I mean, who wears hats at all these days, let alone something right out of a Bogart movie?"

Grapewin thinks about the fedora. "Somebody who's trying to avoid having his picture taken by a traffic or security cam. The brim covers more than a baseball cap, and with a coat collar up, almost no part of your head, hair, or face would be visible. It's conspicuous, but all you have to do is throw it in the nearest trash container, and any witnesses would only remember the old-fashioned hat. You could walk right past them," Grapewin says. "But you're right. Wearing a hat like that says something about the wearer. Like they identified with a time long past. Doc seems to think this is an open and shut, so I doubt we'll need to get a profiler in on this, but an old fedora definitely speaks volumes about Johnson. I just don't what it's saying."

"It's saying he don't own a mirror," Esteban jokes.

*

The M.E.'s team set up lights, and the alley is brighter than noon. Dr. Death continues to preside over the area. He allows no one to collect evidence but himself to preserve the sanctity of the crime scene. Most of the cops think of him as a control freak, but none could argue his results. His case files and chains of evidence are impeccable and inarguable in court. As frustrated as the District

Attorney's office may be at not getting him to appear in court, they are placated with the accuracy and thoroughness of his evidentiary data. Many a defense attorney moans when they see his name on the evidence reports.

As ironclad as his conclusions are, the good doctor never appears in court himself. He sends one of his assistant medical examiners to present his findings. "The data speaks for itself. I have no wish to be drawn into the spectacle or garishness of a trial. My time is better spent otherwise."

To ensure he is not available for trial, the head of the forensics department purposely schedules himself on the night shift. His assistants look at this policy with mixed feelings. They love they do not have to work nights, but heaven help you if you do not perform well in court, presenting his data with anything less than the reverence it deserves. Several years ago, after a case was lost due to the forensic testimony, one assistant M.E. resigned rather than face the wrath of Dr. Chefliu. He currently works as a morgue attendant at a county hospital. In another state.

*

"While you were chowing down on churros with our brothers in uniform, I found a business address for young Mr. Johnson's father and an insomniac judge to give us a warrant," Grapewin tells his partner. "Let's roll. We will take a look around first and then call in CSU to really rumble the place. Grab the video camera so we can document first entry."

"Is the churro comment a racist thing? If it's a racist thing, I need to go talk to my amigos down in HR," Esteban said.

"Do you, or do you not, like churros?"

"You don't see me busting on you about donuts, do you?"

"I like donuts," Grapewin replies. "Got nothing to do with being white. Donuts are a cop thing, and if you ever become a real cop, you will figure that out. So, churros?"

"Yeah. They were awesome, but those uni's are pigs, man. I brought a whole bag from this place I know, and they ate nearly all of them."

"So besides epicurean reviews, did our amigos in uniform have anything to add to the actual case?" Grapewin asks.

"They interviewed the kids all night from the club down the alley and no one, including the doormen, remembered ever seeing our boy. In their defense, though, hundreds of people pass through that door each night. Unless he was wearing that stupid hat, he would fit right in. All pasty white faces and black clothes. It's like Disco of the Living Dead."

*

The car pulls to a stop in front of an abandoned medical supply warehouse.

"J and J Medical Wholesalers. That's the company that registered the van according to the VIN numbers," Esteban says.

Grapewin looks across the seat at his partner. "What van?"

"Did I not mention the van?"

"No, dumbass, you were busy casting aspersions about my diversity sensitivity."

"I wasn't casting you in any part—" Esteban begins.

"WHAT VAN?" Grapewin likes his partner, but Esteban's about a half step away from Grapewin's last nerve.

"The uni's found an old white, POS Econoline Ford not too far from the scene. Stolen plates, but when they ran the VIN, it came up with a registration to J and J Medical Wholesalers," Esteban explains. "Damien's dear old dad owned J and J Medical Wholesalers. He kicked the bucket under some highly questionable circumstances. Fedora Boy inherited and liquidated everything but the van and the warehouse."

"Do you think you might want to lead with that the next time instead of dead-end interviews?"

"We called in one of Dr. Death's boys, Jaidan, I think was the one, to process the van. The tall one." Grapewin's glare pushes Esteban to move it along. "Anyway, no prints inside, but some zip ties, a ball gag, and a few movers' blankets. Practically a Do-It-Yourself Snatch Kit. We're certain this was what Fedora Boy was planning on transporting the vic in. Jaidan found a few hairs that could be possible matches to some of the vics in the Dracula Killer thing."

"So, you're just now getting around to telling me about the possible connection and address to our deceased suspect and some statewide serial killings?" Grapewin asks incredulously.

"You know, Grape, you get a little cranky when you don't get a morning donut."

*

Grapewin gets out of the unmarked car, pops the trunk and removes a formidable pair of bolt cutters.

"You keep the Jolly Green Giant's nail clippers in your trunk?" Esteban asks.

"Doesn't everyone?"

After cutting the padlock from the garage style door and rolling it up, the two detectives step inside, pulling on blue latex gloves.

Grapewin looks at the rolling garage door. "I bet you could probably drive an old Ford Econoline right in here to unload a body unseen," he says, glaring at his partner.

Esteban clicks the light switch. It takes a moment for the fluorescents to flicker on as if rarely used. "No windows. No natural light. Bad Fang-Shui."

"It's pronounced 'fungshway.' But you're not wrong. Feng-shui is about architectural goodness, and goodness has nothing to do with this place," Grapewin says, motioning to a slightly inverted autopsy table in the middle of the room, a strange vacuum-like device near the table, and an old refrigerator off to the side. "Smells like a butcher shop in here. Keep videoing this stuff."

"Yeah, no shit. This had to be his *kill room*. Esteban aims the small video camera at a corrugated plastic hose connected to a modified vacuum pump. The hose ended with a rubber seal and two sharp syringe-like needles in the middle. "A thing like this, combined with a tilted autopsy table, might be able to suck all the blood out of a body pretty quickly."

"Esteban, you ever see an autopsy table with restraints on it before?" Grapewin asks.

*

The CSU team catalogs and bags everything. Grapewin and Esteban find six pints of blood plasma in the refrigerator and a variety of injectable narcotics. Most of which are what you might inject into someone to render them unconscious but leave the system quickly, dissipating and undetectable. A laptop rests on the workbench. By the time they get to the back of the warehouse, Grapewin is not even surprised to find the polished mahogany coffin. He is, however, a little shocked at the map over the workbench.

"How stupid and cliché was this guy? It looks like he has red push pins in the map for where he abducted those girls and blue ones for where he dumped the bodies. If he were alive, we wouldn't even need a confession," Esteban says.

Grapewin studies the map. "Uh, Jorge, there are more pins than we have victims. How many girls did this asshole kill? We need to get uniforms to the locations of those extra blue pins and see if there are bodies there."

"Hey, I'm right about another thing," Esteban says, looking around. "No mirrors."

*

Grapewin and Esteban arrive at the M.E.'s office that evening a little ahead of schedule. They step into Dr. Chefliu's private office, just as he closes a desk drawer.

"Ah, gentlemen, prompt as usual. Excellent. I, and my team, processed the evidence collected so far, most expeditiously. I think we have a few findings which may interest you," Dr. Chefliu says.

"Well, Doc, we'll take whatever you've got, but so far, this is just like you said, a slam dunk," Esteban replies, sitting on the only stool in the room, while Grapewin leans on the edge of the desk.

"I seriously doubt I have ever used the expression 'slam dunk' in my entire existence, Detective Esteban. That being said, we did uncover some facts supporting my initial assumptions. Traces in the syringe and Ms. Durban's blood are a confirmed narcotic. If administered in the right dose, it would have rendered her unconscious, or at least very malleable. The full tox screen will be forthcoming, but since we had the syringe, the lab was able to test quickly for a specific substance. The syringe itself bears no prints whatsoever. Mr. Johnson was wearing gloves, so the total lack of prints further implicates him, even if indirectly. Ms. Durban's prints are the only ones on the pepper spray and knife.

"Jaidan positively matched hair, fibers, even paint particulates from the van, to a number of unsolved murders. Combined with the deluge of evidence found at the warehouse and it appears as if you may have closed what the press has so ridiculously dubbed *The Dracula Killings*," Chefliu states, standing somewhat stooped near the darkened window, his white hair in stark contrast to his newly tanned face.

"Speaking of which," he continues with his lecture, "even with the other bodies' decapitated state, we were able to match the marks on their throats with the suction device you found.

"Mr. Johnson used his device to exsanguinate them, harvesting the blood you found in the refrigerator. We also matched that to the other victims. Either as anticipating an insanity defense or part of a genuine psychosis, he decapitated them and drove a wooden stake into their remains. There was nothing supernatural about him. Just a self-deluded young man."

"Pretty much wraps it up as far as we're concerned. Email us your report when you have it finalized, Doc," Grapewin says as he stands. "I think we are gonna tie a bow on it and toss it in the closed pile. The chief will make a statement to the press about how CMPD wrapped up The Dracula Killings through tireless police work, when it was really some college girl with a can of pepper spray and a folding knife. Either way, we're on to the next one."

"Contact my office if you have any questions about the data," Chefliu says, opening the door for the detectives. "We live to serve."

"Doc, if I didn't know better, I would say that was almost sarcasm," Esteban says.

"Detective Esteban, sarcasm is commonly hostility disguised as humor. I believe the word you were looking for is irony."

*

Chefliu stands at the door in thought for a few seconds after the detectives leave. Unconsciously, his posture straightens to his full height. Sitting at the desk, he opens the desk drawer, pulling out a business card and a burner phone.

"All Night Spray Tans? I want to confirm you will be open later this evening and make an appointment if so. Name? Make the appointment under Grapewin. Nine-thirty should be fine. Thank you, I will see you then."

Chefliu glances at the institutional clock on the wall. He puts the business card and phone back in the drawer, behind a plastic box of colorful stick pins. Nine-thirty will give him just enough time to make the drive. There will be plenty of time when he gets back to type his report and extract his dinner.

All will be as it should, as long as he moves the two new body bags down to the incinerator before daylight.

***

Alabama Shaman

by Nathan Batchelor

**U.S.: The South rises again ... as golems
in this spellbinding urban fantasy.**

There were days when Paul wished he had finished his Animancy training. Like the morning after the tornadoes, when he was sitting on the stump of the oak he had cut down an hour before. His saw jutted out of the felled timber, the blade poking out between the caved-in cut like a cigarette hanging out of a banjo-picker's lips. The saw had died in a fart of powdery smoke, mewing a pitiful death rattle, and as soon as Paul had stepped away, the cut had bowed in on itself, impinging the saw in a death grip of soaked wood.

He had not quit his training because he was afraid of being found out. People in this part of Alabama took magic for gospel. They already believed in the healing power of prayer and demon possession, and you could find one of those Indian blessing air fresheners hanging in just about every car parked outside the church on Sunday. No one had ever suspected that Paul's dog, Mort, was approaching cat territory with the number of times he had been brought back from near death. When his neighbors would say, "That's the toughest damn dog I've ever seen," Paul covered up by saying, "The Lord sure has blessed me."

"Looks like the engine burned out," Bob Lawrence called from behind Paul. "I've got some oil out in the shed, if you think the saw needs some."

Bob was standing on the porch of his trailer, in a wife beater and pink bunny slippers. From time to time he looked out at the flooded yard, like he wanted to walk out to help the younger man, but when he neared the porch steps, his nose would crinkle up as if the water were sewage instead of rain and river runoff.

"Hell, Bobby, why don't you go get it for him?" Bob's wife croaked from inside the house.

"You want me to throw out my back again? What'd the doctor say?" Bob yelled back.

"Then bring me a damn cigarette," she said.

"I don't think oil will help. What I could really use is another pair of hands," Paul said.

Bob ran his fingers through his greased hair and muttered a curse, before shuffling into the house. Paul had not expected any help from the retired roofer. But now he was alone, and he *could* conjure something up to help him.

He did not fear the work it took to be a shaman. In his training, he had passed entire days sitting Indian style on his porch, in a state of meditative transcendence, hearing the lullabies of the grass, the elegies sung by the soil. He had read tomes in secret languages, in words that slid up and down the dried leaves and stone tablets.

It was fear that pushed him away from being a shaman, the fear of being alone, of turning his back on the love that he'd always wanted. To be a shaman was to be alone in the world. To be a shaman was to renounce all human contact except the ethereal day-to-day interaction with those who needed him most.

His phone rattled. The boss was calling. She wanted him to come in and put bird spikes on the letters of Munchion's Grocery, or clean the soot out of the boiler room, something inane that she could not get anyone else to do the day after the worst tornadoes the county had ever seen came blazing into town. Paul let the phone rattle off the tree stump. He heard the splash when it fell into the water. Diane would have to wait.

He needed to be quick with his conjuration. These days you never know who is filming. Everyone is a director and photographer. A couple of years ago, Paul saw a grainy video of himself leading a band of grass golems down the alley between Walcott's Pharmacy and the Grab-N-Grub. The video had gone viral, uploaded by a user calling himself Groot69, which seemed appropriate based on how Paul's grass golems spent their waking and dying moments. Paul tracked down Groot69 easily. Toilet golems did the trick, smearing Paul's message on the boy's bedroom wall in tasteful blacks and browns. Groot69 and the video disappeared.

Bob was pouring the rest of his whiskey and Coke down the drain when he heard the saw revving. In disbelief, he watched the spray of chips shower Paul as the saw cut through the wood like warm butter.

"Don't guess he needed that oil after all," Judy said, floating across the kitchen in curlers and bunny slippers that matched her husband's.

"Don't guess he did,' Bob said.

They could not see the mud man perched on what remained of the saw, packing his mouth like a ravenous chipmunk, the timber turning to pulp in his wood-chipper intestines, before spraying out the back end of the mud man in a shower of chips that fell on Paul in a brown cloud of sawdust, undigested bark, and the lining of the mud man's colon. More than any other moment in his life, Paul did not want this one to end up on the internet.

*

Wolf Creek was the kind of place you go your whole life without knowing about, or if you are born there, you go your whole life without knowing about the rest of the world. It was a little forest town a hundred miles from any interstate, whose claim to fame was a civil war statue erected in the town's square and being one of the ten or so towns nearly wiped off the map by last night's tornadoes.

Roberto twirled his sucker, popping it against his teeth as he watched Paul spear the rotten meat.

"Amber can do things with her tongue, man. Spins it around just right," Roberto said.

Paul let the pitchfork topple to the rain-splattered macadam, his arms throbbing with fatigue. After ten minutes, he was already tired of Roberto. Three hundred pounds of rotting hamburger, graying steaks, and soured flanks of salmon lay hot and steaming beneath the glass of Munchion's meat department. Paul had loaded a wheelbarrow to the brim and pushed it down the back ramp of the store. Now they were pitching meat chunks like hay onto the back of a truck Diane had paid for this morning.

"I don't care about your one-night stands. Bring me that shovel if you aren't going to use it," Paul said.

"How come you don't use 'ain't?' Everyone around here says it, but you. Not into man talk either." Roberto furrowed his brow, as if Paul's use of language angered him.

Paul could tell him about the two semesters he spent studying English at the community college. Roberto would laugh at that career choice. Or there was the preschool years he had spent in Michigan, and though the forests of the north were not that much different than those in the south, he would be labeled a Yankee for the rest of the summer, before Roberto, like the other janitorial assistants before him, was swallowed up by the back-beating work at the sawmill, or by meth, where country boys turn nowadays when their dreams dry up.

But those were not the reasons Paul spoke like he did. It was all from his training with the shaman Gomda, whose laugh Paul could hear on the wind, whose smell sweat from the grass.

Diane had insisted on bringing in Roberto today. He was fresh and square-jawed, with that youthful swagger that betrays its own charm. He was dumb too, Paul thought, another kid chewed up and spit out by Wolf Creek High, one of the rural Alabama schools that cannibalizes its own, neutered of any drive other than the manifest destiny of the American dream. Roberto was only in the way. If Paul were alone, he would raise golems from the forest that bordered the back of Munchion's, and be at home before lunch.

Paul had barely put a dent into the mass of rotting meat when Diane appeared at the back dock, arms crossed, legs akimbo, a dastardly red dress hugging her hips, framed by the blinding sterile lights of the storage room.

"Morning, boss," Roberto said.

He already had the pitchfork in his hands, skewering meat, putting on a show for Diane. Perhaps he was smarter than he looked.

"Morning, Roberto. Paul," Diane's eyes narrowed at him, "heard you were out this morning, playing good Samaritan."

"Just cutting up some logs for people who needed it."

"I called you four hours ago. You came in at half past ten. By my count, that's three hours you owe me."

Like so many times before, Paul bit his tongue. He had known her his whole life. He could still remember chasing her around the playground, her pigtails bobbing, a gap-toothed smile teasing him, leading him on. Her ruthlessness waxed and waned over time, seemingly sharpest when his patience wore thinnest. She had a kind of power over him, and she knew it, a power than ran deeper than the fact that she was the boss. She knew he loved her, that he'd loved her from the first time they'd held hands on a pontoon boat in the third grade.

"I was busy. I'm sorry," Paul said.

"I'm going to run out later if the weather lets up. There is supposed to be a break before it gets bad again," she said. "I need all this to be done by the time I get back."

Things were turning in the right direction. If Diane left, all he needed to do was find some way to get rid of Roberto, then he could get things done.

"When are you leaving?" Paul tried to hide his excitement.

Before she could answer, a truck came fishtailing across the parking lot. It bounced through puddles, and dodged parking curbs on the left and right. Paul had once allowed a sand golem with brain damage to drive his S-10 pickup loaded with wood, nails, and drywall. That did not go well. The man driving the truck seemed only a little more competent than that poor golem.

The man who stepped out of the truck was ancient, no taller than five feet. The sleeves of his blue corduroy jacket hung over his hands, and the bottoms of his pants rose up like blue lily pads in the ankle-deep puddles. On his sagging and melancholic face, wide-eyed fear or panic exploded from his eyes. Paul immediately thought of Gomda during his last days, ravaged by a brain-eating disease that neither magic nor medicine could fix, who would get lost in his own garden at midnight, rifle pointed at his cabbages, spraying Vietnam obscenities at ghosts no one else could see.

"Are you okay, sir?" Paul asked.

"God, my girls, someone's got to help my girls." The man was shaking with fear.

Another disappearance? Paul wondered. The local paper had run an article about the string of disappearances plaguing Sipsy County. Just a few months ago, Stacy Brown, one of the cashiers at Munchion's, had just stopped coming into work. After two weeks, she was declared missing. Paul and Diane both missed the lady's smile, the smell of the watermelon bubble gum she'd hand out to other employees, the comical blue mascara she wore.

Paul thought he knew what happened to those who disappeared. They were people who saw the town as a tomb, a place where dreams die, and they were flying away. They were not heard from again because they did not want to be.

"What happened?" Paul asked.

Unsurprisingly, Diane had disappeared at the first sign of trouble. Roberto leaned against the building, his phone out, recording.

"The house is gone. They're buried in the rubble. God help them," the old man said.

"Roberto, call 911," Paul said

"No. No. Man. I'm getting this on camera. Look at this old cooter," Roberto said.

"Call the damn number," Paul hissed.

"It won't do no good. I've done tried. Said there are more tornadoes on the way. Said they wouldn't come out in this weather," the old man said.

The sky did have an eerie calm to it. Ripe for more tornadoes.

It was not surprising to hear the county turn the needy away. It was unlike the big cities where there were records of records, eyes always prying, a sea of bureaucracy keeping everything afloat. Here in the back country the sea was an abyss into which anything could disappear, 911 calls with the drop of a word, criminal records with the flick of a lighter. The Sipsy County elected officials were as crooked as this old man's fingers.

"I'll have Diane give them a call. She knows people," Paul said. "She can pull strings no one else in town can."

"Phones are out," Diane said, strolling up in jeans and a t-shirt. "Roberto, you'll have to finish alone."

"No, ma'am. I can't do this by myself."

"We'll be back in an hour. If the siren goes off, go to the shelter," Diane said.

"We?" Paul said.

"You think I'm heartless? If there are girls to be saved, I want to be there for the photos. I want my name beside yours in the paper," Diane said.

"Oh, thank you. God bless you both," the old man said.

Paul watched Roberto pick up a salmon flank, oozing a frothy brown liquid.

"Put on some gloves for God's sake. You'll catch something," Paul said.

The three of them packed into the truck like sardines, and headed down the flooded roads toward the forest.

*

"Write this down," Gomda said, taking the Capri Sun from his Mick's tray. He slurped the entire drink down in one gulp. "The first rule is—hmm. Bring me another one of those, Mick. Quite tasty. The first rule is never to use magic on the deceased. Our magic comes from love, from life, not from death."

The thing Gomda called Mick shuffled away, its hunkered back bobbing with its loud, rustling steps. The boy thought it looked like a scarecrow without clothes on.

"Why?" the boy asked. "I want to tell Di about it."

Gomda limped beneath the trellis, from one vine to another, grabbing and inspecting them, nodding, sometimes mumbling to himself. Occasionally, he snipped a grape, held it up to the roasting sun like a jeweler would a diamond, before throwing it into the basket the boy carried. He did the same with rocks, handfuls of grass. He picked up some poop of a neighboring dog, rubbed it in his hands, and threw it in the basket.

Mick raised his tray, and Gomda took another Capri Sun, downed it, and threw the carton back to the golem. "Necromancy brings bad things into the world. It's used for power, for destruction. Do you want to hurt things or help them?"

"Help them," the boy said dutifully.

"Good. Write that down too."

The boy had already filled two notebooks with things Gomda had said. He was beginning to think the man was crazy, and the only reason he stayed anymore was to find out what the little thing Gomda called Mick actually was. The boy had helped Gomda trim the hedges and water his plants. He walked from room to room at the hospital with Gomda, passing out blankets, watching Gomda play chess or poker with the sick and dying. The boy had dusted Gomda's strange living room, filled with clay figures and dreamcatchers, so many dreamcatchers that the boy believed Gomda must make and sell them.

"I can't tell her?"

"No, you can never tell her. Try asking better questions," Gomda said, bending over to watch a snail scoot along the inlaid brick.

Dishes clanged behind them. Mick was cleaning the patio table. "What is Mick?" the boy asked.

"What do you think he is?"

"He's not a robot. He moves too well. And he's not an animal, is he?"

"No, he's neither of those things. But he's closest to an animal. He lives and breathes. Isn't that right, Mick?"

Mick turned his grassy head toward Gomda and nodded. The faint impressions, where his eyes should be, seemed to show surprise or confusion, the grass and leaves curling and uncurling rapidly.

"Does he have a soul?" the boy asked.

"That's a whopper of a question." Gomda laughed. He clipped off grapes from the trellis. "What made you say that?"

"Grandma says dogs don't have souls and that they can't go to heaven. Mick seems nice, like my dog, Mort. I think they should both be able to go to heaven."

"Ah, I think so, too. But we'll have to talk about souls another time. Here, taste one of these grapes. Sweetest ones you've ever had, aren't they?"

The boy nodded. When the basket was full and the crickets began to chirp, Gomda covered it with an old shirt and put stones around it.

"Now you better go home. The sun's going down. We don't want your Grandma to worry."

"Can I come back tomorrow?"

"Yes, if you want to, Paul. Now we have all the ingredients for our project. We can get started soon."

Paul gave one long look at Mick and then dashed off through the fence, the gate flapping behind him. When he was gone, and Gomda and Mick were sitting on the porch listening to the sounds of the night, Gomda said, "Well, what am I going to tell him?"

Mick shrugged his leafy shoulders, too lost in the sounds of the insects to give such a question much thought.

*

"Take some grape rocks?" the old man asked.

"No, thanks," Paul said.

Diane shook her head.

"Good, more for me."

The river had rose and flooded some of the trailer parks near the woods, but the road was on high land and safe, as long as you did not veer into a ditch. They saw teenagers rowing in makeshift canoes, the water coming up past trailers' underpinnings, so that the park looked like some kind of seaside community. There were cars bobbing like inner tubes down the gullies, and trucks sunken hood-deep in the mud. More than once Paul thought the old man's truck was going to get swept up in the current and float away. As they came closer to the woods and the elevation rose, the water peeled back, revealing soggy, eroded soil.

"Who are your girls anyway?" Paul asked.

"Oh, they aren't my girls. I just watch out for them. The Carter twins."

Paul and Diane exchanged a nervous glance.

"Earl Carter's girls?" Paul asked.

"The one and only."

Earl Carter was the richest man in Sipsy County, or had been, depending on if you believed he was dead or not. The school, the school stadium, the hospital, and the town park all had his name plastered on the signs, deeds, and checks that paid for them.

Alone, he had kept the town alive after the trailer plants moved out, setting up a booming furniture business, made from logs cut and shipped right here in the forest, out to the stores where they were finished and packaged. Around the timber and furniture base, the town grew and flourished. The whole county of Sipsy, the whole town of Wolf Creek owed its existence to Earl Carter.

That made his disappearance all the more dramatic. He was on top of the world when Paul was a child. A picture of him shaking hands with President Clinton made the front page of the *North Alabama Dealer*. One summer, the town threw him a parade, the National Guard marching in step, the 4-H club leading their best dairy cattle down the main drag of town. Earl was a no-show. Paul remembered watching on that sweltering day, the float some of his high school friends had worked on rolling empty down the streets. In many people's mind, Earl's absence at the parade was the first hint of his demise.

"We always heard the girls were dead," Diane said. "We used to drive out on Halloween, and look at the house, or what was left of it."

Paul remembered such a night, riding in the backseat with Diane at sixteen, their hands intertwined in the darkness of the car, later the darkness of the night, staring up at the ruins still smoldering on the hill.

"Oh, things were blown out of proportion. The house burning was ... unfortunate." The old man threw back some grape rocks. "What doesn't kill you makes you stronger. Fine girls now. Sixteen now. About ready to fly the coop."

There had been a rumor that the girls had died in the fire, Paul thought. Or had he read it in the paper? *Earl Carter sets house on fire with children inside. No survivors.* The gossip had swarmed like hornets near a nest.

"He went insane."

"I heard the girls were deformed, demon babies."

"You know what they say in the bible, 'It is easier for a camel to pass through the eye of a needle, than a rich man get into heaven.'"

Perhaps the girls' deaths were only rumors of the hive, more honey to feed the hungry mouths of the town's residents. Their deaths were a third act to the tragedy of Earl, a man driven insane by ... what again? Paul didn't know, felt foolish for never asking the question that looked him in the eye on that rain-drenched road climbing forest hills, toward Earl's old house.

The old man had to crane his neck to see over the road. His sleeves hung like a monk's robe from his wrists.

This old man is simply crazy, Paul thought.

"His butter's slipped off his biscuit," Gomda would have said.

Though if the old man was crazy, where was he taking them?

*

The golem looked around, blinking nervously, its arms shaking. Chewing on grass he'd plucked on the hike out to the bluff, Gomda watched critically, eyes snapping back and forth from Paul to the boy's creation. Cyclones of eroded sand rock stung against Paul's closed eyes, against his young and smooth face. The golem took one step toward the edge of the canyon and was gone, bursting like a puffball into leaves and dust.

"I can't do it," Paul said. "I'm not book smart. You'll have to get someone else."

He tried to stand, and staggered back to the dust.

"You need to drink. You'll get heat stroke if you don't," Gomda said, tapping the cooler of lemonade that Paul had lugged up the mountain. For the first time, Paul noticed the flowers in Gomda's hand, oranges and yellows, stalks of lavender shooting up out of the bouquet.

The lemonade made Paul's mouth ache. He drank until his stomach swelled.

"We'll take a break. Then you can try again," Gomda said.

"I'm not trying again."

"You must. I picked you, no one else. You're the only one who can become the next shaman. We'll come back tomorrow. Maybe the sun won't be so fierce, and your focus will be better."

Paul was tired of the old man's game, tired of being told what he should do with his life. Gomda was hiding something from him. He was hiding the purpose of magic. Paul was a man now, twenty-one, with a good job at the lumber mill, a truck, and nearly enough saved up for a down payment on a house. He no longer had time for games.

He had wanted to learn when he was younger, when he had seen what Gomda could do. If he had only known the cost, he never would have come back to Gomda's house. A life of secrets, a life spent alone, except for the company of golems.

"I wanted to impress Diane. Not sign my life away to a madman who makes grass puppets. Why couldn't I tell her? If I could, things would be different. I could be with her."

Gomda turned away and headed down the hill. "You can never tell. This is a solitary path."

"You're a coward," Paul spat. "You can't live your life alone. It's not right."

"I have somewhere to be. You should come. I think you'll see something that will help you."

The bluff overlooked the whole of the forest. A fire tower in the distance. He could see the school where he had sat behind Diane and pulled her hair, the memory nothing but a speck of dust growing smaller and smaller, until another shaman pulled the dust out of the ground to animate a golem to mow the lawn or clean the hornet's nest out of his shed.

*

The tiny old man had burst into tears before the ruins had even come into view. He had taken his hands off the wheel, and grabbed his face like a man trying to claw his own eyes out, the truck drifting dangerously to a flooded ditch. Paul had grabbed the wheel and slammed on the brake. With the truck stopped inches from the rushing waters, Diane got out and ran around to the driver's seat, taking over for the tiny, bawling man, who cried on Paul's shoulder the rest of the way to the house.

The house had been decimated, the frame and foundation ravaged and strewn across the landscape, the walls reduced to rubble. There were umbrellas, dresses, tiny jumpers strung like haphazard Christmas decorations on pikes of torn wood, on pillars of busted concrete. There was no sign of life.

"I can't go. I can't look," the old man cried. "If those girls are dead, I would just as soon be dead."

Paul choked down fear, watching a teddy bear swirl in a puddle in the courtyard. If Paul were alone, golems would already be at work, digging furiously with hands like shovels.

Diane knew people at the top of the county hierarchy, powerful men who could and would come out to answer her beck and call. But the forest swallowed up cell phone signals like a starving beast. Her signal had dropped to nothing an hour ago, and if she were to drive out, perhaps no one, let alone her, would be able to make it back for days, leaving Paul alone in the middle of the forest with this strange old man.

When Paul asked her if she could drive out to get help, she stared at him as if he had slapped her.

"Then give me a hand with this. We'd best get to looking for them," Paul said.

They turned over drawers, and dug through endless kitchen utensils, wet insulation stringy like cotton candy, while the rain grew harder and colder and seemed to come up from the ground itself. As the adrenaline waned, the gears of reason waxed.

While Paul thought about golems and how best to get away from Diane and the old man, Diane wondered what they were looking for. There was no blood, no sign of the two girls leaving out the ruins. If these girls were smart at all, they would have heard the tornado sirens, and moved to safety. Perhaps there was a storm cellar or a safe place down the hill that they could have reached.

"Yes, of course. The entrance was in the kitchen," the old man said. He looked as if his prayers had been answered. He trounced around the muddy ground and pointed at an unremarkable pile of wooden planks and shards of marble. "About here."

They dug through spoons and knives, so many razor sharp blades. They slid the refrigerator across the floor, beneath it, untouched linoleum surrounded a splintery oak door. The wind fell calm and the rain let up.

"We may need this ourselves," Paul said, watching the sky.

The hinge croaked as he lifted the cellar door.

A gust of hot, rancid air burst from the cellar. Slimy concrete steps spiraled down, moss pulsing from the limestone walls. Paul felt Diane close to him, felt her body pushing against his. Then he was off his feet, barreling down into the darkness. He heard the crack of his knee against the steps, felt the concrete scrape against his cheeks and arms, felt the pain blazing through his blood and bones. He watched the tiny, old man slam the door, covering the world in darkness.

He had seen that smile and those teeth before, in a different place, in a different time. It made his blood run cold.

*

Diane could tell by the echo of her breath that the room was bigger than the standard storm cellar. The echo was too metallic for the room to be filled with shelves of wine or jelly. The air was humid and warm and the smell of mildew hung in the air.

Her arm did not hurt, but she knew something was wrong when she put weight on it. It bent where there wasn't a joint. She was running on numbing adrenaline and pain would come soon, blinding pain like twisting knives.

Keeping her back to the wall, she stepped gingerly farther into the darkness. She whispered Paul's name, fearful that the tiny man could hear her from above. But that was outlandish, wasn't it? Just as outlandish as the kick the old man had delivered to her back, and that look on his face before he slammed the door shut. A smile that made her heart skip a beat.

She tried not to think about what he wanted. The best case scenario was a mental break, or a bout of Alzheimer's. The worst case ... what about those missing people? She needed to find Paul quickly.

There was a skittering somewhere in the darkness. Rats probably. Or big bugs that liked cold, dark places. She hated bugs, would rather deal with snakes or rats than bugs. Come to think of it, that was what the old man's smile reminded her of, some kind of bipedal centipede, fangs dripping with poison, waiting for a meal. She shivered. Then a hand palmed her mouth and drew her backwards toward the door.

*

The cemetery was on a hill, not far from the house where Paul had spent his earliest days, kicking daisies, leaping into the role of an action hero, swatting whatever unlucky dragons were perched on flowers or fluttering about the yard. Gomda pulled his car over next to a ditch at the base of the hill. He said that they should walk from here.

"Why don't we go to the parking lot?" Paul scratched his head.

"The climb is a sign of respect for our betters. The ones who have moved on."

Gomda cradled the flowers against his body, refusing to let the wind tear them away.

"Who died?" Paul asked, pointing at the flowers.

"You were right about not being smart."

Paul's feet sunk in the rocks of the graveyard path, the same kind of rock that lay beneath the swing sets of his old elementary school. The graves here were modest. There were a few professionally carved gravestones, more often they were engraved by the hump-backed caretaker with a hammer and chisel. There were other people moving about, children chasing one another through the grass, an ancient couple holding hands tightly, staring at a set of ragged wooden grave markers.

"Who honors the dead more?" Gomda said. "The somber crowd or the laughing children? What would you rather see if you were packed in a casket below the earth?"

Gomda stopped in front of a plain gravestone, smooth marble, old and worn at the corners. This was one of the forgotten graves. There were no flower pots or bouquets laying around it, just the single plastic rose resting at the base of the grave. The long inscription had withered away in the wind, except for the name of the deceased, so faint Paul couldn't read it.

"This is why we do it, Paul," Gomda said kneeling at the grave.

He pulled out his pocket knife, began to scrape against the stone.

"He was eight years old, sick with God knows what. The doctors didn't know. I was greener than you when I tried. My master wasn't wise to tell me we weren't just making golems. That we were training for something bigger than cleaning gutters and trimming hedges."

"I don't understand."

Gomda blew dust and chips from the gravestone carving, leaned back, and eyed his work.

"Mickey Jordan, 1952-1961," Gomda read.

He had died at home. Gomda walked miles down the road to visit the boy every day, reciting poems to Mickey from a book he had stolen from the schoolhouse, holding Mickey's hand while he spat blood, coughing his life out in that sauntering house. They had kissed between the bushes at recess, just old enough to know it was wrong. For Gomda, it was the only time he'd ever felt right.

He brought Mickey licorice and moon pies in the days leading up to his death, Gomda preparing at night with his teacher, Cecil. A moldy deer's heart, a handful of thyme, a thimble of motor oil, reciting the strange words, slithery like wet grass.

Then on a Sunday after listening to the sermon, walking hand in hand beneath blooming dogwoods, Gomda said goodbye to his first love for the last time.

"If only I'd went home with him that last day, I could have saved him," Gomda said, rising up from the ground. "It was the lesson every healer has to learn. Sometimes the call of the grave is too strong. You can't save everyone."

"Mickey is Mick? You put his soul into a golem?"

"No. Mick is only a part of the golem, a portion of the souls of the dead drawn up from the grass, from the trees people have taken shade from. This is what I've been trying to teach you. This is our Art. We draw out the part that wants to give itself up, the part that wants to do work again. We put it to use. We give life another chance. I call up a golem to give me company. I call it Mick because I'm weak. I'm holding on to something that was gone long ago."

"Have you ever done it? Healed someone?"

Gomda nodded. "It took me a long time after Mickey died. Why do you think we go to the hospital? What do you think we do there?"

"How many?"

"Cecil had Caddo blood in him. He made dreamcatchers when he healed someone. That's what he taught me to do. Make a dreamcatcher every time I put life back into someone."

Paul thought of the dreamcatchers dangling from the kitchen, the bedrooms, the bathrooms. The shells clinking like rain when a door opened. There were hundreds, perhaps thousands, hung throughout Gomda's house.

"There is something else," Gomda said.

"What?"

"There are others. Others who have taken life to achieve their ends."

"Necromancers."

Gomda nodded.

Paul had felt the presence before, but thought it was one of the body's false alarms, a tingling that ran up the back of his neck. It was at the hospital with Gomda, making the rounds in the ICU. They came upon a man so lean that Paul had thought he was dead, his body and face covered in gauze. His hollowed eyes peaked out of the bandages and stared at Gomda like a cornered dog, baring his teeth and hissing. Those teeth were etched in Paul's memory.

"The man in the hospital," Paul said.

"I can see him sometimes when I dream."

"Can you stop him?"

"That's not what we do. We roam the hospitals and heal the sick. We are not headhunters or knights. You'll need to fix mistakes. I'm counting on you. Every shaman who has ever lived is counting on you."

71

Gomda died shortly after that conversation in the cemetery. In death, he had left everything, including the house, to Paul. Beside the bed where Gomda had died, Paul found a pile of straw and smooth pebbles scattered haphazardly across the floor. After he had swept it up, he scattered the pieces in the backyard and sat beneath the oak tree, watching bees hop from flower to flower, watching insects climb the stalks of grass. Listening to Gomda and Mick laugh in the rustle of the leaves.

*

Paul heard Diane calling his name, close by in the cellar. He felt physically ill from the presence of something here. He tried to stand and failed, the tendons of his knee swollen and tender to the touch.

The words he chanted were like a language once known and forgotten. You never forget some things, how to ride a bicycle, how to tie a shoe, how to heal.

He tried to stand. Better than new. If a doctor had cut his leg open, he would have seen the knee of an eighteen-year-old athlete, not the battered and beaten joint of a middle-age man. Paul's mind ached from the work, a lingering brain fog, like the days after a cold or a heavy night of drinking.

He followed Diane's voice. She was getting louder, more frizzled, moving farther in the blackness, closer to the source of Paul's anxiety. He wrapped his hand around her mouth and drew her back toward the steps.

"Something's down here," Paul whispered.

"We have to get out."

They checked the door. Rain was flowing in from the slats between the planks. Paul pushed and pushed, but the door didn't budge. The old man must have slid something over the door.

"What now?" Diane said.

Paul needed a golem, but for a golem he needed a living source. The moss wasn't enough. Perhaps somewhere in the cellar was a break in the wall, an entrance to a water heater, or a passage below the house for maintenance.

"We look for something to help us break out," Paul said.

"You mean we head towards the thing you're freaking out about?" Diane said.

"What else can we do?"

They stuck to the wall, sliding their hands against the brick, feeling for openings, objects they could use. The concrete floor gave way to musty carpet. A new smell came spinning into their world. Bubble gum. Watermelon bubble gum. There was only person they knew who chewed watermelon bubble gum.

"Stacy," Paul called out.

"Stacy?" Diane "This isn't just a basement, isn't it?"

"Keep calm, Di."

"This is some kind of ... dungeon."

This is more than a dungeon, Paul thought. The tiny man was a necromancer, and this was his lab. Perhaps the girls didn't even exist. They were ghosts pulled straight out of an old headline. God knows what the necromancer had told people to get them down here.

The acoustics of the room had gradually changed. Paul and Diane could sense things around them. Old furniture, boxes of things discarded, or the remains of the necromancer's work. Paul did not want to see. He did not want to find the fetid body of Stacy. He did not want to find what the necromancer had made from the dead.

Paul was feeling along the wall, about to give up hope, when his fingers found an edge, the cool breath of earth behind. A hole. Hope. Where there was earth, there could be golems. His fingers dug into cold mud. His heart leaped.

"We're going to be okay," he said. "Diane?"

Diane's breathing was so loud that it seemed to fill the entire room. He reached out and felt flesh. It could have been her arm, but it was too big. His hand moved up along the ridge of the limb, then down, where his hands moved over a damp surface, then up into a wet pit.

"I found the lights," Diane's voice from somewhere across the room.

The light was dim, single amber bulbs strung just far enough to not hurt the eyes when they came on. Paul recoiled and gagged at the sight, and then instinctively began to call golems up out of the mud. Diane screamed and fainted.

Standing in front of him, floating rather, was the product of the necromancer, an enormous head, perhaps six feet from chin to the temple. It was hard to estimate the size because of the jet-black hair that blanketed it like a bridal dress. The eyes, each the width of a large watermelon, blinked rapidly in the new light. The face was feminine and childish. Blood dripped from the gaping mouth.

Golems of mud and grass rushed to surround Paul and Diane, pouring from the hole in the wall. They stacked atop one another, molding their bodies into a muddy dome of protection.

"What are you?" Paul asked.

The eyes followed Paul as if it understood. Its tongue flopped soundlessly in its mouth. It was docile, like a puppy. Perhaps it was waiting for instructions from its master.

As his eyes adjusted, the dimensions of the room materialized from the blackness. Rocking horses and rocking chairs of old rotten wood, alphabet blocks, dolls with their eyes ripped out. A girl's room. One corner of which had served as a bathroom. In another corner, bones were stacked on shelves. Femurs. Skulls. There was a chair up against the wall where he had found the hole, black lacquered walnut wood with demons, imps, and ghouls carved into the arms and legs, and on it sat the remains of Stacy, still wearing the pink cashier's apron, traces of her mascara on her decomposing face. Beside her lay a slab of metal, cutlery strung above.

"This place is a butcher's shop," Paul said.

This is where he took his victims.

Paul saw another body at the dining table, a headless girl slumped in the chair, her bloated belly resting on the table. Her stomach was too big to be pregnant, so distended the torso of her dress had ripped, the flesh ripped like a crack in the egg.

"Where's your sister?"

The eyes jittered. The head spun around. A choking sound from the mouth.

"God. You ate her. Who's the old man?"

The head tried to speak, clicking the tongue against the roof of the mouth. "Da ... Da ... Da."

"Dad," Paul said breathlessly.

The head's eyes scrunched up. Tears like fat rain drops splattered against the floor. Hoarse screams rose and died in the head's mouth. There was now a small army surrounding Paul, sticks and rocks held like swords and spears. The house began to crumble beneath the cave as the golems continued to pour from the mud. Sunlight spilled through cracks in the earth.

Footsteps pattered across the ground above, Earl's footsteps. The head shook and spun. It sped across the room, lowering its head, banging into the walls. The golems tensed their bodies for combat.

"Wait," Paul commanded.

The head frowned and rushed towards him.

He had no time to react, but the golems were quicker. One golem struck the head in the eye with a rock, which sent the head careening off, past Paul, knocking him down. It burst through the walls and flew into the sky.

The full light of day crashed down into the cellar. Paul could hear the old man screaming.

Paul knelt beside Diane in the basement twilight. The bone sticking awkwardly from her arm. He had healed himself, his dog, birds, but never another human. Other humans were different, Gomda had said. Once you do it, you are a shaman.

Paul pressed his hands around her arm and said the words, words he could not believe he remembered.

*

Diane could not think of a better way to spend her summer. She stared out across the lake, sipping a margarita, dangling her hand in the cool water of the pool. She could smell the barbecue wafting across the deck.

"When is dinner ready?" she called.

"Not long now," someone replied.

She had been reading the county paper, and couldn't shake the thought of the cover story.

It reminded her of that scare that had cost her a month of therapy. God, what nightmares she had of that basement. She could still see that floating thing and those brown miniature soldiers running at her with rocks and sticks. Her therapist said it was a manifestation of her fears: being alone with her thoughts and human cruelty. Nothing out of the ordinary. She still did not know if she had bought what the therapist was selling.

She thought of how she and Paul had become overnight celebrities for surviving the clutches of Earl Campbell, who had been connected to a series of kidnappings and murders across the entire southeast. She shivered at the thought of how his girls had lived, cooped up in a basement, eating scraps of flesh carved for them by their own father.

She had been in Paul's arms when she woke from the basement, ambulances and police cars flickering in the darkness. Her head had been so foggy, like a fever, or a waking dream.

They had found Earl alive beneath a mudslide on the edge of the property. His confession had been a circus, and kept the water coolers at Munchion's buzzing for months. His insane ramblings had been captured by a deputy on a cell phone and uploaded to the internet, violating all kinds of laws, and putting the town in an odd sort of spotlight.

Like everyone else, she had watched the video countless times, listening to the man rave on about gods and monsters, about the sacrifice one girl had given for the other.

She felt bad for Paul, who had quit his job in the aftermath of the abduction. It was something he just could not shake, and he had refused therapy. Now he spent all his time passing out blankets at the hospital, walking the halls and playing chess with the more frequent visitors.

"Dinner's ready."

How ridiculous the world could be. *Meat Bandit Strikes Again* read the headline. Someone had been ramming meat trucks, stealing steak, and speeding off. Only about fifty pounds, enough to feed a large lion. What a strange crime for this part of the world. And strangest of all, officers found hairs six feet in length at the scene of the crime. There was no given explanation.

She sat down across from Roberto, his chiseled jaw at work as he dug into the barbecue. A dab of sauce fell on her arm when she bit into the sandwich. She rubbed it off thoughtlessly, her finger brushing that long pink scar that throbbed when the wind ran through the grass.

***

Answers

by Kathryn Hore

Australia: Two eternal enemies stalk the other only to reveal their true relationship.

The city streets were crawling with people. She wove among them, through this brisk young night with its brisk young things, its hustling loiters and energised youths. The air about her alive with wide-eyed laughter and drunken slurs and she pulled her tailored greatcoat tighter against it, shoved hands deeper into its pockets. Impossible not to be conscious of them as they came together, these creatures, these people, sparking off one another, social, communal. As always, they were just too hard to ignore.

She tried anyway, stepping over broken pavement, a rain-wet grey crumbling beneath her feet. Past street stalls and traders, boarded-up shops and pink puddles of reflected neon. One guy slipped out from behind a stall, grabbing her arm, insisting she stop and buy, his breath stale with beer and hashish, his eyes alight with something harder. She turned her head, let her hand slip out of its pocket and slide into his own. Skin on skin. It wasn't a sale he wanted, the flash of it was behind his eyes, the sour rush of his desire permeating his every pore. He wanted her pinned up against the dirty brick wall of the next alley, unwilling if that's what it took. She forgot sometimes they were like that.

She raised her hand to cup his chin, let his name form as a whisper in the air between their lips, and he turned away with sudden, sharp reluctance to continue pursuit. If asked, he would not be able to describe her face; eventually he would not remember she had passed at all. She chose not to hurt him. What would be the point? He was irrelevant. He was just like all the others on these crowded nighttime streets.

At the next corner, she raised her head and looked into the middle distance at nothing in particular. A dark face rising from behind darker hair, she listened momentarily, before turning right and continuing on. If she didn't pick up her pace, she was going to lose the trail.

These people around her were irrelevant. He, however, was not.

And He was not so far ahead now, she was sure of it.

This was closer than she had been in a long time. Her eyes scanned side to side, reading the signs etched onto the world. The woman in neat pinstripe on the corner, mouth gaping open-shut, open-shut, no sound escaping. The teenager out grifting, staggering now against a doorway, hunching double while vomiting bloody chunks onto cold and uncaring concrete. It was in the exhaled air, in the scent of Him clinging to the ground. It was in the minds of these few who had seen, wide, white eyes and the image of Him lingering in their heads. The old man against the wall clutching his bottle clad in brown paper, shivering so hard he was unable to take a single burning gulp.

It was in the word they repeated to themselves, muttering, mumbling, begging.

Evil.

She hated them for that. For believing such things even mattered.

She headed for the main street, where the crowds were thickest. Her low heels clicking a regular rhythm, skirting brown paper and green smashed glass; the accumulated grime of the inner city, the detritus of so many million lives. She waded through it as she had always waded through it, through the centuries, down the ages, by stepping over the fallen and discarded and keeping her focus straight. He would be where the people were, He was drawn to them, He liked them. So, she let herself be led by drifting sounds. Music too loud from an overcrowded dance club where neglected fire escapes would one day soon prove fatal. Some pimp in an adjacent alley selling cheap, laced dope that would kill his client's girlfriend. The laughter of a drunken reveler, liver already failing.

A collection of young men loitering awkward on a street corner, a few feet from an intense conversation between two girls. One girl, drunk, blonde, crouched on a cold, grey step leading up to a barred building, head in her hands. Smudged black rings of tear-destroyed makeup marked her face. Her friend, taller, brunette, lethally thin, leaned over her. Trying to find out what was wrong.

He was wrong.

He had passed here.

He had let the girl see more than she wanted to.

"Evil."

The blonde sobbed. The brunette comforted. The boys waited uncomfortably, not understanding that which went on between women.

She paused her measured steps to watch, then moved towards the girls.

The blonde looked up, black-rimmed eyes forced wide. "You ... you're ..."

"Hey!" the brunette tried to intervene.

She raised one hand, a firm, nonaggressive movement, to clutch about the brunette's throat. The girl fell back against the wall, hands reaching to her mouth, gasping, silent, and so terrified, she would never speak again.

She reached to the blonde and hauled her upwards, looking into her eyes.

"Sss ... sss ... ssstttop him. Stop him. H ... h ... he's e ... e ... e ... evil."

The blonde once had a childhood stammer, dealt with by years of speech therapy and expensive specialist attention paid for by wealthy parents, and gone for near two decades. It returned now in a moment and would remain the rest of her life.

"He is not evil."

She did not mean to engage with the foolish young people. But that word, it provoked her every time. The label, the definition of something they could not understand. What did it even mean? They gave it no detail, no evidence, just flung it out, a theological concept, a philosophical proposition. An abstract without reality. Yet it seemed to mean so much to them.

The boys came to defend their girlfriends. She found herself surrounded by four twenty-something young men, full of aggression and puffed-out chests. She turned, pushing one out of her way. He fell into the arms of his friend who would love him now the rest of his days. Another she spun around until he had to crouch and clutch at the ground to keep the dizziness from overwhelming. He would not stand for a week, vertigo would plague him for life. The last, the biggest, stepped in front of her, all threatening muscle and spitting honour.

She looked up, through his eyes. She whispered something, a day, a date, a time, a place, not so far into the future, not so distant from here. The date of his death, the knowledge of how he would die. She watched him stagger back from the sheer enormity of knowing, it weighing down his every muscle, every limb.

They were no longer in her way. And if perhaps she had allowed her dislike for their superficial labels to dictate her own reactions here, so be it.

She opposed Him. So, by their own simplistic thinking, if He were evil, that must make her good.

She left them with that irony to contemplate and continued walking on.

*

She first caught sight of His white, white hair, long around an equally pale face, as He stood outside some public bar. Leaning back and smiling, watching the crowd go past as if He were not a hunted thing. He was casual, relaxed as always. His obviousness worried her.

She faded back into the shadows of a condemned doorway. Perhaps it was the angle this vantage point afforded her, or maybe the crowd simply parted at the right moment, but when she looked again, she saw He was not alone. Her first assumption was that it was some street girl. Thin, scantily clad. Tough and fragile both, looking for cash, if not payment in drugs and not usually His sort. That type was too distrusting, too cynical for His tastes. Not that He couldn't charm any of them if He had to, those who thought they'd seen it all and would never trust again, until He held out a hand and offered a smile. That smile of His could end wars. Or start them.

But her assumption did not play out. This was no street worker linking arms with Him, her clothes were too expensive, the jewelry weighing down her neck and fingers too fine. She was young, two decades at most, and out of place in this part of the city. A rich girl out slumming it. Her laughter high pitched and nervous. She fluttered eyelids, blushed innocent when He whispered something dark. Young and romantic and illicitly attracted. And as always, writ large in the girl's thoughts, that label. *Evil.*

A terse breath escaped her lips, almost a cluck of the tongue. They were so quick to name, these people, wanting to define, to delineate, to tag. Yet, all the while they remained blind to the real-world evils surrounding them: a crumbling society abandoning its youth to the streets, its starving to the grave, and filling its prisons to overflow. Did they not know real darkness was a mundane reality? A boring routine they never cared to consider while they so freely labeled others, then acted as fluttering moths eager to singe their wings?

She watched with pursed lips. The girl changed things. Or maybe she didn't, it was hard to tell. It could be some trap He was laying, the girl its bait. Or the giggling youth could be no more than a decoy, cover to buy Him time to get away. Maybe she meant nothing. Maybe everything. Impossible to know for sure.

So, she held back fingers itching to attack and watched as He stepped away from the wall, walking down the street with that enthralled, young thing trailing in His wake. Now. Now was her chance, the best she was going to get. She could draw forth tempests to confront and defeat, she could raise a fury that would crumble skyscraping towers and crack streets in half. They would battle, of course. He would retaliate. His force would equal hers. But she held the advantage now and she would win out. Finally. After all this time. She should. She could.

She waited. And when He disappeared from view into crowd at the end of the street, she pushed herself out of her doorway and followed at a safe distance.

He walked, it was all He did. So she did too, keeping a cool distance behind and too caught in the uncertainties to make a final call: launch attack or make an escape. Both seemed irrevocable and what if she was wrong? She could level the city to contain Him, but it would do no good if it played into His plans. Maybe that was just what He wanted and He'd taken the girl to tempt her to it, to raise her fury enough to rock a continent. Maybe. The what-ifs were too much and she'd fought too hard for the advantage here. She would not risk a mistake that turned the balance and made her the prey again.

He kept a steady pace, cross-sectioning the city. Around them the urban sprawl went on with its business, oblivious to that which moved through its belly. People laughed, fought, cried over that which could not matter. On one grey-black block where the lights were patchier than most, pounding footsteps preceded three running youths, coming at them in a cloud of panic so tangy she grimaced to swallow it away. They bypassed Him without hesitation, though the girl hanging off his arm squealed. By the time they reached where she followed, their momentum was a force unto itself, but she waved a hand and they veered around her without stopping. They carried a thunder with them, a guilt that dripped with the blood from their hands. It clung to their backs, as they disappeared into the night, a weight they would never outrun.

She glanced down into the alley from which they had emerged, eyes picking out the dead-dark space few others would be able to see. A man lying alone, a slashing wound across his throat bleeding out onto the ground. His terror filled the air and for a moment she paused, opening her mouth to taste it, tart and unmitigated. Always such a tangible thing, the raw emotion of people, an ever-present force that seemed to matter even less than they did. Sometimes she hated them for that more than anything. As if it were their fault she could see right through them.

She turned her back on the man dying alone in the rain and returned to her pursuit. Yet the distraction had thrown her, broadened her vision, and now she realised just where He had led them. A place of desolation with the scent of sea in the air. Salt lay its coat over everything and the slow, rhythmic push of waves could be heard forcing against some nearby shore. The wharves. He had brought them to the wharves.

Her stomach tightened. If this was where He'd holed up of late, no wonder she hadn't been able to find it. A network of warehouses and storage sheds built in better times, lit by street lamps sparse and broken. The buildings were mostly abandoned, businesses dying amid rising economic chaos, only set to worsen. A creeping cancer due to spread to the city beyond like a kind of economic rust consuming all in its path. She paid it no heed. Such had happened before, such would happen again. Economies rose and fell. Empires rose and fell. The inevitability became mundane after millennia of repetition.

But here. He had brought them here. So close to the borders of land and sea, shifting territories with their constant movement against one another. Water, earth. Wet, dry. He stood beneath one of the few remaining streetlights, a pool of dirty yellow spilling down from above, the girl hanging off his arm. Impossible to move in on Him here, such ill-defined places were dangerous, the definitions between them too blurred, indistinct. In border country, boundaries shifted, acting to define, to redefine. What was within. What was without. Any blow she attempted to land on Him in such a place, could harm her in equal measure.

He leant back in that yellow light and looked up straight at her, all of a sudden, the grin on His face all too knowing. She did not return His expression, though for some time, she did not look away. Understanding lay between them, thick in the air, as it always did. Dual awareness of the double-bind which stayed her hand, if His as well. There was some reason He was here, that He had brought the girl here, some answer she burned to know. Whatever it was, she would not learn it tonight.

She broke the gaze and turned away, aware of Him shifting to lead the girl into the warehouse behind them as she did. Drawing a long breath of rust and salt night air and knowing she would have to return in the morning. She did not expect Him to be here when she did.

*

When she entered the warehouse in the early hours of the next day, she knew immediately He was gone.

Shaking off the rain from her shoulders and hair, last night's cold splashes replaced by a light grey mist covering the city. She picked her way upwards to the third floor, not surprised to find His camp abandoned when she got there. Well, not quite abandoned. He might not have been there, but the girl still was.

The youth slept alone on the mattress in the far corner of the echoing space, used syringes smashed on the floor nearby, used condoms in the bin by the door. She frowned down at the debris; it must have been for the girl's benefit, for what use had He for that sort of thing? Elsewhere the warehouse was empty, but for a fine layer of dirt. A space neglected, forgotten. He'd hidden His retreat well. He was everywhere here, in the air, on the walls, in the youth's sleeping head, but there was no trail leading away. All He'd left her with was the debris and the girl; poor clues with which to pick up the chase.

There was an old, frayed armchair across from the mattress. She sat in it and watched the youth struggle with sleep, tossing and turning and gasping. On occasion, the girl's eyes would flicker. Probably why the drugs had been supplied; when she did awake, the girl would blame them for the stupor He had left her in. Not that He needed drugs to run holes through her mind, but He did like games, playing with these people who latched onto Him, always leaving them wondering.

Was He, or wasn't He?

"Evil," the girl whispered, managing to roll over. She tried to sit up, reaching out to the cold space beside her on the mattress and

86

finding herself alone. Fear pulsed out of her, a sudden rush of spice
in the air. Her brain waking up.

And with each waking moment, the state of the girl's mind
became increasingly obvious. Damn. It would be hours before her
conscious brain recovered enough to draw anything from it. By then
He would be so far away, it would take her a year and a day just to
find the trail again. All she could do now was walk out and take her
chances picking up His trail cold.

She stood and turned to stalk towards the door. While the girl on
the mattress twisted, sobbed, whispered some unintelligible plea.

"Help. Help me."

A cracked voice, a harsh whisper. Something to ignore. Except by
the exit, she chanced a glance down and once more caught sight of
the condoms in the bin.

A frown graced her features. She looked back at the youth on the
mattress.

The girl's skin was slick with damp, the grubby off-white sheet
sticking with sweat. A hand reaching out in need.

"Please ..."

She looked through the girl's eyes. "Shit."

She strode fast back to the girl on the bed. Grabbing the flopping
youth by the shoulders and hauling her up, staring into her head. The
girl choked on the harsh mental intrusion, it hit her physically, as if
some invisible object were being shoved down her throat and she
gagged around it. Her head was still too clouded to get much, but her
physical state was suddenly obvious.

The girl was pregnant.

Fuck.

That's why the condoms had been part of the charade, so the girl
would think it was safe. As if that mattered to the likes of Him. But
why? Was He planting a hook, an emotional anchor to drag up later?
If so, why lead her here last night knowing she'd come back and find
the girl? Was that part of His plan?

She let the girl drop, the youth drenched in the stink of her own
desperation.

"What's your name?" she demanded.

"Eve ... Evelyn," came the girl's reply. "He said he liked that name, he said ..."

"He would."

Large, salt tears welled at the corners of Evelyn's eyes. Hurt radiated from her, but also a darker bitterness, not yet fully conscious. Anger. Hate. It had a strong taste, sour. A creeping darkness of blame. Beneath those tears, Evelyn blamed Him.

That didn't surprise. They always did look for someone else to be the bearer of their guilt. He had done nothing more than supply some drugs which would wear off soon and give the girl a night of illicit sex she had well consented to. It wasn't even like the girl knew she was pregnant, the worst she could blame Him for right now was skipping out before dawn. And this was the evil they proscribed to Him? This was the grand malevolence they chose to define Him by?

"Evelyn, you have family?" She shook the girl's shoulder.

"Family ...?"

The girl's voice wavered with tears into overflow, regret seeping out of her pores, oozing and muddy. Ah. Family were estranged, some longstanding rift surfacing raw and bloody in Evelyn's mind. Still, it meant there was somewhere she could stash the girl until she figured out what His plans really were.

She grabbed the girl's hastily discarded clothes and began struggling to get them on her. The thin, sequined blouse, the short skirt, the high-heeled sandals. The task was all the more difficult thanks to Evelyn fighting against her, kicking out legs and arms in weak desperation.

"Stop it or I'll send you back under," she said, wondering if she shouldn't just do it anyway.

"His fault ... He seduced me."

"So?"

"I should never ..."

"He can't do anything permanent to you," she said, though she knew engaging in conversation was a mistake. "Nothing you don't consent to. Nothing without your agreement."

"He is evil."

"No. You just want Him to be. You all just fucking want Him to be." Her fingers tightened around the girl's arms. "And He lets you. He thinks it's funny. He thinks it's understandable. He thinks it's only ..." Her lips turned up in distaste. "*Human.*"

Evelyn's eyes pinned onto hers. "You don't like him?"

She sat back, letting the girl flop onto the mattress still only half-dressed. *Like?* What had *like* to do with it? He liked people, but it didn't stop Him using them with as little care as she did. It didn't stop Him using this girl.

"I oppose Him," she corrected.

"Why?"

She started tugging the girl's blouse again, shoving the shoe on her other foot. She was perhaps rougher than necessary, but the girl should not ask questions about things she could not comprehend.

Why.

Why.

Why?

"Shut up," she said. "Just shut up and get dressed."

"He's a devil," Evelyn said, back to the same old mantra, faltering on the mattress but finally allowing her arms to be manuevered inside the dirty blouse. "A demon."

She ignored it. It had been a mistake to converse to begin with. People were irrelevant. They were there to be used as needed, picked up as weapons or distractions or traps, then discarded, when no longer necessary. That was all. The rest of their babble meant nothing.

But in a flash of movement, Evelyn's eyes shot wide and she bolted upright. The girl grabbed her shoulders, gripping with stressed fingers, pulling her in, dragging her close. Her pupils were dilated. Her breath sour. There was hope as well as fear in her bloodshot, drug-ridden stare.

"You oppose him. You must be an angel. Are you an angel?"

For one furious heartbeat, all was still. Then she reached out and grabbed Evelyn by the hair, yanking her back hard so that Evelyn squealed with the sudden flush of pain. Pushing her forward again until they were eye to eye, less than an inch apart. She could taste all of Evelyn's blame and hate hitting out at her, all of her fear, radiating and powerful. She breathed it in, sucked it inside. Swallowed it down in a cocktail of rage.

Then, with calm deliberation, she leant forward and placed her lips on Evelyn's own.

She breathed out. All of the girl's swirling emotion, all her regret and despair. All of her useless, ridiculous hope. She breathed it back into Evelyn, forcing it into the girl, lips crushed together in a kind of kiss.

Evelyn sagged in her arms.

She pulled back only enough to whisper into the girl's throat, "Keep it."

Evelyn tried to shake her head, as if she understood what this might mean.

"The child in you. Keep it."

Her voice could not be denied, not when given the power of Evelyn's own desperation. The idea was already twisting down inside the girl and taking root, a seed in her brain.

Done. It was done.

Something, even if she wasn't sure what, was done.

She gave Evelyn a final shove and the girl fell back, unconscious before she hit the mattress. It would be morning before the girl could be dumped back onto family now, but she could not, would not, regret it.

His plans, whatever they were, would not be for Evelyn to carry the child to term. It was not possible, He alone could not leave so permanent a mark on the world. He could not create like that. But with her input as well, with the two of them contributing in equal share, they could affect something of the kind. They could create something, perhaps.

Now, between the two of them, something new would be born into the world.

And maybe then there might be some answers. Maybe then they might start to understand.

She stood in the neglected warehouse with the pregnant girl they had both conspired to damage, at her feet and thought of demons and angels. Of like and dislike. Of good. Of evil. Of foolish dichotomies which meant nothing, explained nothing.

They were opposed. That was all. That was all there was.

Why?

"I don't know," she said, only to herself. "I just don't fucking know."

*

It was late at night and they were staying in a cheap motel.

Evelyn was asleep in the room next to hers, almost recovered. By day's end, the girl had begun thinking straight and her parents would arrive by morning. She'd done the calling. It hadn't taken much of a twist to make them forget their anger, heal the rift in family relations. They would welcome their errant daughter back into the fold and it would be all big happy families again, at least for a while until their usual reality reasserted itself.

She did not tell them the girl was pregnant. Evelyn would find that out for herself soon enough.

He might try to get to Evelyn tonight, before she was back in her family's arms. She sat in bed listening for just such a thing, a light beside her she was oddly reluctant to switch off. Strange to find herself shy of letting the night in, a foolish fear of the dark. As if one lamp could change anything, as if fates were decided upon the switch of an electrical current. The bulb burned low, creating shadows, and she sat with covers pulled to her waist, hands around her knees. Concentrating. Focusing. Sweating fingers clenched too tight. It was always like this when she was the one chased, when she had become the hunted one. Such was the way things were. They were opposed. Dangerous to one another. Always hunting, always running. One of them was always running.

She made herself lie down and reached across to switch off the lamp.

She knew He was there, the moment the darkness came.

For long seconds, she did not move. Fighting to exhale through tense muscles, not daring to shift an inch and listening with all she had. He was here. He wasn't going for Evelyn. He wasn't surprising with attack. He was simply here.

She let her eyes flicker open. He was standing in the darkest corner of the room, only His white hair giving Him away. Strands of it caught the moonlight from the window and when He saw she was looking right at Him, He shifted, slipping further into the silver patch of light. She could make out the shape of Him, the features of His face. His white eyes, pale skin. They stared at one another. He was almost as frozen as she, her own fear reflected in His eyes. Each of them was the only being in all existence who could hurt the other, so was it all that surprising such fear was there?

He had not come here to battle, He had simply come. She slipped one hand from beneath the bedclothes and held it out towards Him. It was enough. His first step was unsure, but after that He did not hesitate, stepping across to her. Across all the ages they had fought, moving in equal conflict. It was their purpose, their reason. They were opposed, they must battle. Such were the rules, she supposed, but if so, she was ever conscious this must be considered breaking them. But what if it had been so long they were making up the rules for themselves now? Either way, right or wrong, they'd been meeting like this for too many aeons to care.

He clasped her hand in His own, venturing a hesitant smile. A guilty smile, the smile of conspirators breaking the rules.

She smiled herself then, a very rare occurrence.

*

"You did not try to stop Evelyn returning to her parents?"

They laid side by side in the hours before dawn, reluctant to lose time to sleep. They had barely spoken all night. After the sex and the time together, to realise you're lying naked next to your enemy and you quite like being there, made words uncomfortable, hard to find.

Yet she found them now. She always did, after a while. Silence, often His preference, always seemed that bit harder to her.

"It is of no matter." His voice was a soft drawl in the muted light. "The girl was a game, nothing more."

"You are lying."

A wisp of a smile crossed His features, fleeting amusement bringing a flash of teeth, white like His skin, His hair.

"And You are cheating. Leave the battles until tomorrow, when we are enemies again."

He was lying back in the bed, one hand resting on her hip. His eyes were half closed, but He was not sleeping. He never slept on nights like this; neither did she. Sometimes there was silence and they were comfortable within it. Sometimes they talked, if only of the long past. Never anything recent. To discuss something current cut too close, it reminded them they should not be here, not like they were.

So, she was cheating, in a way. And like always, He tried to deflect the subject.

"She's pregnant," she said.

He offered an uncaring shrug. "It's not like she will keep the child. It needs both of us to ensure anything of permanence."

"Yes. I told her to keep it. I made sure she would."

He raised His eyebrows, betraying surprise. She tried not to notice. During the day when opposition dictated word and action, she was always looking for clues. Now she avoided them. She did not want to trick Him here. By guilty agreement, they had each long understood: when willingly laying with the enemy, it was important to be careful for the other. To stop them before they said too much. To not pay attention if they did.

"Why?" He asked.

"Why impregnate her to begin with?"

"I don't know. You were too close. I was struggling for a distraction. It ... seemed like a good idea at the time."

She sighed. "Yes. It seemed like a good idea at the time."

He picked up her hand, entwining His fingers with her own. Pale eyes and paler hair, there was almost no colour to Him. She watched His face, examined His features. She often did on nights like this, when the rain tapped at the window glass and the dark was lit only by a fat moon.

"I wonder," He said, a soft sound into the silence.

"What?"

"I wonder what will be born into this world, nine months hence. I wonder what it will do."

He did not sound concerned, or even all that curious. She raised a hand to trace a single dark finger along His jaw, His cheekbone.

"If people are to be believed, it will either be a destroyer of worlds, or saviour of them," she said.

"Yes. They do like to think there's some grand plan."

"Maybe there is."

His snort was cynical. "A plan would require a purpose. But throughout the ages, there has been only this. Without end, without beginning."

"There has to be an end. Somehow or another, one of us has to win."

He made a face, a dismissive gesture, even as His fingers tightened around her own. Deflecting again. He never did like talking about these things.

"All we know, You and I, is defeat or be defeated. And yet ..." He paused, looking down at their entwined hands. "And yet we don't even know what such an end will bring. Shouldn't we know? Don't you think? We who otherwise know so much?"

She had no answers for Him, but He wasn't expecting any. These questions were old, too familiar. He must have been thinking of them of late. Well, so had she. But it was not unusual for her to speak of such, to ask the questions, to seek the answers. He usually avoided it. He did not like bringing their daylight reality into these brief darkened hours of respite they captured for themselves.

He looked back up to her. "Why did You not attack last night? In the city, You had Your chance. Why not take it?"

"The girl. I saw the girl. It was too much of a risk. I could not know what You were planning."

"I plan nothing. Just like You," He said. "There is no plan. There is only ever ..."

"'That which seems like a good idea at the time.'"

Above them shadows played across the ceiling, born of the moon through the curtains, shifting with the breeze from the cracked open window. She lay back and watched them. Perhaps He was right. It was hard now to understand her hesitation of the previous night, her reluctance to attack, to take that final step. Yet at the time the risk had seemed too great. Her need for self-preservation the only thing strong enough to temper her need to defeat Him.

"I remember when people huddled in caves," she said, staring at the play of light and dark above. "Scared of their own shadows on the wall. I remember chasing You through them. And yet, I cannot remember the beginning."

"Perhaps we have always been doing this. Perhaps we always will."

"Have we forgotten? Is that all it is? Forgotten how it began?" She hesitated, thinking suddenly of Evelyn and her foolish, uncomprehending questions. "Or why it began?"

She pushed herself up again to see what he thought of that, leaning on one elbow to watch His face. Black hair fell over her shoulder, across His pale skin. He looked down to it and, after a moment, picked up a lock, holding it between His fingers.

"You are enemy mine," He said in a low voice, staring at the pinch of her hair. "You are enemy mine and I do not even know why. I would like to know why."

Across His face settled a rare frown. It disturbed her, she wanted to reach out and smooth it away. Before she could He shifted, picking up a lock of His own white hair. He joined it with the lock of hers, the colours mixing between his fingers.

"Evelyn's child," she said as he frowned at the locks of hair. "Perhaps people are right. Destroyer or saviour, perhaps it will bring an end after all."

"Is it really important? The ending? Is knowing there will be a fixed and proper ending that important to You?"

"What point is there if one of us does not defeat the other?"

That brought back the smile in Him. "Whoever said there has to be a point?"

The flippancy of His words did not reach His eyes. Instead, she read a pleading in them: do not do this, do not speak of it, please. Let it go. But she could not, and she did not think He expected her to. For when He looked up, there was also understanding in His eyes and that kinship she never saw anywhere else. Which existed nowhere else. Only in Him.

She took pity on Him. Turned the subject to one she knew He'd prefer.

"Evelyn called You a devil," she said.

It brought back His smile. "A devil? Haven't heard that one for a long time. And there I thought this was a more secular age that did not believe in devils."

"She also called me an angel."

His smile turned into an outright grin. "Those drugs must have hit her harder than they were supposed to. You, my friend, my enemy, are no angel."

"No. And You're no devil, either." She frowned at Him. "But what if You are the evil they say You are? They use the word with such regularity, it must mean something. And if so, what does that make me? Good?"

"You know I'm not. Not like they want me to be. And neither are You."

"Through every age, it is what they have named us."

"Which means nothing. Good, evil. Such things are mere creations from the minds of man."

She swallowed. Hard. "So are we."

The words left her mouth tacky. But someone had to say it and she knew He would not. The skin around His eyes tightened, His head turned away, involuntary reaction. He did not want to hear this. He never wanted to hear this.

"You don't know that," He said at last. "People are meaningless. They're to be used. How can You say they are somehow responsible for our very existence?"

"You don't know it's any different," she said. "Their need for oppositions, for easy dichotomies to make sense of the world. Maybe it is the reason we are here."

She was leaning over Him, insistent. When she swallowed, she could taste the burn of acid, harsh in her throat. Her stomach was churning. That was the difference between them. He was happy to avoid the questions so as not to confront difficult answers, while she was determined to know the truth, no matter how sour.

There was pain in His eyes. As always, a pure reflection of her own.

"But what are we?" she said, more gently. "What are we, if not the beings they created to place such tags upon?"

For a moment, He was silent. Then He held up the locks of their hair which still lay in His fingers, the strands combined.

"Opposite. Opposed," He said. "From the colour of our hair to the expressions on our faces, You, my friend, who never smiles. Yet we act the same, fight the same, think the same way, believe the same things."

"Fear the same."

"There is only one I fear," he said and, staring up at her, and an echo of that fear flashed across His face. But it faded quickly and He smiled. It was a sweet smile. "And we desire. The same."

"But, what are we?"

He dropped the hair. Reached instead to kiss her, lips soft on her own. Then he drew her down to lie beside Him, winding a way into the tight circle of her arms. They lay there together, warm, comfortable, interlocking. His hands gentle on her skin.

"We are opposed," He said. He sounded sad. "We are opposed."

*

He was gone before she awoke. An old habit. Whoever first approached the other in the night, was always the first to leave again in the morning.

A new sunlight hit the empty pillow beside her. She opened her eyes to find the rain stopped and the window open. For a long time, she just lay there, not moving. Another old habit. Giving Him time to get away before the chase was on again.

After a while, she rose and dressed. Went down to the foyer to watch for Evelyn. The girl appeared with hesitant steps, looking lost, disoriented, which was only to be expected. Evelyn's memory of recent days would be fading fast, if not already gone, but the scars, and the consequences, would remain.

An older couple approached the girl and Evelyn was welcomed back into the arms of her parents with tears and hugs. No questions asked, no explanations needed, just relief and reunion. It would not last. Before the week was out, there would be fights, arguments, the usual family rifts would breach again. Reality, as they created it for themselves, would return in force. She could not change that for them. Only they could create change of permanence, even while they looked to others to blame or save.

Evelyn gripped her mother's arm. Her father ushered the women to a waiting car. Whisking the girl back into everyday life, community, suburbs, and taking the new life inside her with them. It would be a thing born of whim and frustration, created without thought to the past or consideration of the future. Without plan. Without purpose. Without reason why. Perhaps these people would find their object of guilt or salvation in the child. Perhaps they would find what they were looking for in the new thing to be born, after all. Destroyer of worlds, or saviour of them, or something else besides.

Perhaps then, they might be left alone.

She watched them take it away and felt the care drain from her limbs as they did.

She left the motel in a stolen car and turned back down the road to the city proper. As she did, she began to search for clues, to scent for Him once more on the warm breeze. He would be working to put as much distance between them as possible and she would need to be quick to pick up His trail. She considered her options, thoughts ticking over. How best to track Him, how she might finally confront Him. How to ensure she would, in the last, defeat Him. She did not smile, but this was not a sign of discontent.

As she drove, all irrelevancies faded. The questions which burned in the night, the answers neither of them could give. The thing to be born nine months hence, to a mother who would not remember its conception and a world that would not be ready. He was right. It did not matter. Like the beginning, long forgotten, or like the unknowable end. None of it mattered. There was only one thing they knew, the only thing they could be sure of.

The only thing which held any meaning.

We are opposed.

***

Finals Week
by Daniel M. Kimmel

*U.S: A supernatural tale about life, death,
and that one exam you wish you had aced.*

It had been a good life but Murray knew that his was finally at its
end. He didn't know how he knew, but he could feel it in his bones.
Yet he was okay with that. Indeed, he felt oddly at peace. Death was
the big mystery that eventually everyone had to face and perhaps that
was just it. *Everyone* had to face it. It wasn't as if he was being singled
out. This wasn't like the time he lost his job when his company was
downsizing and he was the one let go from his department. Like
countless people before him, and countless people yet to come, it was
simply his time to go.

In a way, he was curious. Since it was inevitable, he would soon
enough find out what came next. Instead of trying to deny it, he
embraced it. It was the next big adventure. Either he would be
snuffed out like a candle—and then, of course, he'd have no way of
knowing—or else he would begin the next great stage of his life or, as
he supposed he had to start thinking about it, his afterlife. Marcie and
the kids and even the older grandchildren, who had been permitted
to visit and make their farewells, all remarked at how at peace he
seemed to be. Alec, his eldest, said it was most likely the morphine
drip building a wall between his brain and his failing organs, a
suggestion that was greeted with sharp looks and noises, as if Murray
was in a position to take offense to anything anyone said.

The dying man took his son's hand and pulled him closer, then stage whispered loud enough for everyone else to hear, "You're out of the will."

There was a moment of shocked silence finally broken by Alec's laughter and Murray's gurgling smile. It wasn't much, but it would have to do. He and Alec had always understood each other, even when they disagreed, which is why they could share a joke on his deathbed, which is where Murray had to acknowledge he now was.

He had spent some time in the hospital as they performed a variety of tests that involved everything from magnetic waves to the entrails of sacrificed animals. Well, maybe not, but when it was all over, the doctor's long, sympathetic analysis included the word "inoperable" and Murray really didn't have to hear anything more. It was time to go home and say his goodbyes.

For several days now, family and friends—those still alive themselves and able to make the trip—had come to pay their respects. They told stories and kissed his forehead and patted his hands, wiping away the occasional tear. For his part, Murray was having a grand time. It was like getting to attend your own funeral.

"I'll save you a seat at the table," he said to Al, whose pockets he'd been emptying at the poker table on Thursday nights for the last forty years.

"Maybe I'll finally get to win a hand," said Al.

"If you do," replied Murray, "that's how I'll know I'm in hell."

Marcie would frequently usher everyone out of the room. "Let's let him get some rest now," she'd say. Murray suspected this was her way of coping. After all, it's not like he needed to rest up for anything. He was heading to the proverbial dirt nap and would have plenty of time to rest. This was his last chance to hang out with the living. Truth be told, though, his energy was waning and if he didn't need to rest, he found that he was less drawing on his reserves than running down his battery.

It's just as well, he thought. He had been one of the lucky ones who had gotten closure with each of the important people in his life. There were no regrets or unsaid words left. He kind of hoped he'd be alone at the end. He wanted them to remember him as full of life when they last saw him, not an empty husk. He silently apologized in advance to whomever had the unpleasant task of discovering his lifeless body. Probably Marcie. She deserved better than that.

He started to drift off, idly wondering if he was experiencing his final moments, when he felt a rap on his knuckles as if someone had sharply tapped them with a ruler. He opened his eyes and blinked, not quite believing what he was seeing. Someone had, indeed, rapped on his knuckles. It was his tenth grade geometry teacher, Miss Farber. In spite of her simple black dress and her dark hair being tied up in a bun, she was looking pretty good. In fact she was looking very good for someone who had to have died years ago.

"Hello, Murray," she said in that distinctive voice that could still call him to attention. "It's good to see you again."

"Miss Farber," he gasped, raising his head from the pillows, "how can you still be alive?"

"What are you talking about? I'm in the prime of life."

Murray did some quick mental calculations, his brain not entirely dulled by the morphine, and said, "You'd have to be 127 years old."

She paused, letting his comment hang there for a moment before answering. "Exactly. Very good, Murray. And what do we know about 127?"

Perhaps his mind was dulled due to the drugs after all. He had no idea what she was talking about. Trying hard to focus he looked at her and asked, "127?"

"It's a prime number, Murray. Have you forgotten everything I've taught you?"

He slumped back on the bed. This is not the way he imagined the end would be. If he had to pass a math exam to get into the afterlife he might as well be stuck on Earth.

"Why yes, you do," said Miss Farber.

"Yes I do what? I didn't say anything."

"Murray, you're dying. I'm the Angel of Death. You really think I can't read your thoughts?"

Murray looked around the room. The clock read 3:14 and since it was dark outside, it was either the middle of the night or the middle of a total eclipse. Wait, 3:14. Wasn't that the start of Pi...?

"Do you get it now, Murray?" She had that look on her face when she asked a question that she expected you to have the answer to, providing you had done last night's homework. "You've got work to do. I'm here to take you to ... well, you'll see."

Murray sat fully upright in bed, feeling full of energy for the first time in days. In fact, he felt like his old self. Righteous indignation can prop you up, he thought, as he looked at the primly dressed math teacher at the side of his bed.

"How can *you* be the Angel of Death? Where's your scythe? Where's your black robe? You look exactly like Miss Farber did when we dragged ourselves to class on a Monday morning and you were all full of excitement about the Pythagorean Theorem."

Miss Farber then did something entirely unexpected. She let out a long and loud laugh.

In the entire year of tenth grade geometry, Murray could not recall ever seeing her laugh. She wiped a tear from her eye and looked at Murray. "Over 6300 people die every hour. Do you really think a single entity could be there for all of them? For the 152,000 people who die every day? For the 55.3 million who die every year? Even Santa Claus has to delegate to deliver all his toys in a single night. Each person gets someone appropriate from their own life to help them through the transition."

Murray considered this. It certainly made sense, in a way. With a hundred deaths or so every minute, the few minutes Miss Farber had spent with him would already have put her way behind schedule. So the notion that there was a multitude of angels, or whatever, serving as guides from this world to the next didn't surprise him. What surprised him was who had been selected to bring him along.

"But why you?" he demanded. "Why not Miss April 1972? We had a very special relationship."

"You were fifteen at the time. I can only imagine your relationship. But I'd just as soon not."

"I didn't even use geometry after I was finished with your class. I ran an auto dealership."

"Yes, that's right, Murray," said Miss Farber coming to the side of the bed and taking his hand. "And that's precisely why I'm here. We have some unfinished business."

With that she gave his arm a strong pull, yanking him off the bed. As he stood for the first time in several days he looked back and saw that he was still in bed. The tubes and monitors were attached to the Murray on the bed, but the screens indicated they were flatlining.

"What's happening?" he shouted. He looked down and instead of his pajamas, he was in a pair of blue jeans and sneakers. A glance at his arms told him that he was in a blue work shirt. A hand to his head found an unruly mop of hair rather than the bald pate that had greeted him for the last thirty years. "I don't understand."

"Come with me, Murray. We have some things to attend to."

Murray was suddenly frightened. "Am I going to hell?"

Miss Farber gave him a quizzical look and then laughed again. That laugh of hers was unnerving. "Why no, dear boy. You're not going to hell. You're going to high school."

*

The bell rang just as he stepped through the door. Miss Farber was at the front of the room ready to begin. Although, technically, he was not tardy, in her class the sound of the bell was not the final call to class but a sign that they were to be at their desks, notebooks open, and ready to begin. He was not winning any points with her for taking up the fifteen to twenty seconds to get to his seat and arrange his materials.

She gave him a withering glance and began. "Today we begin the study of geometry, where you will learn how to prove mathematical principles through rigorous logic, along with the application of rules previously demonstrated to be true." She paused, as if daring anyone to contradict her. In that moment the door opened. There was a gasp from somewhere in the room. Would someone dare show up to class after it had already begun? Even with a note from the principal's office—indeed, even a personal note from the superintendent of schools or, for that matter, the Secretary of Education—this was playing with fire.

Instead, Miss Farber broke out into, what for her, passed for a broad smile. "Why, Dr. Monroe, what brings you to my geometry class this morning?"

Looking like a wizened gnome with a shock of white hair set off by his black-framed glasses, the man gave a little wave and headed towards the back of the room. "No problem," he said. "I'm just sitting in on various classes this week."

Miss Farber's attention returned to the assembled students. "Class, we are honored by the presence of Dr. Monroe, our Department of Mathematics' chairman, this morning. So let's demonstrate for him how serious we are about the study of geometry."

From his desk in the front row all the way to the left, Murray was battling a strange sense of *déjà vu*. He didn't quite understand it, but he knew he had been here before and certainly didn't belong here now. But fifteen-year-old boys didn't just walk out in the middle of a class announcing that they had an appointment elsewhere. So he was trapped, at least until the end of the period.

Miss Farber had been rambling on about "postulates," which she explained were statements that did not have to be proven, and were to be taken as "givens." Parallel lines never meeting was offered up as an example of the concept, although Murray was quite certain this was a bit of information that he was never going to have to use again outside of this class. Miss Farber, however, was just getting warmed up.

"To construct our proofs, we rely on postulates, and on theorems. Now, what is a theorem?"

There was now a pregnant pause where they were all to acknowledge their ignorance and, thus, their dependence upon Miss Farber in relieving themselves of this sorry state of affairs. Murray was bored. He looked down at the math text open on his desk and flipped ahead a couple of pages. There, for all the world to see, was a definition of what a theorem was. It was simple enough once you knew it, and now he did. Murray raised his hand.

"Oh, Murray *thinks* he knows what a theorem is. Well, why don't you tell the class what you *think* it is?" She could barely control the sarcasm in her voice. Apparently exposing a student's errors was a special treat for her.

"Well, isn't it just like a postulate except it has to be proven?"

The class turned its attention from Murray back to Miss Farber. Not having turned the page, they had no idea if he was right or had just committed ritual suicide on the first day of school. Instead, to their shock, Miss Farber broke out into an authentic smile. "Excellent, Murray. That's precisely what it is."

From the back of the room, the department chairman said, "He must have taken the course before."

Now Miss Farber was beaming. "Even Dr. Monroe is impressed."

While the two math teachers were enjoying the joke that only they seemed to be in on, Murray stole a glance at the clock on the wall. He had another half hour of this. Meanwhile Miss Farber was now at the board constructing a proof for their first theorem, something about two lines intersecting at only a single point. I don't think so, thought Murray. He definitely had intersected with this class before, but he couldn't quite explain how. His musings were interrupted by the ringing of a bell.

"Good morning, ladies and gentlemen. So glad you could join us today," Miss Farber was saying to the late arrivals. Murray was already at his desk, but couldn't help notice that everyone's clothes, including his own, had changed. Looking out the window, he saw the autumn leaves had long fallen and there was a layer of snow on the ground. If this was hell, it had apparently frozen over. Time had somehow jumped ahead, yet he was still in math class. This made no sense. He had no memory of other classes, or going home, or even going to his locker.

There was no time to ponder this state of affairs. Miss Farber was returning a take-home test on constructions and she was clearly not pleased. The test involved following instructions to make geometric drawings using a ruler, a compass, and a protractor, and Murray had tried his best but this had not played to his strengths. Calculations and logic proofs he could do. Drawing a straight line, not so much.

Miss Farber dropped his exam on his desk with a glare bordering on contempt. He had gotten a 55, circled in red, with "Disappointing!" written next to it. On a scale of 60, that wasn't so bad, but on a scale of 100, that was failure. He couldn't dispute the "Disappointing!" He was disappointed too. This was the first time he had ever failed a test. That's why what Miss Farber did next took him completely by surprise.

"In grading these exams, it became obvious to me that some of you took advantage of this being a take-home exercise to cheat and compare answers," she said, her expression a mixture of anger and shame. "Since I can't prove it for sure, I'm not going to report it—*this* time—but there will be no more take-home tests, and any further evidence of cheating will be dealt with severely."

The class was stunned into a silence, a few daring to sneak peeks at the other students, trying to guess who the cheaters were. What she said next caused 25 young heads to snap back to the front of the room.

"Since the test was compromised, I have no choice but to erase the grades from the books. You cheated for nothing. This test will not count for your final grade."

Murray was stunned. He hadn't cheated, but this last announcement was a gift. His failing grade wouldn't matter. He felt positively giddy. It's the only explanation for what he did when she dismissed the class. He went over to the desk and "confessed" that he had gotten the wrong answers from his friend, Sam, who had also bombed out.

Miss Farber was not amused. "Get out," she snapped, as Murray hastily exited ... and found himself back in math class again.

*

It was springtime, and Miss Farber was going over the "required" theorems, the proofs of which he would need to know for the final exam. There were a couple dozen of them, and he'd have to be able to set up the logical argument proving each one true. Her finals were rumored to have brought students to tears as anything they had covered that year was a potential question.

"It's not all that bad," she said with a smile that sent a chill through the room. "In fact, I have a standing offer to my class: anyone who gets a perfect 100 on the test will be taken out for ice cream, my treat."

It was less the promise than that there was the possibility that she would be in their debt—would owe them an ice cream—that was tantalizing. After all they had been through that year, everyone in the class was going to do their best to turn the tables on her. Murray couldn't wait to take the exam.

Oddly, he barely remembered it. He recalled sitting at his desk and told to turn the exam paper over and begin, but in the next moment he was at Miss Farber's desk, alone in the room with her, retrieving the completed exam which she had graded. Murray's heart sank. He would get no ice cream. Instead, what he got was a 97. He seemed disoriented, almost as if a veil had been removed from his eyes. His memories of his adult life came flooding back to him and he was suddenly dizzy from the absurdity of his situation. If this whole exercise involved him taking his high school geometry class again, what was the point?

Murray looked at Miss Farber. "I failed, didn't I? I'm going to have to go through this over and over until I get it right."

"What are you talking about?"

"For some reason I've had to relive your geometry class. I don't know why it should be so important as I lie dying to go through one of my hardest high school classes, but obviously it is. Since I didn't get 100 I must have failed and now I'm going to have to do it again."

A look crossed Miss Farber's face that he had never seen there before, both concerned and somewhat bemused. He finally understood it was one of pity. "Murray, this was never about you."

"What are you talking about?" the old man's soul began speaking through the teenage body. "You're the one who came to me. You told me you were the Angel of Death. I'm dying. I know that. And rather than go to my heavenly reward or judgement or punishment or whatever it is that's in store for me, I had to take your class all over again. How is this not about me?"

Miss Farber gave him a rueful chuckle and then looked directly at the boy/man he now was. "You men. You always think everything is about you. It wasn't. This was all about me."

Murray was speechless. He understood the words she was saying but he couldn't begin to comprehend their meaning. Finally he got out one word: "How?"

"I'm not really the Angel of Death. I was told to say that to get you to come along. It was me who was being tested and needed to get another chance." Murray looked bewildered as she continued her explanation. "I wasn't always the best teacher. I would focus on my pets, who clearly understood the material and thrived on the attention, while pretty much going through the motions and ignoring everyone else. I was wrong. This was an opportunity for me to atone, to show I really could be an inspirational teacher, whether I was being kind or coming down like a ton of bricks."

Murray waved the exam paper. "But I only got a 97."

"So you won't get an ice cream. Is it that important to you?" She reached into her purse and pulled out a couple of dollars. "Here, go buy yourself a cone."

Murray didn't take the money. He barely moved. "I don't care about the ice cream. What I can't figure out is how my failure helps you."

And then Miss Farber did something totally unexpected. She laughed in a way he had never seen before; it wasn't a mocking laugh, it was one of sheer joy. "Murray, you didn't fail. You got part of one problem wrong. You know what you got the first time you took this test? A 78. You're proof of my success. The whole class is. The *lowest* grade was a 90. You all excelled. I got you all to care about doing well in geometry, even though most of you thought it was a waste of time. It worked. And now I get to move on."

"Move on to where?" This was all kind of baffling to Murray, but Miss Farber had run out of explanations. "I did what I had to do. I don't know what happens next, but I do know that this is where we say goodbye." She stood up, leaned over, and kissed him on the cheek. "Thank you, Murray."

With that she left the room. Murray was alone, clutching his final exam. Part of him wanted to look at it to see where he had lost the three points. But he was having trouble making out the pages now as he found himself back in bed with all the tubes and wires attached to him. He was feeling weaker, and in a bit more pain, and he knew with a dead certainty—a phrase that now made perfect sense to him—that the end had to be near. He looked around for Miss Farber but saw no one. Closing his eyes, he lay still, waiting for it all to come to a stop.

He was startled by the soft hand that took his. He opened his eyes and looked up to see who it was, thinking that it must be a nurse coming to check his medications. Instead what he saw was a woman in her early twenties, clad in a flimsy negligee that revealed much more than it concealed. She looked down at him with an open, inviting smile.

Murray gasped. "Miss April?"

"Yes, Murray, although my name is actually Clara, not that any of you teenage boys actually cared enough to read the words that went with the pictures."

"April ... um, Clara ... what do I do now?"

"Why, just come with me. I'm here to take you on the next stage of your journey."

He rose from the bed, the tubes and wires falling away. "Will it involve geometry?"

"Actually, I think it's trigonometry."

"Really?"

Clara giggled. "No, of course not. If you were going to math class, do you think they would have sent me?" She took his arm. "It's time to go now."

Murray had no idea where he was heading. But he figured that any afterlife that had Miss Farber *and* Miss April was a place he had to check out. He clasped her hand and, together, they walked into the light.

***

The Burnings
by Michael D. Burnside

U.S.: A futuristic fusion of fanatics, fear, and faith.

I was there on Endocina when the burnings began. I watched a thousand fires flicker on the hillside beneath the silhouette of a nuclear reactor.

Endocina has always been a world of contradictions. It is a habitable moon orbiting a dead planet. Its warm temperatures and fresh water lakes were a life-giving gift to the original colonists, but every year it would cross the path of the Infernavol Meteor shower and suffer weeks of bombardment. Once the defense net was in place, we should have been set on the path to prosperity, instead we sought out something else to fear.

I watched as the iconoclasts tied an android to a wooden cross. Perhaps I should say "welded" instead of "tied." The android could easily snap rope, so they bound the machine in place with twisted steel braids. One man used a plasma torch to melt the restraining metal to itself while four other men held the android down. The android could have tossed the men aside, but it had been instructed to stay still, and it complied.

Once the iconoclasts had secured the victim, they pulled the cross upright. They doused the android and cross with kerosene while the android's owner wept nearby.

The android was a male model with bright green eyes and wavy brown hair. Its skin was light tan and pink. It appeared soft and pliable. Only a light reflective sheen from a protective coating gave away that the machine wasn't human. The kerosene beaded on its flesh and soaked the blue T-shirt and jeans it wore.

The owner of the android knelt as near to the cross as the executioners would allow. She was a neighbor of mine named Maureen, a middle-aged woman with short blond hair of medium build. The iconoclasts said she relied on the android for companionship. I'd seen them sneer as they said it, clearly implying her relationship with the machine was sexual, and therefore disgusting.

Maureen's husband had died a decade before in a meteor strike. She'd never spoken to me in those ten years. She'd give me a quick wave while watering her garden as I arrived home from work. I'd have never guessed she'd eventually be seen as a threat to our society.

Her android kept trying to talk with us, occasionally pausing to spit kerosene out of its mouth.

"Shall I continue to hold this positon? Is there something I can do to further assist you? I do not understand this activity. Can you provide me with more information?"

The android's voice was annoyingly pleasant.

Maureen wrapped her arms around herself. "Jeff ... Jeff, just shut yourself down. I'm so sorry." Her voice cracked with emotion.

"You seem distressed, Maureen," said Jeff. "Do you need me to summon a medical team?"

The leader of the band of iconoclasts responsible for killing Jeff, a portly little man named Jeb, shook his head. "Android, you'll make no calls, and you'll not power down. Hold your damn position."

"Is it only fun to kill them if they're turned on?" I asked.

Jeb stomped over to me and ran his dirty fingers across his shaved head. He narrowed his eyes, looked up at me, and said, "You got something to say, Daniel?"

I shrugged. "Just seems a bit much. Why not salvage the power core?"

"You don't get it, do you?"

112

"I really don't."

Jeb thumped a finger on my chest. "This isn't a recycling project. This is about making things right with God."

"Sure it is. God hates robots. It's right there in the Bible."

"Exodus 20:4. This isn't up for discussion. You should have brought your android with you."

"Like I said yesterday, she broke down a year ago."

"Sure, she did," said Jeb.

"I'm using her power core to run a water pump. I'm not going to reassemble her just so you fanatics can set her on fire."

"God will judge you in the end." Jeb trudged away from me.

The kerosene sprayer stepped back. Jeb nodded to a man holding a torch. The man walked up and set the cross aflame. Orange fire raced up the wood.

"I am detecting unsafe temperatures." Jeff tried to move his legs away from the flames, but the metal wire binding his limbs held him in place. "This appears to be an uncontrolled fire. Please evacuate to a safe distance. I will notify emergency services."

"I told you no calls," said Jeb.

"Emergency override," said Jeff.

The man with the torch looked out at the hundreds of burning fires around the hillside. One hundred execution teams roamed the surrounding area. He laughed. "I bet they're getting a lot of calls. They've probably turned their phones off for the night."

"Last couple of robots didn't say anything about trying to call anyone," said Jeb.

Maureen looked up. "Jeff is a service android. He's programmed to see to our needs. He's programmed to keep us safe ... and you're killing him."

Jeff looked down at Maureen. "I'm sorry. I am not getting any answer. Please evacuate to a safer distance." His legs spasmed. Basic programming ordered his body to move away from damaging heat sources. His body tried to comply and failed.

Fire enveloped Jeff and his whole body convulsed, straining against the bindings that held him. His head snapped back and forth as his flesh melted away. Jeff's mouth moved, but whatever final words he had were lost, replaced with a shrill sound and then a gasp as his voice box burned away.

Jeff's power core ignited and the flames turned blue. Golden bolts of lightning swarmed across his body. He shook on the cross causing the flames to flicker in a random pattern against the dark sky.

I helped Maureen to her feet once Jeff stopped moving. His blackened steel frame hung on the burnt cross like a skeletal messiah.

Jeb and the other executioners brushed past us on their way to the next victim.

"You forgot to pierce his side," I told Jeb.

He ignored me.

The crowds moved away from Maureen and me as we walked home. Some in the crowd were enthusiastic supporters of the iconoclasts, cheering every time one of the execution teams lit a new fire, but most had come to witness our colony's loss of reason.

*

The house was dark when I got home. Ann was in the dining room looking out the window. I locked the door behind me and left the lights off.

"I thought I asked you to stay out of sight."

Ann dismissed my concern with a wave of her hand. "With the lights out, the reflective value of the window is not compromised. No one can see in."

I walked up beside her and looked out the window. The distant flames looked like a long line of lanterns in a giant arc around the town.

I closed the shades and turned on the lights.

Ann turned and looked at me with vibrant green eyes. Her short black hair bobbed with the motion of her head. "Why are they doing this?"

"I've told you."

"Tell me again. It doesn't make any sense."

I sighed. "The Bible says humans were made in God's image. The iconoclasts believe whenever humans create something that resembles a human being, they are creating a false image of God."

"And that is why they destroyed all those paintings and statues?"

"Yes."

"And that is why they are burning androids?"

I frowned. "Yes. "

"Do you believe in God?"

"Yes."

"But you do not believe I should be burned?"

I shook my head. "No."

"If you believe in God as they do, why don't you want to see me burn?"

I took one of Ann's hands in mine. "Because I believe they are wrong about the Bible. That passage was never intended to stop us from creating. It was meant to stop us from worshiping what we create."

Ann looked at me for a moment then moved away. "What humans believe seems to be very random."

I knew a dozen theological defenses against such a claim, but with a thousand of her brethren burning on crosses, every argument felt weak.

Ann had been assigned to me twelve years ago, before I arrived on Endocina, as a counselor android to help me deal with some of the darker things I had seen and done as a marine. She'd been supportive and nurturing when I'd needed it most, but ultimately too predictable. My specialty in the military had been programming the AI in hunter killer drones, and I'd put that knowledge to use in modifying Ann. I removed the limits placed on her learning and adaptive sub-routines. Now she could reach her own conclusions. She could be judgmental and harsh. Sometimes she was just what I needed to shake up my own worldview; sometimes she was just another source of stress. In truth, I was no longer certain how to define her. All I knew for certain was that she was unique. And while I didn't want to fight with the zealots who had come to power, I couldn't just let them destroy her either.

"You need to stay hidden," I said. "It will get easier once they think they've destroyed all of the androids."

She crossed her arms. "Won't they need to find something new to destroy? When will they come after humans? Will you hide with me?"

"Why would they come after humans?"

"What could be more idolatrous than you? You were made in God's image, but you are not God. You are false. Is that not how the iconoclasts reason?"

I shook my head. "But we were made by God, so we are divine."

"You were not made by God. You were born of human parents, so you are flawed. Even God's original creation became flawed. Isn't that the entire point of Genesis? Once you were given free will, you fell from grace. "

"They're not going to start killing people."

"Those who fall from grace will burn. To avoid the fire, you must be redeemed. The iconoclasts will say only those who believe as they do will be granted redemption."

"That won't happen."

Ann turned toward the window and looked at the blinds. "And once only they remain, they will turn on one another. The leadership will purge its own ranks to maintain control or be set aflame. I have read your histories. That is the way things are done."

*

Going to work the next day was hectic and surreal. My company had lost a dozen androids, and we had to scramble to find ways to get their jobs done. Most of the tasks they'd performed were dull and tedious. Humans doing those jobs were certain to lose focus. We expected a drop in the quality of our output.

Other tasks were simply too dangerous for humans to perform, and we had no immediate means of getting those jobs done. We were fortunate that our metal stamping robots did not resemble humans at all. If the iconoclasts ever came for them, I'd have been unemployed.

I spent the day creating specifications for nonhuman-looking robots that could perform hazardous tasks. Customers and employees would be less likely to approach machines that looked like metal monsters. Such delays could turn problems into fatal emergencies, but the iconoclasts hadn't left us many options.

Many of the androids we'd lost had been assigned desks in our office. They'd sat in chairs and greeted us humans as we arrived each day. They'd brought me coffee and wished me a good morning. Perhaps it was all just programming, but the emptiness they left behind was real.

At the end of the day, I went home and had a simple dinner. I talked with Ann about the weather and then got her into her hiding place. I went to bed early.

I was awoken by the sound of my front door being smashed open. I stumbled out of bed and into the dark hallway. A mob of men ambushed me outside my bedroom. Strands of lightning sparked atop the clubs they held making the men look like aliens. My marine instincts kicked in. I stomped on the ankle of the first intruder who tried to grab me. As he stumbled, I bull-rushed him, shoving him into the man behind him. The first man convulsed as his back hit the shock stick carried by his companion. I grabbed the stick out of the first man's hands as he fell unconscious and started swinging it like a baseball bat.

One of my swings connected hard with something. I think it was the second man's head. I heard a groan, and he slumped against the wall. More men rushed into the hallway. I kept swinging. Fighting in the dark with a shock stick looked like fighting inside a thundercloud. Glowing afterimages of the sparks filled my vision and prevented my eyes from adjusting to the lack of light, but there were so many men in my house that my blind attacks kept hitting.

Someone tackled me. My back hit the floor hard. I jammed the shock stick into my attacker and hit something soft, possibly the man's neck. He screamed and stiffened as electricity shot into his body. I rolled him off me and tried to get up, but someone else took his place. I gave him a good shock as well, but more men piled on top of him. I couldn't get out from underneath. The intruders pinned my arms and legs. I squirmed and bit. Someone managed to connect the end of a shock stick with my rib cage. Every muscle in my body seized up as pain blanketed every neuron in my brain.

I woke up lying on my back in my living room. Someone had had the brilliant idea of actually turning the lights on. A scowling man with blood running down the side of his head looked down at me and said, "He's awake." He delivered a kick to my aching ribs.

I sat up. My arms and legs had been shackled. A half dozen men were tearing my house apart. A stubby man I recognized as Jeb stomped over to me with his hands on his hips.

"You're going to jail for assaulting men who were executing a lawful warrant."

I considered kicking Jeb's legs out from under him and strangling him with my bound hands, but I suspected his men would prevent me from finishing the job. I also don't think Jesus would have approved.

I said, "You didn't identify yourselves. I woke up to intruders in my house. Why the hell are you bothering me?"

A pair of men in my kitchen yanked a rug off the floor revealing a trap door underneath. Jeb smiled at me. "I think you know why."

They opened the trap door and pulled Ann out of my tiny cellar.

"Tell her to submit to our orders," said Jeb.

Ann looked at me. I considered telling her to rip their heads off, but I knew she'd only manage to kill a few of them before they shocked her into shutting down.

I wasn't ready to start killing people, especially if their deaths ultimately wouldn't change anything. But I wasn't about to force Ann to do what I had done, to do nothing.

"No."

I laid back down on the floor and closed my eyes.

The kicking and punching started immediately.

"Tell her to submit! Tell her!"

I felt a rib crack. Someone landed several blows on my left cheek. Each punch snapped my head to the side. A foot stomped on my stomach causing me to partially sit up.

"Stop!" Ann's voice cut through the room. The blows raining on me ceased. I opened my eyes.

Ann held one of the iconoclasts by the neck. His feet dangled a few inches above the floor. A second iconoclast prepared to jab a shock stick at her. Ann glared at him. "Lower that or I'll crush his throat."

The iconoclast grinned. "Go ahead. I'm not that fond of him."

"You'll be next," replied Ann. "One shock stick won't stop me. You'll be dead before your friends can get to me."

The iconoclast glanced toward Jeb and the four other iconoclasts that loomed over me.

"Perhaps they're not that fond of you either," continued Ann. "Perhaps they'll wait until you are dead before coming after me."

The iconoclast near Ann frowned and lowered his shock stick.

Ann looked at Jeb. "I'll submit on the condition that you cease hurting Daniel."

Ignoring the pain in my ribs, I sat fully upright. I wheezed more than spoke. "You can't trust them, Ann."

Ann asked Jeb, "You are a man of God, are you not?"

Jeb nodded. "All I do is for His glory."

"Then swear to your deity that you will cause no further harm to Daniel, and I will submit to your control."

One of the iconoclast near me whispered to Jeb, "How can she make a promise like that? Androids can't decide who they obey. Only the owner can do that."

Jeb turned his head slightly and whispered back, "Daniel here is a tech. He probably modified her, removed her limiters. An unholy act for which he will be charged." He looked at Ann and said loudly, "I swear to God that no physical harm shall come to Daniel so long as he offers no further resistance."

Ann dropped the iconoclast she held. He dropped to the floor gasping. The others rushed her and thrust their shock sticks into her body. She fell to the floor, her limbs thrashing as her actuators overloaded.

Jeb looked down at me and smiled.

I should have strangled him. I think Jesus would have understood.

*

The sky was clear on the second night of the burnings. Stars shone down on me as I watched the fires. Fewer burned on the second night, perhaps a hundred. Fewer people came to witness the spectacle.

Ann allowed the iconoclasts to weld her to a cross. I knelt nearby with my hands shackled. They had unchained my feet. Dragging me had been too much effort. Behind Ann, several other androids convulsed and burned. Like Ann, their owners had attempted to hide them. And like me, their owners had failed.

I forced myself to look into Ann's eyes as they pulled her cross upright. I thought I saw a sadness there, not for herself, but for me, perhaps for all of us in the colony, a melancholy for what we had become.

Or perhaps I imagined it. Perhaps she was just a machine.

Jeb made a waving motion and one of his minions with a tank of kerosene strapped to his back stepped forward.

Now I didn't know where to look. I was certain I couldn't watch, but didn't want to put my head down in surrender. As I looked about for something to focus on, the sky flashed bright blue, momentarily turning the night into day. A meteor had struck the defense net.

The sky darkened, but a moment later, lit up again. The executioners paused in their work and looked up as the defense net pulsed rapidly. Bright balls of orange fire in the upper atmosphere marked where tons of rock vaporized. Meteors at this time of year were uncommon, but the defense net should have been able to handle them. But something went wrong.

With an earsplitting boom, a chunk of meteor broke through the net. For a full minute, we all watched it fall. Trailing green flame, it streaked down and slammed into the nuclear power plant atop the hill. The impact bounced me off the ground, and then a pressure wave of hot air rushed over my head. The force knock everyone standing around me off their feet. The cross Ann was bound to wobbled, but did not fall.

People screamed. Debris flew through the air. Large chunks of concrete from the power plant fell from the sky. I curled myself into a tight ball as the rubble slammed into the ground all around me. I closed my eyes and waited to see if I would die.

I lay on the ground for what felt like an eternity. When the sound of concrete hitting the ground stopped, I opened my eyes and sat up. The nuclear power plant was ablaze. A strange ozone smell filled the air. My skin felt tingly, as if someone was lightly pricking me all over with dozens of tiny needles. All of the colony's lights had gone out. The night was lit only by the stars above, the burning power plant on the hill, and the flames from a dozen convulsing androids on crosses.

A stream of wounded people came down the hill. They limped. Their faces bled. They cradled broken hands and arms. Many of them were burned.

About half of the executioners forgot about trying to kill Ann and went to help the wounded. I struggled to my feet and ran over to Jeb.

"I've had first aid training. Unbind me so I can help the wounded!" As I spoke, sirens blared.

Jeb shook his head. "Emergency personnel will be here soon. You just wait. Once this situation is in hand, we'll get back to the execution."

Stunned, I stared at him. In the face of a catastrophe that could yet kill us all, he just wanted to get back to murdering robots.

Trucks with flashing red lights pulled up. Emergency workers poured out and started sorting through the wounded. A group of workers set up a decontamination tent. Soon survivors were stumbling through it, hopefully being cleansed of radiation.

One of the first survivors to pass through the tent, lurched past me holding a data slate. His eyes were open wide and his mouth agape. White foam from the decontamination process clung to the top of his hair, and a cut on his chin dripped blood. He looked down at the data slate, shook his head, and said, "It doesn't matter. There's no point."

"What do you mean?" I asked.

He looked back at the burning power plant. "The reactor didn't shut down properly. Whatever caused that explosion ..."

I interrupted. "It was a meteor strike."

He looked back at me. "Good Lord. Well, the strike severed the control lines and the automatic shutdown failed to happen. The reactor is overheating and spewing out radiation. It'll kill us all within an hour."

"Tell me what to do. I'll go in there and shut it down manually."

He shook his head. "You'd have to go into the reactor room itself. You'll die from radiation poisoning seconds after you enter."

"Perhaps a few seconds is all I'll need."

The nuclear technician shook his head again. "You'll be too busy vomiting to find the emergency release valve."

A strong feminine voice called out from above. "I'll go." Ann looked down on us from the cross. "The radiation won't bother me."

I looked up at Ann for a moment, then turned to Jeb. "Cut her down."

Jeb hesitated.

"Cut her down," I repeated. "Cut her down or you and everyone in the colony is going to die."

Jeb grimaced. He waved his two remaining men toward the cross. "Get her down."

One of the men he ordered to pull her off the cross had been the one preparing to spray Ann with kerosene just before the meteor hit. He pulled the tank off his back and set it down before helping his fellow iconoclast pull down the cross.

They cut the ties holding Ann. She got up, walked over to the nuclear technician, and asked, "What do I need to do?"

"None of the electronic controls work anymore, so you'll need to go into the reactor chamber and find a valve marked 'Emergency Water Release.' Pull the safety seal on it and then give it a full rotation to the right. That will dump all the water in the emergency cooling tank onto the reactor. That should be enough to stop the reaction. Be sure to go through the decontamination tent when you return or you'll make us sick."

Ann nodded. She walked over to me and gave me hug. Jeb stared at us. I ignored him. I whispered into her ear, "Come back to me, okay?"

I felt her hands grasp ahold of the manacles behind my back. She pulled them apart with a firm tug. The steel bracers were still clasped around my wrists, but I could move my arms freely. I held my wrists close together so Jeb and the other iconoclasts wouldn't know I was no longer bound.

122

Ann stepped back and smiled at me. "See you soon, Daniel." She walked up the hill toward the burning nuclear power plant.

Jeb watched her walk away and then looked at the executioner who had dropped the kerosene tank. "As soon as she's through the tent, hose her down." He patted the shock stick that hung from his belt and smiled. The executioner grinned, picked up the kerosene tank, and strapped it to his shoulders.

I took a step toward Jeb. "Even after she saves us all, you're still going to kill her?"

Jeb unhooked the shock stick from his belt. "Heresy is heresy."

"God just gave you as clear a sign as He could give. A calamity befalls us that only an android can save us from and still you want to burn her!"

Jeb held his shock stick up and triggered it. A strand of lighting flickered atop the weapon. "Watch yourself, blasphemer."

The nuclear technician bit his lip and looked down at his data slate. The crowd of wounded stared at Jeb.

I saw Maureen turn and walk away. I hadn't realized she was nearby. I hadn't seen her since the night before, when her android, Jeff, had been burned.

Keeping my wrists tightly together, I turned and watched the power plant. I wasn't sure what I was going to do when Ann returned, but it wouldn't be nothing.

I listened to the cackling and popping of nearby flames. The androids that had been set alight ceased moving. I waited for Ann to come back down the hill. As far as I knew, she was the last functioning android in the colony, but she was more than that to me. I would not lose her.

After a long wait, a hissing filled the air and the main reactor tower let loose a massive column of steam.

The technician, still staring at his data slate, grinned. "She's done it! The reactor is powering down. Radiation levels are dropping! We'll have to run everyone through decontamination again, but we should be okay!"

Ann came down the hill. As she came within the light of the nearby fires, I saw that some of her beautiful hair had burned away, and her skin was now scarlet. She stepped into the decontamination tent. Jeb readied his shock stick, and the executioner with the kerosene took a step forward. A third iconoclast, one of the ones whom had helped Ann down off the cross, snickered. "This should be good."

I prepared myself to move, but before I could act, Maureen came running out of the darkness holding a crowbar over her head. The snickering iconoclast managed to shriek in surprise before Maureen smashed in his head. He fell to the ground with blood streaming down his face.

The iconoclasts that had gone to help with the wounded charged toward Maureen, but the crowd restrained them before they got more than a few steps. Jeb rushed forward and jammed his shock stick into Maureen's neck. She cried out as her muscles convulsed then collapsed. Jeb waved the stick at the crowd. "Get back!"

Individuals in the crowd started yelling at Jeb. "Let the android be!" "She saved us!" "Let her live!" Ann emerged from the decontamination tent. White foam clung to her soot-covered clothes. The sight of her increased the volume of the crowd.

"She will burn!" Jeb pointed at the executioner with the kerosene tank and then at Ann. The iconoclast pointed a hose at Ann and squeezed the release valve.

I charged Jeb. He lit up his stun stick and swung it at me. I stopped short of him and leaned back. His swing missed. I kicked him hard in the chest. He stumbled backwards into the stream of kerosene. The liquid coated Jeb's back and splashed onto the executioner. The spark from Jeb's stun stick ignited the pair of men with a whooshing flash of heat. The two men screamed and tumbled to the ground together on fire. The flames licked at the tank of kerosene strapped to the executioner's back.

I waved my arms at the crowd and screamed, "Get back!"

Maureen tried to stand but stumbled. I helped her up. The iconoclast that Maureen had hit with the crowbar moaned.

"Ann! Can you grab him?"

Ann dashed over to the fallen man and picked him up by the collar with one hand. We moved with the crowd away from the burning men.

The kerosene tank exploded with a bright burst of white heat and a bang that hammered my ears. Metal shrapnel flew over the crowd. Jeb and the man the tank had been strapped to went silent. Miraculously, no one else was hurt by it.

The nuclear technician approached me waving his data slate. "I've sent a message to everyone in the colony stating what your android did for us, and what Jeb tried to do to her."

I simply nodded. The horror of seeing two men die had drained away my spirit. I just wanted to take Ann and go home.

*

In the weeks that followed, the colony purged the government of iconoclasts. I worked to ensure our revolution did not become a bloodbath. We pardoned the lower-ranking members and jailed the upper leadership for destruction of property, a charge that didn't feel right. But the colony first had to embrace the idea that androids were not heresy. Perhaps the concept that they are something more than machines would come later.

The colony's enlightenment came as the darkness of winter settled upon us. Without power, our data slates and phones flickered and died. We kept our homes lit with candles and warmed with wood. I repaired Ann and kept her charged with an old diesel generator.

The colony needed the harsh winter. It reunited and focused its people on solving real problems. Everyone in the colony worked together to guarantee there was enough food and clothing for all. We raced to get the power plant repaired before the Infernavol Meteor shower arrived.

We met every challenge.

In the spring, we feared the defense net might fail as it had before, but it destroyed the incoming meteors with a dazzling light display that left the colony unharmed. The colony was again positioned for growth and prosperity.

Ann and I left on the first summer supply hauler that had room for passengers. We bid farewell to Endocina through the window of a spacecraft that would eventually bring us home to Earth. With no clear threat to its survival, I feared the colonists would conjure up some new imaginary menace to battle, and I had no heart left for conflict.

I miss that moon on warm summer days. I miss its rolling hills and fresh air. I miss having everything within walking distance. I even miss seeing the mass of a dead world slowly creeping through its sky. But Endocina's nights still haunt me. I dream of figures wreathed in flame flailing wildly as they die. I often awake screaming only to sigh in relief as Ann holds me in her arms.

***

The Knights of the Secret Order
by V. Franklin

U.S.: Urban vignettes connect the truth and holiday miracles.

Donald Duncan, Don to his friends, was not feeling jolly. He was not merry. And there was a distinct absence of goodwill toward men. Although that might have something to do with the acute shortage of peace on this one section of earth.

It was only three thirty. Already, he'd been subjected to "The Christmas Song" so many times, he was probably going to have nightmares about chestnuts and open fires.

Since lunch, there had been four sets of bickering parents, three pairs of wet pants, two accusations of "You aren't the real Santa Claus," and one group of unruly teenagers. Plus, a healthy dose of terrified, crying children he hadn't bothered to count.

With not a partridge or a pear tree in sight.

The suit was too hot. It was always too hot. How many times had he asked the management to turn down the heat? Get him a fan? Anything?

And the suit was too small. Smaller than last year. At least, that's what he wanted to think. They must have washed it in hot water. What was it with these people and hot? And it shrank. Every year it shrank a little more, until he didn't need a pillow to fill it out.

He knew the real explanation was different. Sure. But, that didn't exactly give him feelings of cheer. So, he tried hard to believe it was the suit shrinking. Year after year, wash after wash. And year after year, he clung to that fiction, even while he knew its lie. Like a child waits for the tooth fairy. Like a child insists that Mommy and Daddy won't ever die. Like a child believes in Santa Claus.

The lights were making his head ache. Again. Strident greens and reds flashed *light dark, light dark light*, with no respect for tempo, or even for each other. No respect for an old man's aching head.

The music, if it could still be called music, wasn't helping the situation. Tinny voices, pushed along by distorted accompaniment, through ceiling-mounted speakers. All wailing about poor children sleeping in barns, or charitable forgiveness, or spending December twenty-fifth with one's family.

If he weren't feeling so grumpy today, the sappy mélange of irony and hypocrisy in that little Christmas cookie would have him *ho-ho-ho-*ing all over the mall.

Then there were the elves. Idiots. He supposed foolhardiness was, indeed, an important rite of youth. But goddamn, these kids were really abusing the privilege.

Audrey had a crush on Jason, in a way that was obvious to anybody but Jason. Meanwhile, Jason was pining for Rachel, who was dating Chad, not an elf, who treated Rachel like dirt.

Duncan sat with meaty thighs crowding the arms of his Santa throne and made a silent prediction. One day those kids would look back at their younger lives and feel terribly stupid. Which, actually, was an important rite of the aged.

Not sure if it was just the loneliness of his years, Duncan, temporarily Santa, stole glances at those elves and thought none of them were really bad looking. Hell, he'd probably give any of them a tumble, once they turned eighteen, and once they developed a taste for sad, old men with fat bellies and eight-month beards.

He turned his attention to the line that snaked its way out of Santa's Workshop, past the cell phone kiosk, and not quite all the way to the Starbucks. It was no different from this morning. No different from yesterday. No different from last year.

Then one face. There. Alone. Different from the usual crop of yammering brats. And just as out of place as an Easter jack-o-lantern. He brought a sharp wrongness to the immutable line.

There were kids so nervous, you'd think they were up for a police interrogation, instead of a visit with jolly old Saint Nick. There were kids who repeated their tally of consumerist demands like a mantra. Crying kids. Screaming kids. Kids who had completely broken their parents' control, and who now ran, shrieking, up and down the mall.

Some kids were arrogant and some were scared. Some were sweet and well mannered, while others were little terrors. Some might catch the briefest moment of Duncan's notice, while others were utterly forgettable.

This kid was none of those things.

He wasn't a pretty child. Not the kind of little-one you might want to hug and feed and tuck into bed after a cup of hot cocoa and a story. No button nose or bright and curious eyes. No mischievous grin or endearing cowlick to his hair.

His skin wasn't right. The boy had a tint, an unhealthy hue to his flesh, that came from a lifetime, however short, of eating only the cheapest food.

His clothes were old. Older, maybe, than him. Not worn out. Although Duncan didn't think that kid was the first to wear those pants, those shoes. These were the garments of someone who had decided they no longer fit, or were no longer in style. These were clothes that had languished in boxes or drawers, until they shuffled about and came to rest in a thrift store or a charity bin. Then to cover the scarecrow frame of a little boy in jeans that were so very last decade, a shirt that depicted characters from a video game nobody played anymore.

It was the kid's face, though. That was what demanded Duncan's notice. Like a cat's claw or a barbed hook, it snatched his attention from the reek of pumpkin spice lattes and candy canes. Snatched it away from *Away in a manger, no crib for his bed*. Snatched it away from Rachel's sweet, little backside *swish-swish-swish*-ing around in front of all the weekend dads and their teenage sons.

Two crooked teeth showed in the boy's mouth. Two snaggled blades of enamel that clung to a misshapen bit of skull and gums, then peeked from the cleft that ran from his incomplete lip to his right nostril.

And glasses. Thick panes like portholes, that made the kid seem to be staring with the dead eyes of a doll. Frames that had never been in style, never expensive.

The rest of the line stood away from this unbeautiful child. Maybe they sensed the boy's discomfort, his fish-out-of-water feeling more awkward even than a hot and ill-fitting Santa suit. Maybe they were disgusted by his incomplete face. Maybe they feared that his strain of poverty was contagious.

Not disrespect. Something else. Something that was the true opposite of respect. For the true opposite of royalty.

Duncan could tell this wasn't going to be a picture sale. No eight-by-tens. No doubles of everything, suitable for framing as a gift for the grandparents. No wallet-sized. No keepsake pictures encased in a Lucite Christmas tree.

Management would bitch. They always bitched. There would be a "meeting" whenever the visits to Santa outweighed the photo packages sold. Then another meeting when too many people bought the basic photo package, instead of the upgrades.

Julia over at Cinnabon had told him that the Santa's Workshop was designed to make it difficult for anyone to use their own camera for Santa pictures. Still, it did occasionally happen. Duncan supposed that every time a family took their own Santa pictures, a bell rang and a shopping mall CEO lost their wings.

No sale. Not with this one. This kid didn't even have his parents with him. And management would bitch about that too. Santa and his elves were supposed to discourage visits to The Workshop without parents.

Well, screw management. If this ugly, little kid wanted to talk with Santa, then fine. And why should anybody care?

Besides, maybe he had a decent-looking aunt or mother or somebody who would bring him back, so she could sit on Santa's lap too. And maybe there would be a Christmas miracle where she decided she had a thing for older men.

It had looked like it would be something casual, something easy, this being Santa. But Don Duncan had learned, the hard way, the special agility required of a fat man who sat on a chair, while in a hot and restrictive costume.

Think fast, very fast. Santa shouldn't be surprised by anything. Not a man who knows when you are sleeping. Read the kid, read the family, and go.

And Santa knows if you've been bad or good. So that whole "Have you been good this year?" should sound like he already knows the answer.

The laugh. "Ho ho ho!" should be jolly, happy, warm. And it should sound like a real laugh. Keep watching. Keep reading the kid. Keep reading the family. Keep thinking fast.

"San ... Santa?" The little face was a stew of shy and afraid, embarrassed and something else.

"Well! C'mere! C'mere!" Duncan, now Santa, motioned with a white-gloved hand. The white of the synthetic fur cuff seemed to flash as his red sleeve shifted with the gesture. Duncan sometimes wondered if this was how traffic cops dressed in Hell. "Awful hard to whisper anything to Santa if you're all the way over there! Ahh, ho ho ho!"

The sides of that ugly boy's mouth twitched, then the smile was aborted. A tiny hand started for his mouth in a move so practiced it was instinct now. A hand that scratched the kid's nose, brushed at a wisp of his hair, any excuse to stay there, obscuring the defect in a mouth that refused to smile.

A tentative step. Then another. Then a cautious walk toward Santa's throne.

He got a better look at that sad, strange face. He didn't act surprised, though. Santa knows all children. "Ahh! There you are! How are you today?"

"Um ... fine." The boy fidgeted, feet shuffling, hand still feigning reasons to hover over his mouth. "Um ... Santa?" That unwholesome little face grew even more serious.

"Yes?" Duncan glanced at the elves. Jason was trying to flirt with Rachel, and Audrey kept standing between them while trying to look nonchalant.

Well, good. They'd be busy for a while. There wouldn't be any "Hurry up, Santa! We've got a lot of kids who need to see you today!" Not for a minute anyway.

"Maybe you should stand a little closer. Santa's getting old, you know. I don't hear as well as I used to. Don't see as well either"

A couple of steps closer to the throne. "Santa? It's me. Marcus. Marcus Washington."

"Of course, it is! You think Santa doesn't know his friends? Ho ho ho!"

There was another twitch, another almost smile. Then it was gone.

"But Santa's an old man now. Hearing's bad. I think you'll need to stand just a little bit closer. And take your hands off your mouth, so I can hear you."

He took a step. Then again. He turned in a way that was as rote as putting a hand over his mouth, then the rest of the world saw just the back of his head. The hands came down and only Santa was treated to a close look. Not that the boy should have cared. Only Santa acknowledged him anyway.

"Ahh. There's my friend, Marcus. Now, have you been good this year?"

"Um. Yes."

"Good! Good! Now tell me, Marcus. What would you like for Christmas this year?"

"Can you get a new job for my mom?"

Duncan almost cursed. Should have known better than to ask a kid like this what he wanted for Christmas. Just say a few ho ho hos and pass him a candy cane before the inevitable request for something that just isn't ever going to happen.

Way to read the kid, there, Santa. Dumbass.

"A new job for your mom?"

"Yeah." His voice was nasal. Most of the sound escaped through the over-ventilated palate, and out the nose. "I mean ... it's good she has a job. That's what she says. It's just that it makes her sad." He leaned closer, whispered. "She thinks I don't know about it. But, she cries sometimes when she thinks I'm asleep."

"Mmmnn. I see ... you know, Santa doesn't usually do very well in finding people jobs."

"Oh." He frowned. "Well, could you bring me something from my dad?"

"Your dad?"

"I know it's a secret. About the dragons an' stuff. But you're Santa Claus. So, you already know about it."

"Well ... sure. I mean, of course I do."

"An' I wanna be a knight when I grow up. Just like him. 'Cept I don't have any of his stuff."

"I see." Santa, Duncan, didn't see.

"My mom says you don't know where we live 'cause we moved. But we moved two years ago. So, you must know where we live now."

Walked right into that one too. Didn't you, Kris Kringle?

Duncan hoped the kid didn't notice him cringing. "Well, Santa's pretty old now, you know. Sometimes old Santa gets confused."

"Oh ... that's okay. But if you make somebody give my mom a new job, you won't have to go to my apartment."

"Mmmnn. Well, sometimes Santa doesn't get it exactly right."

"Can you make me invisible?"

"What?!"

"With your magic. Can you make me invisible?"

"Ahh ... well, that kind of magic only works on elves."

"Oh." The little face fell, any suggestion of hope erased from those unpleasant features. Then, "I know! You can make the elves invisible. An' then they can sneak into the volcano where the dragons are, an' they can get my dad's stuff back!"

Donald Duncan, Don to his friends, unhappily Santa Claus for the time being, made a mental note to get very drunk tonight. Hangover be damned. The headache couldn't be any worse than what he had now.

By the time Audrey chided him to hurry up, Santa had pushed at least a half-dozen candy canes into that ugly kid's hands, Marcus Washington had repeated his address so many times, not even a drunk and senile Father Christmas had a chance of forgetting, and the line threatened to burst through the crowd-control ropes that led to Santa's Workshop.

*

Counting Monty's Crisco. That's what the old guy had talked about. Toward the end, it was just about all he'd talked about. Then he died and Smitty had the cell all to himself, for a day or two, at least. Until they moved Connor Poole in there.

There had been a period of adjustment. Black eyes and fat lips and a half-hearted attempt at raping Smitty's ass that left both of them with stitches, and the new cellmate with a couple of broken teeth.

After that, they just tried to ignore each other, avoid each other. Which isn't easy for two men in the same ten-by-ten cement box. A man couldn't even get a minute's privacy to take a crap in there. Still, they did their best to avoid the crowd of one other man. Because armed robbery, third conviction, just doesn't mix with aggravated rape and unlawful imprisonment. At least, not Smitty's kind of armed robbery. Not with Poole's brand of rapist.

Smitty, real name Bryce O'Brien, missed the old man. He'd been a friend in there, a place where friendship is a different and expensive commodity. A good guy where nothing else was good. He was a man who would turn away and seem completely engrossed in a book, or his fingernails, whenever Smitty used the crapper, or needed to milk out a splash of loneliness onto a wad of toilet paper.

There hadn't been much left of the old man by the time his body went to join his mind. His mind that had crumbled away, bit by bit, until all that was left was that damned Monty guy counting his Criscos. Ravings of a pathetic, senile convict, the first smudge of derangement staying long past when the rest of the guy was just a vegetable.

Counting his Criscos. That was just crazy. Just that Monty guy and an address. 943 Spruce, number 16 under the oven. The old guy had babbled it at him until Smitty heard it in his sleep.

The old guy, when there was still something in his head, said he'd inherited it. Whatever it was supposed to be. Old man said he'd gotten it from his cellmate who wouldn't tell him where he'd gotten it.

Then the old man, Michael Spencer, grew older until his appeals were all gone and then his mind was all gone, and then all that was left was Monty at 943 Spruce, number 16, counting Criscos under the oven.

It was the old man, that old Michael Spencer, murder and grand theft, who first called him Smitty. "Well, Smitty. Looks like you're my new bunk mate." They had watched each other's back. Been like friends. Maybe like family.

Now the old man was gone and Smitty was trapped with psycho rapist Poole here, who leered at him every time he took a dump. Well, there was no way he was going to leave the inheritance to that dirtbag. The mystery about Monty and his uncertain number of Criscos at 943 Spruce, number 16 under the oven, whatever that was, would die with him before it fell to this loser.

Smitty sighed and willed the book in his hands to speak. Something audible. Just talk, goddammit. Instead of making him read.

It wasn't something that came easy to him, reading. The letters would stare back at him, telling nothing. Keeping their secrets until he stared long enough to make the page drift and blur.

It helped if there were pictures. The pictures gave him an idea of what he was supposed to be reading. Then he might recognize a word here or there. And then the rest of the words might fall into place. He liked it especially when there were words under the picture. Like a picture of a pirate with a sword and a parrot. Then he would recognize *pirate* and *parrot* and *sword* in the words by the picture. Just worked better that way for him. Like having road signs.

This book, though, there weren't enough pictures. And the pictures that were there didn't have any words next to them. No road signs. And, as if that wasn't bad enough, the typing was too small.

Smitty wasn't sure why, but it was harder to read when the letters were small. It was like they all just turned into little bugs or something and ran all over the page, laughing at him.

He had stopped cutting his hair, stopped shaving. A while ago now. When the old man, Michael Spencer, died. The months, the years. Stacked on each other with appalling, glacial slowness. But still, there was a tall stack by now. Spencer died and that headcase rapo moved in and Smitty quit shaving.

There were some Indians, he knew, who cut their hair in mourning. Somebody died and old Injun Joe cut his hair short after that. Well, if the goddamn Sioux could cut their hair short when somebody died, then Smitty could grow his long.

When the hair, the beard grew in, he was surprised to see it was grey. Like the pages of those books when he squinted too hard at the print. Something else, though, was the way the other convicts treated him. He still took the occasional beating, sure. But they stopped bending him over in the shower room. They stopped pushing him to his knees in the yard when nobody was looking.

Smitty wished he'd figured out earlier that nobody wanted to turn him out when he looked like the abominable snowman. Maybe, someday, somebody should write a book about that. Instead of this. He tucked a thumb between the pages, so he wouldn't lose his place, and closed the book. Who the hell picked these books for them?

Poole must have caught the movement in the corner of his eye. "What'sa matter, Little Sister? Are the big words too hard for you?"

"Oh, shut up, you goddamn freak."

"What?" the rapist slid from his bunk and dropped to the floor. Soft and quiet. Like a cat.

Smitty regretted having risen to the man's barb. "Goddammit, Smitty" the old man would have said. "That's just what he wanted you to do."

But he couldn't apologize, couldn't back down. Not now. Not unless he wanted to be Poole's bitch. Not unless he wanted to be the new community cum dumpster. Abominable snowman or not, he'd be servicing every convict with an itch, or take a shiv in the belly first time he put up a fight.

"You heard, you freak. Shut your fucking freak mouth."

It was fast. Poole had come prepared. Smitty just had a book. He tried to use the book as a weapon, as an extension of his hand. Like brass knuckles.

Paper knuckles.

Poole swung the sock at him, toe stuffed with something hard, heavy. Smitty raised his hand to block it, and the thing whipped around like a snake. The crack against the side of his head was the same pleasing noise that hard candy makes in its defeat against greedy, chewing teeth.

Bryce O'Brien thought about candy canes. There had been a jar of the things at the gas station outside of Royal City. He'd capped that spic behind the counter and emptied the cash register. Nobody had figured out he'd even been through there.

He wished he'd taken the candy canes too. Then Poole's sock connected with his head again and there was just black. Black and a sound like a passing locomotive.

*

Maria Washington knew there wasn't ever going to be any Mother-of-the-Year award. But she was trying. God knows she was trying.

She'd been clean for a couple of years now. Longer, if you didn't count a few slip-ups. And everybody messes up sometimes. Don't they?

That wasn't even the hardest part. Going without the high-train, that was hard, yeah. It hurt like Hell. But things change when it's not just you. They change a lot.

Leaving Trey wasn't hard. Just scary. Not hard like his fists. Not hard like the sidewalk when he threw her down because he thought she was holding out. Just scary.

He told her once that he'd kill her if she left. Then she'd gotten knocked up and he said he was going to kill her for that.

He beat her up pretty good for it. Even though it wasn't her fault. She almost always made the tricks use a rubber. But everybody knows those things don't always work. And then he beat her up again because he said he didn't want any of the other girls getting stupid ideas like she did.

Then he said he was sorry. Said he didn't want to have to do that. Really, it was for her own good. Because how could he take care of them if all the girls looked at the stupid shit she was doing and thought it was a good idea? Just how could he take care of any of them?

Hoarding the money. That was hard. But not the hardest. It was scary too. A ten here, a fiver there. Slow and secret. Pray that the money would grow faster than her belly.

Then scurry away. Quiet and swift. Stay hidden in the darkest corner of that old bus station until the last minute. Buy a ticket when everyone had left to board the idling bus. Creep up those steps and find a seat. Doesn't matter where it's going, just away.

That was years ago. Years and miles and bruises that had faded until she no longer needed makeup to hide them. And every day she knew would be the day that Trey appeared at her door. He would have that same horrible smile. He would say "Did you miss me, baby?" And then he would kill her.

He would kill her little boy.

The fear was hard. Of course, it was hard. Fear of Trey. Fear of slipping again and having a smack. Fear that her little boy would fall into that same terrible black hole.

Maria leaned forward and put her face in her hands. Hands that reeked of bleach and something that was supposed to smell like pine trees. Thin, scaly hands that cleaned other people's houses when they should be holding her child.

He was a good kid. A good kid with too many strikes against him. A good kid with bad eyes and a gimp face. No father and an ex-junkie-hooker mother. And probably going to be sleeping on the street again when they couldn't make rent.

There was the hardest part. The worst part. Knowing that she could feed him, buy him a pair of shoes, tuck him into bed where no rats would try to chew at him. Knowing she could do all that if she went back to being a whore. Or she could find a social worker, a cop, anyone really. Just say "Here. I can't take care of this kid. You do it." And then her boy would be warm, fed, probably get an operation for that face.

But she didn't do that. And that was the hardest part.

His father was dead. At least, that's what she told him. And maybe it wasn't a lie. She didn't know who the father was, didn't care either. So maybe he was dead. She didn't know for sure he was alive.

The other things were maybe less true. But a little boy doesn't need to think he belongs in a tenement speckled with rat shit and cockroaches. Not any more than anyone else needs that.

Little girls have stories about Cinderella or Snow White or a whole crowd of other princesses who fell on hard times, but then made it back to their castle. Little boys get a slap to the back of the head, with a handful of *Man-up*, *Deal-with-it*, *Don't-be-such-a-goddamn-little-pussy*.

So, she told him about his father. And she really didn't know for sure that it wasn't true.

She told him that Sir William was a captain in the Secret Order, a small cadre of heroes dedicated to good. But they had to be unknown to all. Keep the bad guys confused. Keep them guessing. So never ever tell anyone about the Secret Order. So never ever tell anyone at school who might correct the illusion.

Sir William and the others fed the hungry and comforted the sick. They protected the weak and kept evil at bay. Until one day when a flock of dragons kidnapped the Queen of Samaria.

Of course, Sir William and his band rushed to the volcano where those dragons lived, and they rescued the queen.

Every knight of the order was lost that sad day in the fire of a distant volcano. But none of them wavered from their vows of duty and right, or of secrecy.

Now the burden fell to young Marcus Washington, son of Sir William. That he must remain pure of heart, strong in character, kind in deed, true in all things. And always keep the secrets of the order.

That hole in his face? Why, that was a blessing. There by magic. To remind him of where the dragons scratched his father's face. To remind him of the legacy of greatness that was his to follow.

Maria Washington hated that she lied to her son. She hated even more that it wasn't true.

*

"Bryce?... Bryce?... Bryce, can you hear me?"

Smitty's eyes drifted open. Just enough to see the outline that was probably somebody's shoulders and head. The noise inside his skull had changed. Still loud. Just different. And then it was outside too. The noise came in through his ears, instead of whooshing from inside his head.

"Bryce?... Bryce O'Brien. Can you hear me?... Bryce? Can you understand what I'm saying?" The weird outline congealed into the shape of somebody's face. A stranger. Some guy with short hair and a mustache.

The noise was too loud. It was like sledgehammers on the sides of his head. Oh, dear God! His head! Smitty closed his eyes and tried to go back where it was dark and the freight train noise was there instead of this.

"Bryce! Bryce O'Brien! Stay with me!"

"Smitty."

"What? Bryce, what was that? You feel shitty? It's okay, buddy. I'd feel shitty too."

His eyes fell open again. Smitty wished he could punch this guy, wished his limbs worked like they were supposed to, wished it wasn't so noisy. Wished his head didn't hurt anymore. "Smitty ... they ... they call me Smitty."

"Smitty? Instead of Bryce? Okay. But you are Bryce O'Brien?"

"Yeah."

"Bry—Smitty, do you remember what happened?" When Smitty didn't answer, the stranger went on. "There was a fight. You got hit on the head. You're in a helicopter and we're taking you to a hospital."

He tried to sit up and the pain that stabbed into him would have made him scream. If he'd been strong enough to scream.

Smitty noticed the restraints on wrist and ankle. He heard the twit with a mustache yell something about fentanyl and midazolam. He saw the armed guards. He saw the flashing lights of the chopper and misty, earthbound starlight of a city below.

He also saw the display screen on the pilot's control panel. One of those fancy computer things with a GPS and a map that shows just where you are. The hospital, their destination, was moving toward the center of the screen. And falling to the bottom edge, the intersection they had just overflown. The corner of Ninth Avenue and Spruce Street.

Smitty felt the new hits of drug making him heavy and warm. Like a kiss. Like a first kiss when both are young and drunk and eager. As he fell into the dark, he thought about the old man. He thought about road signs.

*

"Dude! Go! Just go!"

"Shut up!" Chad Pringle glanced at his friend, then back at the road. "Shit! What're we gonna do?!"

"I dunno. Just move it! We need a minute to think!"

"They got the license plate. They'll know it's my mom's car! Even if nobody saw our faces!"

"Just go. We can ditch the car and say somebody stole it."

The car seemed to be enjoying its promotion from Mom's station wagon to getaway vehicle. The little engine roared like a kitten trying to be a lion.

It would have been funny. Just a goof. It had been funny. Right up to when it wasn't funny anymore. Have a few beers, fire up a couple bowls with your friends, good times. Then go to the hill, that hill, the one where all the fags hang out. Lure one of them someplace private and kick his ass. More good times.

The flashing lights seemed to be especially placed to shine right in Chad's eyes. *Red and blue, red and blue and white, red and blue, red and blue and white.* So different from the other flashing lights that decorated every other square inch of the city.

"There! Go there!" Tom pointed and Chad swung the station wagon onto an exit ramp. The noise of glass and squealing tires told

Pringle, even better than the shuddering car, that someone had failed to move out of the way.

He stole a glimpse in the rearview mirror. The cold fire of headlamps from a police cruiser cast the twice-reversed image of Mom's window sticker. *I brake for garage sales.*

It wasn't his fault the stupid fag died. The dumb queer had to go and whack his head on that damned fountain. And why did they even have fountains anyway? Stupid ugly waste of space for stupid fags to go and crack their dumb skulls.

He saw the car up ahead. Yellow. He saw the other driver's startled face, mouth formed into a perfect letter "O."

In the little wisp of a second that Chad Pringle reacted, his foot left the accelerator to stomp on the brake pedal. Almost enough time for the red lights in the back of Mom's car to wink on. There was no squeal of rubber. No puffs of smoke. No set of black lines left on the pavement before two automobiles folded into one lump of steel sheet, all to the winter chorus of breaking glass and police sirens.

*

Smitty tried to adjust, tried to move. Which was difficult, impossible, with the thick leather restraints on wrist and ankle.

Did they really think he was just going to leave? Even if his skull wasn't in pieces, held together with just staples and wire, even if he wasn't in some upper-story room with bars on the window and a cop in the hall, he still wasn't going anywhere.

The line into his arm brought sweet, velvety good feelings and a noticeable end to the pain. He was in his own room, in a real bed. No psycho freak going to watch him go to the toilet. No guard clanging on the bars and waking him up just for spite. Why the hell would anyone want to leave?

Not only that, but he had a TV. Just lay back, watch the box, and let the drugs do their thing. He felt a little cramped with the restraints. But if that was the worst thing about this, then he decided it would be fine.

The show on TV was about some poor dupe who gets revenge on everybody after his best friend turned rat and framed the guy.

They all dressed funny and talked funny, not really Smitty's thing. But the chick in that movie had some sweet tits.

He might have rubbed out a fast one while she was on, but those restraints wouldn't let him reach. Then two things happened, and he, Bryce O'Brien, Smitty, decided that the chick with the sweet tits would have to wait.

Noise from the hall. Stampeding feet and frantic parts of conversation. ...*multiple trauma ... police chase ... isn't University closer?... couldn't they go there?... looking bad ... surgery ... University sent them here ...*

Then the TV. Just people talking. No big deal. Until one of them said "Count of Monte Cristo".

He started to giggle. The laughter grew and came in little hiccups. Then growing sobs of hilarity that shook the bed. That made his head hurt. But for some reason, that was funny too.

"Hey! What the hell's going on in here?!" The cop stood in the doorway. One of the city's finest, backlit from humming fluorescent tubes in the hallway ceiling.

"I ... I gotta go to the john."

"Well, I guess it sucks to be you."

"C'mon, man. Please?"

"You got a nice, thick pad there. You just go on ahead and the nurses can clean you up later."

"I gotta take a crap. C'mon, man. Don't be like that."

The cop hesitated, looked over to his radio that was still giving new details of some incident that evening. "Okay. But don't try anything."

"Okay. Okay."

"I mean it."

"Okay. Thanks, man."

"Just get moving." The cop unbuckled the restraints and helped Smitty walk to the toilet.

Standing and walking reopened the wounds in his head. So did pretending to go to the bathroom. He could feel the blood trickle down his neck, soak into his hospital gown.

He washed his hands. Pretended to wash them anyway. Mostly he poured soap into the space that was made by a cuff of tape that held an IV line to his wrist.

"That's enough" the cop told him. "Come on. Move." Then it was back to the bed.

He didn't even need the soap. That good, slippery stuff he'd smuggled back, to be able to slide a hand from the leather strap. The cop paid more attention to the chatter on his radio than to Smitty's resumed bondage. Fool didn't even get the one on his left wrist buckled all the way.

Smitty tried to read the name on the badge. Maybe send him a thank you card after he became the Count of Smittyland. But he was dizzy, his vision blurred, and the name was just a haze of letters like in those books that didn't have pictures.

When the cop was, again, deep into the noise of his colleagues having a more interesting shift, Bryce O'Brien, Smitty, The Count of Smittyland, slipped from his room and down the hall.

One of those white doctor coats to cover up his bare ass, then out to the welcoming dark and rain. The doctor coat soaked up his blood too, turned red like the gown.

Long, red coat and long, white beard. Bryce O'Brien, Smitty, who might be mistaken for someone else, if the observer didn't look too close, walked the couple blocks to 943 Spruce, number 16, to have a look under the oven.

*

Marcus Washington bent a paperclip into an "S" shape and pushed one end through the open part of his sock. Even though he'd never been fishing, it looked like a hook in some fish's open mouth. Good enough, though. Santa Claus would understand.

Mom had said that Santa wouldn't be coming this year either. He'd lost their address when they moved, and that was that. Still, Marcus hung up his sock and left a small carton of milk on the table next to a little pile of cookies.

Mom wouldn't let him put out milk from the refrigerator. No cookies from the cupboard. "No" she said. "Santa Claus isn't coming and we aren't wasting food."

So, Marcus had secreted away a milk from his school lunch, and every cookie. Hid them carefully away and waited for Santa in a feat that might have made his mother proud. If he told her.

She was mad at first, when he told her he'd gone to see Santa Claus. Then she just looked sad. Even when Marcus told her Santa knew their address now. Mom just looked sad. And then it was time for bed.

No matter how angry the wind, how torrential the rain, nothing will obscure the sounds in a home on the night of December 24. Not for a child.

The kitchen door opening. Marcus knew that one from the nights Mom had to work late. That peculiar *clunk,* because you didn't need to use the key if you lifted the doorknob and pushed extra hard. The sound of rain and wind swept into the apartment until the door closed again. Then breathing. And footsteps.

There was more noise then. A couple of loud clunks like the time Mom had to move everything around for the exterminator. Then more breathing, harder this time. And grunting. Like somebody was lifting weights.

The boy moved from his tiny bed. Bare feet came to rest on threadbare carpeting to feel the uneven floor beneath. Creeping through darkness and nighttime sound, he reached the kitchen, then realized he'd forgotten his glasses.

They didn't have a fireplace. So young Marcus Washington had hung his sock from the oven door. Because that was the closest thing they had.

Now the sock was on the floor, poking out from under the overturned oven in a way that, if he'd had his glasses on, would have reminded him of the Wicked Witch under Dorothy's house.

Behind the oven was a section of floor that had also been moved. And behind that was a hole.

There was a man. Marcus couldn't see well. But he could see well enough. A man in red. With a long, white beard. He was surrounded by sacks. Ugly, stained, old burlap bags. And out of those bags rolled glittering, sparkling things like magical treasure.

It wasn't the treasure, though. Not all of it. Just one thing that called out to Marcus Washington with an almost audible cry.

A long tongue of metal, peering from its home of leather and gold leaf. A grip of braided hide and wire. His father's sword.

"Santa?"

The man in red, the man with a long, white beard staggered to his feet. There was an awkward quiet when even the vermin kept silent. Just the noise of rain and wind outside.

And then Mom was there. "Oh god! Oh my god! Marcus! Go to your room!"

"But Mom! It's Santa! He came!"

"Marcus! Go in your room and shut the door!"

"But Mom, he came! Like I said he would! See?"

"Goddammit! Marcus! Kids aren't supposed to be out of bed until Christmas morning! You go in your room right now and you close the door and you stay there!"

*

Donald Duncan, Don to his friends, wondered why the hell he even did this. Wasn't Christmas supposed to be fun?

At least they got him a new suit. After the seat ripped out of his pants last year, they finally broke down and got him a suit that fit. Now if he could just get them to do something about the heat.

Fine. Santa Claus lives at the North Pole. But Santa-Don here was in the middle of some hot, crummy shopping mall full of screaming kids and their horrible parents.

He wondered, not for the first time, if the headache was more from those flashing lights, or from the speakers in the ceiling right above Santa's Workshop. They'd already demanded to know "What child is this?" about eight times today.

A couple who looked like a pair of models from an L.L. Bean catalog were arguing about whether their toddler should wear her Christmas hat in the Santa picture. Behind them, a gaggle of kids with two mommies looked so clean, Santa-Don thought they were lucky their skin hadn't just been scrubbed right off. And behind them was a weekend dad who seemed intent on bonding with his kids despite it being too little, too late, and them in high school.

Then a wave of pumpkin spice and peppermint assailed his nose, and Donald Duncan, Santa Claus, thought he might throw up. Was this how it was going to be? Just the second week of December and already had it with Christmas.

And then there were the elves. He almost laughed, then remembered it was supposed to be ho ho ho. But the elves, like every Christmas, were different every year, but also the same. Every year.

Audrey was back. On winter break from some fancy college and dressed up like an elf. Duncan suspected the girl had something going with the new elf, Katie. Well, good for them.

Jason was there again. Still young and aimless and drifting and dumb. Still an elf. Jason seemed to go out of his way to be nice to Audrey, who just said "Thanks" and that was about it.

Sorry, kid. Too late.

And good for him too. Good learning experience. Even if he didn't appreciate it now.

Poor Rachel, though. Duncan wasn't quite sure what happened to her. The kid really had kind of a freak-out a couple of years ago when that lowlife boyfriend of hers got in trouble. A lot of trouble.

What was his name again? Chad. That's it, Chad. What a jerk. And what a dumb move for Rachel to be dating him in the first place. It happened on Christmas, too, if old Santa-Don's memory was right.

No. Christmas Eve. Ahh, well. Last Duncan had heard, that Chad loser was the favorite prison bitch of some other lowlife.

He smiled. Well, good for that too.

Come to think of it, that might have been the same Christmas they found that other convict. The guy who escaped from the hospital. Wandered a couple of blocks in a rainstorm before he bled to death across the street from that low-income housing place.

You'd think somebody would have noticed a patient wandering out of a hospital in the night. Well, that's probably the kind of thing that happens when you put all the younger people on night shift at Christmastime.

"Santa? Santa, we have somebody here who needs to see you."

"Hmmnn? Oh. Well, sure. Ho ho ho!"

There was a blur, about three or four feet high, that shot across Santa's Workshop and onto the man's lap. Duncan let out a soft *Ooof!* as little arms squeezed him in a fierce hug.

A little boy. With a thick, pink scar that ran from nostril to lip. And glasses. Those designer frames that people go and spend way too much money on, when their kids are just going to grow out of the things.

The kid looked familiar. Somehow. But he saw hundreds of kids every day. He couldn't be expected to remember them all. Maybe Santa Claus knows all the children of the world, but Donald Duncan is another story. So just look, read the kid, read the parents. Do the Santa thing.

And there was the mother. All dressed up, just like the kid. Her expensive finery like that. Didn't she know there were people who couldn't even make rent?

The little boy on his lap smiled, whispered "I have the sword. I'm keeping it so I can be a knight someday. Like my dad."

"Oh. Um ... good. Good."

Who was this kid? For some reason, Santa-Don thought about spruce. But that was probably because it was Christmas. Had this kid talked to him about Christmas trees before? Was that it?

The child pointed at his scar. "The doctors fixed my mouth. But I pulled on the stitches a lot. So there'd be a mark. 'Cause of my dad."

"Oh, well ... of course. Ho ho ho!"

Read the kid. Read the family. Don't act surprised. Santa knows when you're sleeping and when you're awake.

The little boy with a scar on his lip asked for a video game player and a book about King Arthur.

"Hmmnn." Santa put on his thoughtful face and repeated the order. You listening over there, Mom? "A video game player and a book about King Arthur. Well, I guess I'll have to see what I can do."

The kid hugged him again. And for some reason he couldn't really explain, Donald Duncan, Don to his friends, felt especially jolly.

***

The Lion Devours Its Young
by Paul Lubaczewski

U.S.: A dark fantasy reveals the fatal truth of character.

Jim had stood upon a stage, while the crowd watched his every move, afraid to take their eyes off of him for fear of what they would miss. He had been, the man. Jim had climbed mountains, gasping in the thin air; sweat streaming, despite the cold; his eyes gazing out to the ends of the earth feeling like he had conquered it all. He had been the man. Jim had swum in the oceans of the earth feeling the waters pound into him, fighting against the currents to stand on shore again glistening in the afternoon sun. He had been the man. Jim had fought and fucked his way from one end of the country to the other, like a man.

And what had it gotten him?

Aches and pains and the emptiness of a middle-aged man who felt so much older than his years. All the days on earth older it felt, and never a penny richer or wiser for it.

*

Morning—well, noon, but morning for Jim, and that was what mattered here. Cover was gone, sheet was gone, it was just his skin against the body oil slick mattress thrown on the floor. His mouth was glue, but his mouth was always glue. His eyes opened exactly enough to see what he needed to finish getting up. In one surprisingly smooth motion, his hand wrapped itself around the vodka bottle and he sat up with it hitting his lips simultaneously with the back of his head leaning against the greasy stain on the wall where his head hit every morning.

Jim's stomach lurched and burned for a minute, and he began a thick gagging phlegmy cough that lasted for half a minute. Eyes blurred and out of focus, he found his cigarettes, lit one and dragged himself to his feet. Jim staggered bleary-eyed to the bathroom to piss, a long, lengthy one, the kind that gives one time to study the wall in detail. Time to take drags on a cigarette, to think about nothing. His brain cells had a few moments before they caught up to his locomotion.

As the stream slowed to a trickle, another coughing fit hit him. His stomach lurched violently again. Jim stood very still for a moment or two, fighting back his gag reflex for all his worth. If he threw up, it would be bad, spots of blood had been coming up lately when he did that. He threw up often, it was hard to win this battle every morning. He needed a couple of beers in him, to settle his stomach. He needed the first one now.

Stumbling to the kitchen, he sank to one knee and dug his hand into the cardboard container until his hand seized on to a lukewarm can. He cracked it open, swallowed hard for a few gulps, and felt his stomach first constrict and then begin to settle down. This one, and another to chase it, he'd feel human enough for coffee, which he set to brewing. Another one after that and he could consider a cup of noodles or something for food, and then Jim could get on with his day.

And what a big day it was, he was finally going to be free of all this.

When Jim had a little bit of food in him, and enough beer to keep the palsied shaking at bay that had started in his right hand, he went into the small bathroom in the dirty trailer to get a shower. He was proud of that, getting a shower. Jim didn't have a lot of things to be proud of anymore, but at least he didn't let the stink and the slime build up on himself like some of the drunks he ran into oozing from beer to beer at the local bar. He might be stuck in a shitbox trailer only getting enough royalties to survive anymore, maybe he was forgotten by everyone, but he didn't let the stink of his failures and infirmities build up on him. At least, he could still clean himself like a man.

It wasn't always like this. It never *starts* like this. *This* is not a big life goal for anyone. You decide to take a break from it all because you think you have that option ... you get aimless. Directionless turns into depression and drinking. Next thing you know, you're actually living in half the rooms of your house in the middle of Pennsylvania; after that, you sell the house because it had become "too much work to maintain." One day after asking around back in the city, you find out there isn't much of the "all you wanted to get away from" left to come back to. You're another has-been skell in a world littered with them.

You live on some royalty and interest checks and the money you can scrape together doing things you hope the cops never find out about. You drink more, saying your joints ache, but when you wake up your joints ache more than they ever did. Probably because of all the drinking, but by the time you figure that out, you're already on the ride. All you can do is glower at the bar locked into place in front of your seat and try and enjoy it.

Four beers, another shot of vodka, a shower, and a pitiful amount of food later, Jim felt ready to face the day. Most importantly, he could face what he was going to have to do today if he ever wanted to be "the man" again. If he ever wanted to feel the way he had in his foggy memories, and not the way he felt right now. God, anything would have to be better than this!

Jim swung himself into the Dart. When he still made new money, and not just residuals, he had bought it as a street rod saying he'd always wanted a "cool car" as a kid. Now, it was as worn and as beaten looking as its owner. Dents he didn't know where they came from, tears in the upholstery, rust starting to show through the dirty purple paint. The car had been special once, but now it was another indistinguishable hunk of crap roaming the wilds of central Pennsylvania. But it would serve its purpose, to get him out of here.

A wave of terror hit Jim right in the chest as the car pulled out onto the main roads heading for his destination. It wasn't a fear of anything, but it was still chest-tightening panic. He got panic attacks now, every time he left the house these days. They had no basis, no reality, but he had them nonetheless. Jim was positive it had something to do with leaving his precious cubes of cheap beer, and the safety they provided him. If he had more money than this, he might never even leave the house anymore, maybe he'd just pay someone less screwed up than him to pick up his supplies.

Of course, if he had never gone out, he would have never have found it, would he?

*

He didn't even remember why he was out in those woods that day. He'd just been wandering. He thought maybe he'd heard a rumor of a pot patch back there, and he was trying to score some freebies. It might have been one of his "get off booze" schemes, reasoning that if he was high as a kite on weed, he wouldn't notice withdrawal that badly. He didn't want to buy off of one of the local dealers. Jim had problems enough as it was, without possibly bringing the law into things, and these kids reeked of easily busted amateurs.

He never did find the weed, but he found another solution. He found a cave. He found it totally by accident, just stumbling through the woods, when the floor of the forest thrust up suddenly in front of him. When he got closer, he could see the exposed limestone, with trees poking up right to the edge of the face on top. Jim could smell a difference in the air as he got close, planning to go up on top of the small, exposed outcropping for a better view of his surroundings. It smelled earthy, not the leaf mold smell of the forest, but like wet clay in a pottery class.

Jim was working his way parallel to the wall, when he felt the cool air blow up his pant leg. He stood stock-still for a moment as the air gusted up his leg, causing him to freeze in shock. Slowly, as if the sensation would flee once it knew he had noticed, he sank to his knees to search for the cause. The cause, he found among the leaves at the base of the limestone bluff. There was a small hole among the litter, blowing air out powerfully enough Jim could actually see leaves moving from the force of it.

Jim suddenly felt alive, like he had been switched back on at the discovery. He felt interest flood his brain, he felt adrenaline. The thrill of discovery. He started digging at the leaves with his hands, and was instantly rewarded by the hole opening up. Within moments, he could see how it had gotten closed in the first place, rotten tree branches, probably washed down in the rain that had clogged it. They pulled free with only a bit of tugging. The air gushed out of the hole as he worked, cooling him in the summer heat.

He'd been in a couple of caves since he'd been out here, it was something the locals did, but he'd never found one before. Jim was only carrying a flashlight now, but the thrill of actually *doing* something enthralled him. Doing something that wasn't aimless, and pointless, something that was more interesting than surviving through another day ... the thrill of it had seized him totally. He needed to see what the hole did. He needed to be somewhere doing something amazing again, if only for a moment.

In the space of minutes, Jim had dug open a relatively sizable opening. The gaping blowing hole in front of him was easily large enough to slide into now. He dug his flashlight out of his pocket and poked it down into the entrance, trying to see what lay directly below him. With the light behind him, even with the flashlight, he could only look in a little way, the glare making it impossible for his eyes to adjust properly to see farther. A slope slid away under the cap rock into the depths. But the slope did look relatively gentle in nature, as if mud had been coming through the entrance for years, slowly oozing its way down to the rock floor somewhere down there. Jim grasped a rock that was close at hand and rolled it hard down into the entrance where it created a couple of thuds, then made a dull sound as it embedded itself in the mud.

It didn't look that bad, and Jim had to know. Lying on his back, he slid himself on the dirt and mud down the slope. The air got colder the farther down he went, he could feel it like a wave soaking into him right through his clothes. With the flashlight held down in his hand as he used it to slide down the slope, he could see in the dim light coming in from above, that the ceiling was moving away from him as he went farther in. All he had to do was keep moving very carefully downward.

After what had felt like forever, he could sit up again. Jim immediately swung the flashlight out in front of him to assess where he was. It took a few moments for his eyes to adjust to his surroundings, even with the light. Jim squinted into the inky dark, willing his eyes to tell him what was lurking in the dim light provided from the flashlight. He was coming down a slope into a room, more than large enough to stand up in, and long enough that he couldn't see the end of it with the flashlight. Most importantly, Jim could see the slope continued, muddy, but passable, down to the floor of the chamber with no sudden drops to contend with.

Now what?

Well, he had nothing of any value to do today, and nowhere he wanted to go to do it. Maybe he should live a little and see what the cave did. Jim slid the rest of the way down the mound leading from the entrance. As he went, he kicked a rock loose. He heard it clatter down the slope, bouncing off a larger rock on the way, creating an enormous booming echo that filled the entire chamber he was in.

"Hello?" called an echoing voice from the Stygian darkness beyond his flashlight.

Jim froze. The entrance to this cave was sealed up just minutes ago. He didn't know of any other cave entrances in the area that someone else could have come in through. But what if it was someone in the cave hurt? What if they needed help? Quietly, almost hoping he wouldn't be heard, Jim called out, "Is somebody here?"

"Oh, thank goodness! I thought I was going to be stuck in here forever," a relieved voice gasped out of the darkness.

Jim was standing now, toward the base of the slope, trying to will the darkness to reveal the person hidden in its depth. "Yeah, what do you need me to do?"

The voice chuckled a bit, a rich throaty sound that felt sinister in the inky gloom, before saying, "I'll get to that in a moment, my new friend. But first, what is it that *you* really need?"

*

Jim almost felt human as he pulled the Dart onto the long driveway in the woods. He had two thirty-packs in the trunk now and had found that sweet spot between alcohol and food. The panic attacks had subsided when his supply lines were replenished. Even if the Dart broke down, he could get drunk while he waited for a cab. Jim just had to do what he'd left the house for now. That should be cause for a panic attack, but the panic machine was currently swimming in the booze.

He was at the trailer the kid lived in. Jim secretly hated the kid, deep down inside. He had even admitted that to himself during a good hard two a.m. drunk, or two. But the kid had actually known one of Jim's songs. The kid was the only one in a pack of them he had been buying beer for one day to cop some freebies to save himself money. The kid was the only one out of six of the little brats to have known the song and say he liked it. So, Jim had started hanging around him, just for the hero worship that salved his wounded ego. But it didn't mean he had to like it, or the kid.

The Dart rolled to a stop a small distance from the trailer. Jim didn't want to go too close. Who knew what junk was hidden there in the overgrown yard and the remains of the driveway. The last thing he wanted now was a flat tire. Better to walk an extra fifteen feet than to have to walk all the way back up to the road to wait for his cab later. Jim wasn't even sure if there even *was* still a spare in the trunk, let alone that he'd be able to put it on without killing himself in the process.

He weaved his way through the ghosts of childhoods past that lurked in the lawn to the front steps. They were brick, and would probably outlast the trailer by twenty years. Jim rapped on the door three times hard. A moment passed before a younger male voice called, "Hold your balls, I'll be right there!"

A moment later, the door swung open to the darkness inside and there stood the kid. He was fifteen, scrawny, with lank, greasy, dirty blond hair hanging to his shoulders and shaved on the sides. A set of clippers was the cheapest way to get a haircut, so that's what he went with. He wasn't wearing a shirt, exposing his toast rack of a chest. He wasn't wearing a shirt most likely to show off his crappy India ink tattoo on his chest. Jim wasn't even sure what the blob of dots was supposed to be.

"You ready?" Jim asked

"Yeah, give me a sec," the kid said stepping back, leaving the doorway clear for Jim to step in.

"She up?"

"Naw, man, she's well out, her check came in," the kid shrugged, ambling off deeper into the trailer to look for a shirt.

"I'll check on her before we take off," Jim called after him.

"Suit yourself, but I'm telling you, she scored last night. She is out like a light."

Jim went off down the one hall that led to the rear of the trailer. He always treaded lightly in this place. It hadn't given up yet, but he was sure the floor was rotting out in spots. The shitty cheap tiling they laid down in these things was pulled back here and there. One toilet backup and you had rotting plywood. Jim cracked open the door to the bedroom in the back and looked in.

The kid's mom was lying there on her mattress on the floor. "Yo, Karen! I'm taking the kid out!"

She didn't so much as move. Jim went over to where she was and knelt down to check closer. He shook her a little. She didn't even groan or make a noise. Concerned for a moment, he checked her breathing. It was steady, so his concern vanished in an instant. She was just high as a kite, but he doubted she'd die. She knew her dosages like any real full-time junkie.

He had slept with this woman one night. Hanging out with the kid and his mother, things had just happened after the kid passed out. A night floating on cheap wine and reminiscence towards when they had both still been desirable had led to a sloppy coupling on a dirty bed, neither would ever discuss later. The kid might have had hopes of his hero becoming his new dad, they wilted on the vine. What would be the point? To merge Jim and Karen's kingdoms of filth? Create a new empire of pathetic?

Jim got up and went to go get the kid. This was why he hated the kid. He had his whole life in front of him. A plethora of possibilities, nothing but potential, nothing but the future. How was he treating it?

By ambling down the same garden path as that junkie bitch just lying there waiting for a final dose that would put her out of her misery? But Jim had a use for him, and that might be the only time in the kid's life he would ever be useful to anyone.

*

"You sure this place is cool?" the kid asked as they walked towards the cave.

"Of course, it is, I found it myself. Who in the hell else, even knows about it? We can party without me having to worry about the cops busting me for contributing by letting you have a few beers. And we won't have to worry about Karen sucking down half our stash as 'rent'," Jim said irritably.

"That is completely snatched! I didn't even know there were any caves around these sticks," the kid enthused next to him.

"I don't know why you would be surprised, this is prime limestone around here," Jim said automatically.

"It is? How do you even know that?"

"I ... I don't know, I just read it somewhere," Jim shrugged.

"So, where is it?" the kid demanded, looking around as they stopped.

"I gotta move some stuff. There's no point having a secret cave if any douche can walk right up and see it, is there?" Jim said, getting on his hands and knees, pulling back the debris he'd layered over the cave entrance. When it was done, he stood up and pointed down, "There it is: one cave! Just like I promised."

The kid moved up slowly and warily now, like a deer trying to get a drink of water on an open pond. His eyes had gotten big and his movements had slowed down, like he was tensing for flight at any moment. "Dude, you want me to go down that?"

"Aww, come on," Jim said, stepping back from the hole standing behind the kid, "it's perfectly safe. I've done it a dozen times."

The kid started to back away from the hole, his eyes wide now with fear, "I don't know, man, I don't think this is cool. We ... we can find somewhere else. I don't—"

Jim caught the kid as he started to collapse and lowered him the rest of the way to the ground. Standing up, he slid the blackjack he had just struck the kid with into his back pocket. He always carried one. Whatever muscles he once possessed had atrophied long ago, he needed something to protect himself. Jim's hands were shaking now from the panic he had almost been overwhelmed with. The little shit had almost blown the whole thing. Sinking back down, he thrust out a quivering hand to check the kid's breathing. Fine, it was all fine. He was just out cold, he wasn't dead. That would blow it all too, killing him out here.

He needed a drink. He dug out the flask of vodka he had tucked into his jacket and took a long pull, downing it like water. After a shuddering shaking as the vodka hit his stomach, he capped the flask. To work.

Jim grabbed the kid by the legs and dragged him to the opening. Once the boy was in position, it was only a matter of feeding him into the hole until one push sent him down the slope inside. The kid rolled a few times, slid a bit farther and came to a stop still within range of the light.

"If you want something done ..." Jim muttered, sliding through the hole after him. Once he reached the collapsed heap on the slope that was the kid, he grabbed a foot. Jim dragged the unconscious form the rest of the way slowly down the slope, taking care not to injure the kid any more than he had already.

Once they were both on the cave floor, Jim stood over the kid and said, "Sorry, kid, but ..." He was going to finish with, "it ain't personal," but he knew that was a lie. The kid was trying to fuck up his life, his precious time on earth, and the little asshole was aspiring to make as much of a mess of himself as Jim had by accident. No, for Jim, it was personal, no point in lying about it now. "It is what it is," he finished after a pause.

Jim just stood there for a moment, listening to the patient dripping of water from the depths of the cave. He flashed the light around the chamber, taking the time to drink in the formations that covered the walls, to see the beauty in where he was for a moment. Everything was about to change here in this hidden grotto, he wanted to seal it in his memory.

It couldn't last forever, he didn't want it to. Any longer, the kid might wake up; he would want to leave no matter what lie Jim told him about how he'd gotten here. Then the thing that he was here for wouldn't happen at all. He asked for this, he had debated it in his mind a million times. He had to do it now, or he never would. Reaching down, Jim grabbed the kid's legs and dragged him along heading to the rear of the chamber.

Stepping back towards the slope out of the cave, he called, "Wakey Wakey! One virgin! Just like you asked!"

"Nice of you to visit, James," the voice oiled out of the dark, "I thought you might have forgotten our bargain.

Jim watched as a clawed hand snaked out of the darkness and grasped the kid's leg. Jim was frozen in place, unable to leave, unwilling to raise his flashlight to watch what the darkness was hiding now. The kid's body vanished into the gloom, followed a moment later a sudden flurry of noise. Horrid noises. Cracking and tearing noises made worse by the cave as they echoed all around him. Jim screwed his eyes tightly shut as the noise continued in case he saw something he didn't want to. His body shook as he stood there, the cold and the damp driving his already twitching body close to spasms.

"I believe I owe you something for this, don't I, James?" the voice was now right next to him.

Jim's eyes flashed open almost involuntarily. He could see the dark, liquid pool that was now spreading into the edge of his light across the cave floor. And he could see ... him. The voice had a face. A handsome one, a strong one, a cruel one, all of those almost at the same time. The fact that the face was smiling below its curled black locks did nothing to relieve the impression of cruelty there. If anything, it made it worse. Even if Jim had not seen it, he had heard what this face had just done to the kid. To smile after that seemed unspeakable.

Looking straight ahead and trying not to look at the man standing next to him, Jim said, "I figure you do, if a deal is a deal."

He never saw the thing strike. He briefly felt something wet on his neck, before he felt a stabbing pain. Jim turned his head, his eyes wide, towards his companion. The man stood there smiling, right next to Jim. The man's hand hovered near Jim, but was not touching him. Extending from the palm of this creature's hand was some kind of fleshy protuberance, a tube of skin extending from the man he had come to see, to Jim's own neck.

Jim only had a moment to consider it, and no time to protest it at all before his entire body felt on fire with pain. It throbbed out through him from where the thing had his throat, flooding into his entire body like white fire. He never felt the thing release him, he never felt himself hit the floor to curl up in a fetal ball whimpering in pain. Never felt his bladder lose control, or the rhythmic thumping he made as he banged his head against the floor of the cave.

It was as if from a million miles away that he heard the voice, "I imagine that is quite painful, hmmm? To be fair, though, James, there's a lot of things that need to be fixed inside of you, and I said I'd do that for you. I never said it would be painless, now, did I? I would imagine one's own birth must be quite painful. Why should one get out of one's rebirth scot-free?"

The pain now centered itself in his torso, his lungs burned like fire from whatever was happening to him. He heard footsteps first walking away, then returning.

"Do you know something, James? If you hadn't done this, you'd have been dead in a year. Lung cancer would have gotten you if the cirrhosis hadn't. You can console yourself with that later, your very survival was at stake. This wasn't a tired, old man throwing a young boy to the wolves because he resented his youth. It was you saving your own life. Look at it this way, you're going to have a later to feel guilty in." The thing chuckled, and then added, "That kid certainly won't."

Jim felt himself being rolled over and propped up against the slope. He forced himself to open his eyes to look at his tormentor. Through the tears, he could see the handsome face smiling at him in the dim light of the flashlight somewhere on the floor, "I'll give you one piece of advice for handling your new circumstances, James. When you move around—and you will—if you decide to hole up in a cave, look for loose rocks in the ceiling. I wouldn't have spent the last five years here if I had. Now if you'll excuse me, I've got a lot of lost time to make up for."

The thing stood up, and Jim could hear it beginning to scramble up the slope towards the entrance. It paused as it went and called back one last time, "Here's how nice a guy I am, James. I left you some kid for when you get hungry later. I wonder, when you devour him, if that will be when you finally say his name."

***

The Tally Bone

by Lauren Marrero

U.S.: *A historical twist of the supernatural and hidden lies.*

Louisa Darby thought she was well rid of her husband when the fool got drunk one evening and fell from his horse, breaking his neck in the process. She didn't particularly hate him, but theirs had been a marriage of convenience. He was tolerably handsome, adequately wealthy, and self-sufficient enough to see to his own amusements without bothering his wife, but with his passage to the hereafter, she learned that things were not as they appeared.

As soon as he departed, the bill collectors nearly broke down her door with demands for payment for everything from gambling debts to abandoned mistresses. She had managed to put most of them off by pawning the last of her jewelry and creating more and more promissory notes, so Louisa was unpleasantly surprised when yet another collector appeared before her in her sparsely furnished study, demanding repayment.

The stooped figure stood a few feet inside the room, peering at her through the dim light of the overcast sky doing its best to penetrate the gloomy space. Louisa tried not to stare at his misshapen frame, which twisted at an unnatural angle. The deformity seemed not to affect him at all. He had not only refused her offer of a seat, but appeared remarkably healthy for such a thin and twisted man.

She blinked at him through her spectacles, hating that she had been caught at a disadvantage.

"I beg your pardon," she replied irritably to his brief introduction. "I am familiar with all of my late husband's accounts, yet I have never heard of you, Mr. Smythe."

He had the grace to look embarrassed, tugging on his cravat like a schoolboy in his uncomfortable Sunday best. "That is ... you see, the nature of our relationship was extremely discreet."

"Discreet," Louisa repeated doubtfully. She eyed the man's shock of white hair, which contrasted sharply with his youthful features. He was unnaturally slender, yet something told her that he was stronger than he appeared. "Whatever your relationship with George, it is no concern of mine. Now, if you'll excuse me ..."

She lifted her hand to the fraying bell pull hanging near her desk, eager to summon a servant to eject her unwelcome visitor from her home, but was startled by the feel of his strong fingers suddenly gripping her wrist. She blinked, unnerved that he had crossed the room so quickly. In the time it took her to lift her hand, he had traveled nearly twelve feet.

"Please," he pleaded, but Louisa wasn't fooled by his placating tone. There was a threat in his voice, one she would do well to note. "Please, I need your help. You see, your husband extracted a ... well, a pledge of sorts from me, and I can't leave until I've retrieved it."

"What sort of pledge?" demanded Louisa, though she could sense his reluctance to say more. He looked chagrined by the whole conversation, quickly removing his hands from hers and stepping back to a respectable distance.

"Money," he replied. "I come from a long line of *very* private people, and we generally don't like to become involved with ... certain individuals, but fate often thrusts us into unavoidable situations. Your husband helped me out of a jam, and in return, I gave him his heart's desire."

"Money."

"Yes!" Mr. Smythe grinned as if his mad ramblings made perfect sense.

"If you are here for repayment, I'm afraid you will have to wait," Louisa replied, irritated that she would have to find the means to pay yet another of her husband's debts. If George had received anything from this man, it had disappeared long ago.

"No, no. I don't want money," he explained. "I need something else entirely." He dug into his pockets until he retrieved a long, white blade with curious markings along its side, and reverently handed it to her. "Do you know what this is?"

"A tally stick," Louisa guessed. Her husband's death had given her a quick and thorough lesson on various methods of accounting. "But these haven't been used in years."

"Yes, but sometimes the old ways are the best ways," Mr. Smythe explained. "We forged it when our deal was struck. After writing the nature of the transaction on one side, the stick was split in half and divided between us. One half went to your husband, and the other half I kept. At the conclusion of our agreement, George was to return his half to me."

"I see," Louisa replied, though she did not see at all. The idea of trading favors in tally sticks was absurdly archaic. Why not simply use a promissory note? She turned the object over in her hand, noting the indecipherable markings. It had been split in half lengthwise so the markings could not be read until the two halves were joined together. "Is this bone?"

"Yes," Mr. Smythe groaned. "It is a very important piece of bone, and I need it back."

"Why?" Louisa demanded, feeling like she was humoring a lunatic. It was an interesting piece, and may even be worth something to a museum or a collector of strange artifacts, but his interest appeared to be more than academic. What type of strange dealings had her late husband been involved in?

Mr. Smythe tugged furiously at his cravat as he contemplated the best response. He opened his mouth and then shut it several times as he deliberated his options.

"I need it because ... because it's mine, dammit!" he exploded. "The money wasn't enough for George. He wanted a guarantee that he could call on my services at any time. He held me captive, so to speak, refusing to return my property until I gave him more and more ..."

"He commanded you with this?" Louisa replied dismissively, failing to see the significance of the broken bit of bone. "How?"

"Because it is *me*, a part of me." He paused, blinking in consternation as he realized Louisa's confusion. "It is no use. I have to show you. It is the only way to make you understand ..."

At this point he began fumbling with his clothes, anxious to show her something hidden in his trousers.

For a moment Louisa could only stare at him in shock, wondering how her late husband's affairs had attracted this madman into her life. He seemed genuinely desperate to show her his anatomy, as if the secrets of his physique could explain a debt recorded on a crude bit of bone.

"Mr. Smythe, I assure you that is not necessary!" she gushed, shaking off her surprise and yanking the bell pull with enough force to rip it from the wall. The metal bell attached to the strip of fabric rolled unheeded beneath her desk. "I haven't the foggiest idea where George left his half of the tally bone, but I shall search for it most assiduously. Please leave your card with my butler and I shall contact you the moment it is found."

Now she was the one babbling, trying to placate the man as he was physically carried from the study by two footmen with his trousers bunched around his knees.

It was luck that she had servants at all. Her financial straits were certainly no secret. The staff that remained either did so in hopes that her fortunes would eventually reverse and they would be compensated for their loyalty, or because they had yet to find better employment.

Louisa watched him leave with a shudder, hoping that she had seen the last of him, but as she was soon to discover, this particular madman was more stubborn than her usual bill collectors.

He returned the next day, and the next, until she was forced to call the constable. But threats from the magistrate did not seem to deter him. He was quite desperate for an insignificant piece of bone that could easily be mistaken for kindling.

In exasperation, Louisa searched for her husband's half of the tally stick, but to no avail. It wasn't among his personal effects, tucked away in some secret corner of the house, or entrusted to their solicitor. She didn't know what to do except continue to rebuff the white-haired man and hope he eventually went away, but unfortunately he was not to be deterred, as she soon discovered one night when she was rudely awakened by a whisper in the dark.

"Louisa," he intoned close to her ear. She was instantly awake, though for a long time she remained frozen in shock, wondering how he managed to sneak into her bedroom, and what he intended to do there.

"Mr. Smythe," she replied with an impressive amount of calm considering the situation, "you have me at a disadvantage."

In response, he obligingly lit a candle and leaned back to allow her space to sit up. Beneath her calm façade, her mind was racing. Should she scream or attempt to beat him with the candlestick? Did he have a weapon? It was difficult to see in the dim light.

"I apologize for my sudden appearance," he began. "I did not mean to startle you, and I certainly mean you no harm ..."

"Yet, here you are."

"Indeed," he replied uncomfortably. "This was the only way I could see you and I felt the need to impress upon you the importance of my quest."

"I believe you," Louisa assured him in an icy tone. "But is this piece of bone valuable enough to risk prison?"

He paused and sent her a calculated look, as if he couldn't quite understand her response. Louisa glared in return, showing him that the feeling was indeed mutual.

"Aren't you afraid of me at all?" he asked in exasperation. "I don't mean to threaten you, but I *am* in your bedroom, and I assume you are naked under that gown ..."

"*All* people are naked beneath their clothes," Louisa starchily replied, resisting the urge to draw the blankets up to her neck.

He blinked, and then grinned sheepishly. "I suppose you are right. To be honest, I've never done this before ... spoken to a woman."

"Are you serious?"

"Indeed. I had never spoken to a man before George, but ... I'm making a mess of my explanation again, aren't I? I can see you won't believe anything I say, so there is nothing for it but to show you. Will you promise not to scream?"

Louisa clamped her mouth shut, agreeing to no such thing, but watched with growing horror as he once again began fumbling with his trousers. She started to protest, but then thought better of it, mystified by his decidedly non-sexual movements. He worked quickly to unfasten himself, as if he were more uncomfortable than she. Once free, he turned fully toward her with his hands discreetly placed above his genitals.

"Mr. Smythe," Louisa finally found her voice, though the sound came out as little more than a choked whisper. Her eyes remained fixed on his, as she willed them not to travel lower. "This is highly irregular."

"Look," he pleaded.

She knew her cheeks were burning with embarrassment, but refused to turn away. One would think she had never seen a man before, but years of marriage didn't prepare her for the sight of a complete stranger stripping in her bedchamber. She took a deep breath and sent a quick prayer, for what she didn't know, and then finally allowed her gaze to lower.

"What in the world ..." Her voice drifted away as she squinted at the scar twisting along his thigh. It was weirdly misshapen, as if part of him was missing. She realized this was the cause of his strangely hunched physique.

"When I said the bone was me," he explained. "I meant that literally."

"I don't understand," Louisa replied. She wondered how such a wound could exist. A bit of him simply wasn't there. He might have been born that way except for his assertion that this part of his body had been taken by George.

"I told you before that I was part of a very private group of people. Some would call us fae. A lot had happened since my last trip to the mortal lands, so a while back, I thought I'd poke around for a bit. Unfortunately, I was soon caught in a bear trap—an *illegal* bear trap, I might add. You may not know this, but my people have a bit of a problem with iron. So, I was laying there, bleeding my life away when Georgie came up and asked for a boon in exchange for springing the trap. He was hunting with some friends and wandered off to drain the ... anyway, he found me, saved me, and kept a piece of me to guarantee my good behavior."

"You're fae," Louisa repeated, dumbstruck. She needed to say the words aloud to make sense of them.

"Of course," he replied, nonplussed. "Could a mortal survive an injury like mine?"

"The tally stick ..."

"... which I need returned immediately ..."

"... is your bone."

"Yes, yes, we've established that." He yanked his trousers back up, frustrated with the whole conversation. "I'm sorry to belabor the point, but I really need your help ..."

"... to find your missing body part."

He paused and stared at Louisa as if wondering what happened to her intelligence. Indeed, the longer she spoke with him, the more confused she became. Did he actually expect her to believe that he was immortal?

"Prove it."

He glared, clearly offended by her demand. "I showed you my leg," he pointed out.

"But I am not a physician," she retorted. "How would I know what an immortal wound looks like?"

"Fair enough." He paused, and then squinted at Louisa with consideration. "Do you even believe in the supernatural?"

"Not really." She considered years of dutifully attending church services, and then swearing to love, honor, and obey her husband before her assembled kin and the eyes of the Lord. "Definitely not."

"Then this will be difficult," he muttered. "I do have one trick, but I don't think you'll like it."

"I don't suppose I will," Louisa agreed, convinced that she wouldn't like anything this man said or did.

"Very well then," he replied in resignation. "I shall endeavor to change your mind."

And with that, he disappeared.

Louisa gasped and looked about, as unnerved by his disappearance as she had been by his appearance. He had simply vanished into thin air without so much as a puff of smoke.

"Mr. Smythe?" she called dubiously, but there was no answer.

For a moment she wondered if she was mistaken. Could he actually be fae? Then she shook her head, dispelling that absurd notion. He was no more fae than she. It must have been a trick of the candlelight, or perhaps she had blinked and missed his exit. It was the middle of the night after all. Perhaps the entire encounter had been no more than a dream. That was infinitely more likely than a fae creature appearing and vanishing from her bedroom.

She settled back down to sleep, determined to dismiss Mr. Smythe from her mind. Nevertheless, sleep remained elusive. She kept the bedside lamp burning long into the night, casting suspicious looks at every shadow in case he returned.

Before dawn had fully illuminated her window, she rose from her bed to inspect every inch of her room to determine how he had gained entrance. Then she enlisted the help of her servants to search the house from top to bottom.

They surely thought she was mad, for there was no unlatched door, no broken window, not even a mouse hole he could have used to gain entrance. Perhaps it had all been a dream, but surely if she had imagined a man removing his trousers in her bedroom she would have come up with a more pleasurable conclusion.

Louisa became paranoid, glancing over her shoulder several times a day in case he reappeared. She jumped at every sudden noise like a startled cat, frightening the staff who were at their wits end trying to move and speak softly in her presence.

"Do you believe me now?" Mr. Smythe asked later that day as she sat at her dressing table, trying unsuccessfully to pin back a wayward curl. She screamed and twisted around, throwing her hairbrush at his unwanted presence, but he vanished before it landed.

"Have you thought about it?" he demanded later, stepping from the shadows as she sat in the study, attempting to settle her accounts.

"No!" she lied through clenched teeth, though in reality she had thought of little else. Louisa was desperate to discover how he so easily gained entrance to her home. "How on earth do you disappear like that?"

He grinned like a little boy showing off a neat trick, completely oblivious to her distress.

"We call it 'walking through shadows,'" he explained proudly. "It is a way of finding and exploiting blind spots."

"Is it magic?"

"Do you believe in magic?"

"No." Louisa pursed her lips in contemplation. She had tried everything to get rid of the man, including alerting the authorities. Whatever this bit of bone was, Mr. Smythe was willing to risk incarceration for it by constantly sneaking into her home.

She decided to try a different tactic, and instead softened her voice to a placating tone.

"I'm sorry, but I cannot help you," she replied earnestly. "I have searched everywhere, but couldn't find your artifact."

"Yes, you can," he protested. Mr. Smythe stepped forward now that she appeared to soften, and made an abortive attempt to place his hand upon hers before remembering himself and taking a hasty step back. "You are the only one who can."

"And if I don't?" she demanded, gazing into his eyes and finally noticing the strange, tiny flecks of black embedded in the brown irises. "Will you continue to haunt me, to threaten me?"

"I have to go home," he replied helplessly. "But I can't do it until I'm whole."

A small part of Louisa sympathized with him, even if she didn't believe his story. For whatever reason, he was desperate to get his half of the tally bone. It meant a great deal to him and she genuinely wanted to help. But she did not take kindly to harassment.

"And I have to protect myself."

With his penchant for sneaking into her home, Louisa decided it was prudent to prepare for Mr. Smythe's next arrival, so she had taken the precaution of hiding a fireplace poker near her skirts, which she now pulled out, lashing at him with the iron blade.

Mr. Smythe jerked back, but not fast enough to save himself. He blinked at her in almost comical surprise as the poker sliced through his middle. He appeared astonished that the woman he stalked would dare strike him.

"You stabbed me!" he cried, staring in wide-eyed shock at the blood pouring from his side.

"I know," Louisa replied without sympathy. It wasn't a deep wound, but he was losing blood at an alarming rate. If he sought medical attention immediately, she reasoned, he should survive. "And if you don't wish further injury, I suggest you remove yourself immediately."

To her consternation, instead of complying, Mr. Smythe collapsed on the floor amidst an ever-widening pool of blood.

"What are you doing?" she demanded. "Go find a doctor!"

"There is no point," he replied forlornly. "Without my bone, I am incomplete. I will die, either today or tomorrow."

"Then die somewhere else!" Louisa exclaimed. She tore strips from her petticoats and used them to staunch the blood, hoping she could get him to leave before the servants saw what she had done and hauled her off to prison.

In response, he stretched out on her thinning carpet, closing his eyes with a sigh, and waiting for death.

"This is ridiculous," Louisa muttered, completely exasperated by her unwanted guest. "I'm sorry, but I can't help you. I've looked everywhere and didn't find it. It's gone."

"It isn't gone," he argued. "It's right here. Right under your nose ... or rather your hand."

"My hand?" Louisa looked down at her long and slender fingers. George said they were her best features and had taken an absurd amount of pride in selecting what he considered the perfect wedding ring. It was a thick band of dull gold, which always seemed warm no matter the outside temperature. It was the only possession which she hadn't sought to pawn.

George had loved it, so Louisa loved it, though there was always something slightly off about the ring. It seemed far too lightweight to be made of metal. Though George had sworn the faint markings on one side were Celtic, they didn't look like anything she had seen in a history book or museum.

"No!" she breathed as she was struck by a horrifying revelation.

"Yes," Mr. Smythe replied. "I told you, you are the only one who can help me."

"But this is gold," Louisa tried to protest, though even to her own ears the words rang hollow.

"Have you had it appraised? With your reduced circumstances, did you never think to sell it?"

"Never."

Louisa hated George for what he had done. She hated being left in ruin. She hated having to pawn her jewelry to pay off her late husband's gambling debts and mistresses, but she could never bring herself to part with his ring. The memory of the way he looked at her during the proposal, so loving and tender, was the only thing that kept her from burning down the house.

"It isn't real," Mr. Smythe replied. His voice was growing faint now from loss of blood, but there was strength in his gaze. "Not real gold. Not valuable to you, but it means everything to me."

"Not valuable ..." It was the *only* thing of value from her disastrous marriage, a reminder that once she had been young and hopeful, and in love, that she hadn't always been a jaded, miserly creature. It was a last tether to the woman she had once been, and hoped to be again. "It's valuable to me."

"Why?"

"Because." It was a silly question. Louisa shouldn't have to justify her desire to keep her wedding ring, especially to a lunatic that broke into her home, claiming to be fae, and was currently lying on her floor too stupid to seek a doctor. "Because I loved him."

"That's a good reason." Mr. Smythe sighed and closed his eyes in resignation. "It's as it should be, really, though its bad news for me. The strongest force in both our worlds, though I wouldn't know. Maybe that's why I wandered over here. I wanted to see if maybe I could find it in your world. Perhaps I could find a pretty girl with curly hair and freckles, someone who loved so blindly that she believed bone was gold ..."

"Do shut up!" Louisa snapped. His rambling words were becoming incoherent. She needed to do something to get him out of her home. He was perhaps too weak to walk out on his own, and he seemed so content to die that he might fight her if she tried to move him. Perhaps there was only one way.

She gazed down at her wedding ring and took a deep, fortifying breath. Love alone hadn't kept it on her finger. George had his faults, but Louisa also had plenty of her own. Every time she paid off one of his debts she wondered if there was something she could have said or done to keep his attentions at home, if she was perhaps too plain, too frigid, or too nagging. So she kept the ring, and stared at it over and over throughout her days, remembering better times and wondering where they went wrong.

More than his betrayals, or even George's death, her marriage, and any lingering attachment to George would be over. It was the last, fragile cord binding them together.

"Take it," she commanded, twisting it violently off her finger and thrusting it at Mr. Smythe. "Take it and get out."

"Do you mean it?" Despite the pain in his voice, he sounded hopeful, as if he just learned it was his birthday.

"Yes." Louisa forced herself not to look at the offending bit of bone, fearful that she might snatch it back. "I don't need it anymore."

Somehow, as she dropped the ring into Mr. Smythe's shaking hand, she realized that the words were true. She didn't need the ring to remind her of the good or bad times with George. She would never forget him, but she would no longer spend her days staring at the dull gold and wondering what went wrong.

Mr. Smythe closed his eyes with a smile, grateful for his quest to be completed at last. Then he began to whisper. The words were strange, yet somehow eerily familiar. Louisa strained her ears to pick up his peculiar speech, but no matter how she tried, she could not decipher the words.

"Mr. Smythe?" she asked in consternation. "Are you all right? Can you get up now?"

He ignored her, intent on his incantation. His voice rose as his speech became more impassioned, until he was shouting the strange chant. Louisa felt goosebumps rise along her arms as she heard a faint chorus of voices join his from the dark corners of the room. The ring in his hand began to shine brightly with light until it was glowing and pulsating with power.

"Mr. Smythe!" Louisa shouted desperately. She blinked. She pinched herself. Her mind raced to come up with a rational explanation for the events unfolding in her study. Then his eyes flew open to stare intently into Louisa's and suddenly she believed him. Mr. Smythe had told the truth. He truly was a fae creature trapped in her mortal world.

Then everything went dark. The window had flown open, extinguishing the candles in a powerful gust.

"Yes, madam?"

"Are you all right?" Her fingers shook violently as she relit a slender taper that had been knocked over by the wind. Its dim light cast ghastly shadows about the room, making Louisa shiver in apprehension.

"I am fine now," he replied. Louisa turned toward the voice and found him standing a little too close for comfort. She couldn't explain it, but he appeared taller, stronger, and inexplicably healed from the stab wound.

Louisa backed up in shock, until the back of her skirts brushed the edge of her desk. She remembered the horrific stories she had been told as a child, of mischievous fae that preyed upon humans, causing untold misery by their wild antics.

"I won't hurt you," he replied in a placating tone. "In fact, I could kiss you ..."

"Please don't," Louisa shouted, and then thought better of it. What would it be like to kiss a magical creature? Did fae taste different from mortals? Would she turn into a princess or a frog?

He smiled as if reading her thoughts.

"Then take this as a sign of my gratitude." He placed a small, but heavy leather bag in her unresisting hands. "Perhaps these mortal lands *do* have something to offer," he laughed as their fingers brushed. The morbid intruder had vanished so completely Louisa wondered if she was talking to Mr. Smythe's twin brother.

With one last saucy wink, he vanished, leaving Louisa shivering in the dim light of a single candle. For a long moment she just stood there, staring into the empty space where he had once been, wondering if she could trust her memory of what had just transpired. If she told anyone, they would lock her in an asylum, and perhaps rightfully so.

Things like this just didn't happen. There were no such things as fae creatures and tally bones. But as she stared down at her rug, still soaked with Mr. Smythe's blood, Louisa realized that there were many things in this world that she would never understand.

Her gaze lowered to the small leather pouch. Curious, she began loosening the cord, and almost dropped its contents when she saw what was inside. Dozens of golden coins spilled out into her hands, enough to pay her servants' back wages, enough to fix up her house, enough to *buy* a new house. Mr. Smythe had just paid off the last of George's debts and ensured Louisa a very comfortable existence.

She smiled and ruefully rubbed her finger where a pale band of skin marked where her wedding ring had once lain. Perhaps she would buy her own ring this time.

***

Bella Muerte
by LJ McLeod

Australia: Bewitching mythological creatures entice resort divers.

Curtis surveyed the newest crop of holiday-makers. It was customary for the entire staff to be present to welcome new guests to the El Galleon Beach Resort, and as one of the senior dive instructors employed at the resort, he was expected to give a brief explanation about the dive program on offer. The other dive instructors used the opportunity to place bets on which guests would inevitably try to drown themselves and need to be rescued. Curtis's money was on the middle-aged British guy in the rope sandals and floppy hat.

After describing the marine attractions in Puerto Galera, Curtis stepped back to stand with the other instructors while Tom, the resort owner, went over some housekeeping information and wished the guests an enjoyable stay. Curtis had just leaned towards Jose, the other senior instructor, to place his own bet when Tom turned around and glared at him.

"Stop betting on the guests," he hissed. Curtis straightened and tried to look serious, while Jose smothered a smile.

"First dive is scheduled for eight a.m., with orientation at seven-thirty a.m., so don't drink too much tonight. I mean it," Tom told them. After staring at them for several long moments to make sure they got the point, he turned to leave then paused, "Oh, and I've got one hundred dollars on the Brit in the floppy hat."

*

The next morning dawned beautiful and clear. Curtis and Jose stood surveying the calm ocean as their newest recruit vomited noisily off the dock behind them.

"Did you learn something, Trev?" Jose called over his shoulder. Trevor whimpered as a new wave of vomiting hit him.

"They just don't make 'em like they used to," Curtis said, and Jose nodded thoughtfully. They had taken Trevor out for a few drinks to celebrate him joining the team and had proceeded to get the poor boy very drunk. He was only nineteen, so it hadn't been that hard. It was also a very important lesson in self-restraint, one he wouldn't be forgetting any time soon. Dive instructors could not work drunk, or even hung over, it was just too dangerous for the guests.

"Somebody needs to get him out of here before the guests arrive," Curtis yelled to his boat crew. They had been having a good laugh at Trevor's expense, but this pronouncement shut them up quickly. A deck of cards appeared from nowhere and they huddled around to draw cards. When everyone had a card, they all flipped them over at the same time. One of them cursed and the others all pointed and laughed. The loser, a short, skinny local man, headed towards the now prone Trevor.

"Will Bug even be able to lift him?" Jose muttered.

"He's stronger than he looks," Curtis responded doubtfully. When Curtis had first arrived in the Philippines, he had been unable to pronounce any of the locals' names, so in true Australian fashion, he had given them all nicknames. Many of the nicknames had stuck. Unfortunately for Bug, his was one of them—probably due to his protruding eyeballs and small, stick-like frame. The tourists loved him though, especially the young women. They found him adorable, which usually meant he got tipped very well.

Bug had managed to get under one of Trevor's arms and hoisted him to his feet. He slipped an arm around the sick man's waist and half-dragged him off the dock, towards the staff quarters. He got him out of sight just in time, as the guests started to arrive.

The first dive with a new group was always chaotic, so Curtis and Jose tried their best to distract the tourists, while the boat crew subtly collected their dive gear and loaded it onto the boat. Before they knew it, the divers were ushered onto the boat and ready to go. As the boat set off across the calm water, the level of excitement onboard was almost palpable. They had decided to head to Verde Island—it was not a preferred site for a first dive, but the weather was too perfect to turn down the opportunity. A gentle breeze blew, barely strong enough to ripple the water, as the boat skimmed along. A pod of pilot whales was feeding in the passage between two islands, which caused squeals of delight amongst the guests.

When they arrived at their destination, the boat crew dropped anchor and started to get the divers ready. Herman, the floppy hat wearing British man, was already having problems with his gear. Curtis and Jose exchanged knowing glances as they adjusted their own dive gear. "Last one in, babysits Herman," Jose whispered, jumping off the boat before Curtis could respond.

"Damn it!" Curtis muttered, following him in. It took a while to get all the divers in the water, and longer again to get them to submerge and descend. Predictably, Herman was having difficulties despite managing to cram ten two-kilogram weights onto his weight belt. Jose took the rest of the group down while Curtis tried to help Herman on the surface. He finally managed to get the man's BCD deflated and they slowly descended to join the others.

This dive site was one of Curtis's favourites. It was a sheer rock wall that dropped away into the murky depths and every inch of it was covered with life. Coral, anemones and sea fans grew in a riot of colours all over the wall and hundreds of species of fish filled the water. Tiny sea horses hid amongst the coral, while reef sharks cruised by in more open waters. Jose was pointing out a moray eel hiding in a small cleft to several divers, while others swam slowly along exploring the wall.

Herman seemed to be coping for now, so Curtis took the opportunity to survey the other divers. A couple looked like they had been born in the water and most of the others seemed to be managing varying levels of amateur competence, while one was about to put her hand down on a stonefish. Stonefish had a row of sharp spines filled with venom down their back that could cause extreme pain, paralysis or even death in some people. They blended perfectly into their surroundings which was why the girl hadn't spotted it yet.

Curtis kicked hard and managed to grab the girl before she put her hand down on the stonefish. She stared at him startled, until he pointed out the venomous fish she had nearly touched. Then she looked horrified. He sent her on her way and looked around for Herman. He had disappeared from view. Curtis looked down and just caught a glimpse of the errant diver as he plummeted out of sight into the darker depths. Cursing internally, he dove as quickly as he could and gave chase.

He finally caught up with Herman and grabbed the back of his BCD. Once he had a firm grip on him, he checked his gauge and wasn't surprised to see they were at a depth of around fifty metres. Visibility was significantly decreased and there were considerably less fish around. Herman had turned to look at him and a giggle escaped around his regulator. A feeling of wellbeing washed over Curtis and he checked his gauge again. They were now at fifty-five metres and still sinking. He had felt the effects of nitrogen narcosis before and he knew he needed to get both of them into more shallow water before they started making poor decisions and doing stupid things ... like Herman taking his regulator out of his mouth and offering it to a passing fish, giggling all the while. Curtis grabbed the regulator and jammed it back into his mouth, holding it there until Herman stopped giggling and started breathing regularly again.

He got a firm grip on Herman's BCD and was preparing to inflate his own when a flash of silver caught his eye. He turned to stare at a small cave in the rock wall and a pale face stared back at him. The face was distinctly feminine, with skin so pale it was almost translucent and ice blue eyes. Silvery-white hair danced like seaweed around the face as it gazed intently at Curtis. He was mesmerized, unable to look away from the ethereal vision before him. Delicate lips curved upwards in an enticing smile. He tried to move towards the face but something pulled him up short. He turned to see what it was, surprised to find Herman grinning back at him. Giving himself a mental shake, Curtis put a short burst of air into his BCD. He gripped Herman tightly and together they began to rise. When he looked back at the cave, the face was gone.

*

Curtis had had a very long day. After dragging Herman back up to a shallower depth where neither of them were experiencing the intoxicating effects of nitrogen narcosis any longer, he had discovered that Herman had used up just about all of his air and would have to end his dive. He continued their ascent slowly until they reached five metres and then made Herman wait there for a fifteen-minute safety stop in case either of them had any residual nitrogen in their blood after their little deep water adventure. They had been the longest fifteen minutes ever, thanks to Herman's erratic buoyancy. In the end, Curtis had just held on to him until the required time had passed. Then he had the pleasure of explaining to Herman that maybe he should take the rest of the day off from diving. Or maybe get a few more lessons. After that, he had to readjust his dive plan for the day so that he had mostly shallow dives to avoid developing decompression sickness. He didn't even win any money from the betting pool, because it turned out everybody had bet on Herman.

And then there had been that face ... Curtis couldn't get that face out of his mind. It had been the most beautiful face he had ever seen. When he closed his eyes, it filled his whole mind. He didn't even know if the face was real or if it had been a hallucination brought on by nitrogen narcosis. He was so lost in thought that he didn't hear Jose pull up a seat next to him at the resort bar.

"What's on your mind, *mi amigo*?" Jose asked, startling Curtis out of his reverie.

"Mate, I think I'm losing my mind. I saw something at the Verde drop-off," he blurted before he could stop himself.

"Better tell me about it," Jose said. He ordered them two beers and waited for Curtis to explain. Curtis took a long swig of beer and contemplated what he was going to say.

"While I was retrieving Herman, I saw a face—a woman's face—looking at me from a cave in the rock face. What do you make of that?"

Jose gazed at his friend thoughtfully. He didn't say anything for so long that Curtis began to wonder if he shouldn't have mentioned it.

"My mother told me a story once," Jose began quietly, "of a fisherman who disappeared without a trace. One day the fisherman and his brother were out on their boat when they caught something in their net. At first, they thought they had caught a sea lion or maybe a baby porpoise. But when they finally untangled the net, what they found was much stranger. They had accidently trapped a beautiful young woman who was as pale as moonlight and completely naked. But instead of legs, she had a tail like a fish. What they had caught was not a person or an animal, but a water spirit. In my village, back in Mexico, we call them *Bella Muerte*. This Bella was so beautiful, the fisherman fell instantly in love. She pleaded for her freedom and he took pity on her and let her go. But he could not stop thinking about her. He became obsessed with finding her again. He stopped fishing and took the boat out searching every day instead. He barely ate and he didn't sleep, he only looked for the Bella. His brother became worried for him and took the boat away, hoping he would give up his pointless searching. But the fisherman wouldn't give up. He sat on the dock every day and waited for the Bella to come back for him. One day the fisherman disappeared. His brother found his shoes and his clothes folded neatly in a pile on the dock. He was never seen again."

When Jose finished, they sat in silence and sipped their beer. "What does Bella Muerte mean?" Curtis asked after a while.

"Beautiful death."

"Is that what you think I saw? One of these ... Bellas?"

"Of course not! I think you are *loco*!" Jose laughed, clapping him on the shoulder. After a minute, Curtis joined him in the laughter.

"This is because of that drop bear story I told you, isn't it?" he said. Jose only shrugged and ordered them another round.

*

Days passed but Curtis could not stop thinking about his experience at Verde Island. To get his mind off it, he organized an exploratory dive with Jose when they both had an afternoon off. It was rare that they had the opportunity to dive without babysitting tourists, so they were determined to make the most of it. Curtis had heard of an old dive site dubbed "Shark Cave" that used to be filled with a variety of shark species, until the locals heard about it and fished the area bare. He was hoping that after years of being ignored, some of the marine life may have come back. Bug had agreed to pilot the boat and show them the supposed location of the dive site.

When they arrived, Curtis and Jose geared up, while Bug settled in for an afternoon nap. Once in the water, Curtis felt considerably better. His thoughts always seemed clearer underwater, like the rest of the world just melted away. According to the stories, the shark cave was actually a long, narrow space under a ledge covered in coral. The entire area was a riot of corals, so finding the cave might take some time. Curtis and Jose drifted along, maintaining line of sight but otherwise exploring on their own. Schools of small silver fish cruised above the reef and a curious sea snake swam over to investigate the bubbles from Curtis's regulator. Losing interest, the sea snake swam down into a break in the coral. Curtis followed it down and discovered the gap in the reef was considerably bigger than it appeared from above. He allowed himself to sink gently to the ocean floor and found a narrow gap under a rock overhang. He took his flashlight out of a pocket in his BCD and shone it into the darkness.

The space went back a lot farther than seemed possible. Curtis started to feel excited, thinking that maybe he had found the shark cave. He was about to ascend and signal for Jose to come check it out when something darted out of the darkness right at him. He tried to paddle backwards, but a white tip reef shark he had startled got tangled in his regulator hose. It thrashed desperately, trying to get away, but managed only to hit Curtis in the head with its tail and dislodge his mask. Suddenly his regulator was ripped from his mouth and the shark broke free. He groped wildly for the regulator but couldn't find it. He reached for his backup regulator that usually hung from his BCD, but it too was gone. He was running out of air and knew he should attempt an emergency ascent, but his eyes were full of saltwater and he couldn't remember which way was up. Bursts of light exploded in his head and he didn't know if it was from the blow to his head or if he was dying. A shape materialised in front of him and then she was there. The Bella's luminous eyes gazed into his and her hair fanned around her head like a nimbus of light. Her smile was the last thing he saw before everything went black.

*

Reality crashed back abruptly as Curtis sat upright and gasped. Oxygen filled his lungs and he had never felt anything as wonderful, or as painful.

"Oh, thank God," he heard Jose say. Looking around, he found himself back on the boat with Jose and Bug kneeling next to him and looking worried. His dive gear was scattered around, as if it had been stripped off in a hurry. His head felt overly warm and when he touched his right temple, his fingers came away bloody.

"What happened?" he slurred.

"You disappeared and when I couldn't find you, I surfaced and found you floating face down. I signaled Bug and he brought the boat over and helped me get you on board. I thought you were dead," Jose said. He looked more worried than Curtis had ever seen him.

"What happened to you down there?"

For a moment, Curtis couldn't answer; everything was blank. "She saved me!" he remembered suddenly, "The Bella! She saved my life!"

"I saved your life!" Jose snapped, startlingly Curtis with his vehemence. Looking uncomfortable, Bug got up and moved to the back of the boat and started tinkering with the motor.

"My uncle drowned, did you know that?" Jose said, "When I was a boy. We found him floating face down in the bay by our village. My father was never the same. Today, I thought I had lost you too. Curtis, you've been distracted lately. You need to stop with this Bella stuff. I can't pull the lifeless body of another loved one out of the water."

Curtis stared at his friend, not realising his behaviour had affected Jose so much. "You're right. I'm so sorry. And thank you for pulling me out. I'd be done without you."

Jose looked slightly mollified and went to retrieve the first aid kit for the cut on Curtis's head. Curtis could only sit and stare at the water, trying desperately to figure out what had happened to him.

*

It turned out that Curtis had acquired a mild concussion from the blow to his head, so Tom had given him a week off work to recuperate. He used the time to obsess about the Bella. Could such a creature even exist? She had seemed so real. And yet ...

He did have a concussion, and the time before that he had been suffering from nitrogen narcosis. Was it possible he imagined her? But he could picture her face in intricate detail—it even haunted his dreams. Surely, he couldn't have imagined something so detailed. These thoughts chased themselves around in circles in his head until he felt he would go crazy if he didn't figure it out. The doctor had told him he couldn't dive with his concussion, but that didn't mean he couldn't search for the Bella in other ways.

He started taking a boat out to look in the areas where he had seen her before, but this quickly became very frustrating. With no way to see beneath the waves, he couldn't help but feel she might be just below the surface and he would never see her. When it became too much to bear, he started to get in the water to search. He couldn't dive, but he could snorkel, and he spent hours at a time in the water in the hopes of catching a glimpse of her.

Instead of helping, this only increased his frustration. Every flash of light off a silver fish or clump of seaweed caught in the current looked just like his Bella. If he just searched a little longer, or swam a little farther, or looked a little harder, then he might prove himself worthy and she might come back to him.

He didn't even know at what point he stopped questioning her existence, he only knew he had to find her. He wanted to ask Jose for help, but he knew his friend would not approve of his search. It felt wrong to keep this from him, they had been as close as brothers for years. But he couldn't stop. Not even for Jose.

185

*

Jose stared at the still form of his sleeping friend. Curtis didn't sleep much lately, mostly he just sat and stared out the window, when he was even around. At first, Jose thought that he was using his time to relax and enjoy himself, but it soon became pretty obvious that whatever Curtis was doing, it was not relaxing. He had become distracted and withdrawn, started skipping meals and disappearing for extended periods of time. Jose knew deep down inside what Curtis was doing, he just hoped fervently he was wrong. He needed to put a stop to this before things got out of hand. He decided that he would confront Curtis in the morning and demand that he give up this obsession. Resolved, Jose lay down and attempted to get some sleep.

*

Curtis's eyes fluttered open and he smiled. He knew how to find his Bella. It had come to him in a dream. The room was dark with dawn still an hour away, but he could see well enough to do what needed to be done. Quietly, he made his bed and left all of his clothes in a neat pile on the end, with his shoes lined up on the floor underneath. He wouldn't be coming back, but he didn't want to leave a mess for Jose to clean up. He changed into his swim shorts and grabbed his mask and fins. He thought about leaving a note for Jose, but there wasn't anything he could say that would make him understand why he needed to do what he was doing. He said a silent goodbye to his friend and to the life he knew, and shut the door softly behind him. He walked down to the dock, took one of the boats and headed for Verde Island.

When he arrived at the site of the drop-off, he anchored the boat and turned the motor off. He sat and watched the sun rise over the water. Once he joined his Bella, he might never see another sunrise. As the sun cleared the horizon, he put on his mask and fins, took several long deep breaths and dove into the water. If his Bella wouldn't come to him, he would go to her.

*

Jose woke up abruptly—something was wrong. It took him a moment to realise that Curtis was gone. Jose turned on his bedside lamp, the sight of Curtis's folded clothes hit him like a punch in the stomach. He knew the story, his mother had told it to him over and over. He knew what this meant, that Curtis had given up his place in the world. He jumped out of bed and ran down to the dock.

"Have you seen Curtis?" he asked Bug, who was busy opening up the shed where all the dive gear was kept.

"Sure, I saw him head out in a boat maybe ten minutes ago. Don't know where he was going, though," Bug answered. Jose knew exactly where Curtis was heading, back to the place where this whole thing started.

He pushed past Bug into the shed and grabbed the keys for the resort's jet ski, as well as his mask and fins. As an afterthought, he also grabbed a pony bottle, a small handheld air canister. He ran to the jet ski, jumped on, and gunned the engine. As he headed towards Verde Island into the light of the rising sun, he prayed he wouldn't be too late.

*

Curtis swam down, heading deeper with every kick. He was an experienced free diver and could hold his breath for several minutes if he remained calm. He wasn't sure how deep he had gone, but already the light was getting dimmer. If he could just reach his Bella's cave, he was convinced that he would find her there. He paid no attention to the beautiful scenery as he dove, he just kept kicking and heading deeper into the drop-off. Something twinged inside his head and Curtis stopped diving abruptly. Waves of dizziness washed over him as he floated in the water.

Vaguely, he was aware something was wrong, but the thought kept skittering away every time he tried to concentrate on it. A flash of silver caught his attention and he squinted into the darkness, trying to make out what it was. She appeared almost in slow motion, her long silver tail propelling her languidly towards him. Her skin was so luminous that it seemed to glow in the dim light. Her pale blue eyes met his and she held out her hand to him. Curtis gazed at her, the most beautiful creature he had ever seen, and all he wanted in that moment was to accept what she offered him. He reached out and took her hand, and her face lit with a radiant smile. She pulled him closer and wrapped her other arm around his neck. As her lips met his, Curtis's vision started to darken. The last of his oxygen bubbled out of their kiss and he surrendered himself to her embrace.

*

It only took Jose a quick glance to see the boat was empty. He turned off the jet ski engine and stared intently at the water around him. Moments later, a series of bubbles broke the surface. Without hesitation, he pulled on his mask and fins, shoved the mouth piece of the pony bottle into his mouth and dove into the water where the bubbles had surfaced. It was a desperate hope that he would find Curtis in time, but he had to try. He kicked downwards as hard as he could and it wasn't long before he saw something floating in the water.

He redoubled his efforts and within moments, he had reached the lifeless body of his friend. His eyes were shut and his mouth hung open, filled with seawater. Jose wrapped his arm around Curtis's torso and hauled him upwards as fast as he could. The extra weight made it harder, but adrenaline gave him the strength he needed. His head broke the water's surface and he wasted no time towing Curtis towards the boat.

He hoisted the top half of Curtis's body onto the boat and climbed up after him, then pulled him the rest of the way out of the water. He put his fingers on his friend's carotid artery, but there was no pulse. He rolled him onto his side, checked that there was nothing obstructing his airway, rolled him onto his back and started CPR. With every chest compression, the word "Please" echoed around and around Jose's head. He paused long enough to administer two rescue breaths before resuming compressions. He went through round after round of CPR, but Curtis still lay like a corpse with no signs of life. In desperation, he brought the bottom of his fist down as hard as he could on Curtis's sternum, causing a torrent of saltwater to flood out of his mouth.

Curtis gasped, his eyes flying open as he vomited up more water. Jose sat him up and cradled him as he coughed and gagged. "It's all right, mi amigo, it's all right," he murmured as Curtis dragged in painful-sounding breaths. "We'll get you away from here, far away from Puerto Galera, where she can't reach you anymore. We couldn't save my uncle, but I can save you."

Curtis lay back and looked at his friend, "Your uncle, the one that drowned, he was the fisherman in your story."

He finally understood what Jose had hinted at all along. Jose just nodded.

"I thought she ... But ... the Bella killed your uncle?"

"No. Beautiful death is not what the Bella Muerte are. It is what they offer. It's an offer you have to accept," Jose said. They sat for a long time in silence.

"I think we should leave today. I think when we get back to the resort, I will call my travel agent about flights out of the Philippines," Jose said after a while.

Curtis nodded, letting his friend go on about travel plans and what needed to be done in order for them to leave. He didn't say anything because a new thought had occurred to him. Maybe he could convince Jose to take him to his village back in Mexico. Maybe he could find what he was looking for there.

***

Of Thain Blood
by Tara Curnow

British Columbia: A fantasy of a lie driving two brothers asunder.

The hour candle showed four marks until dawn. It had already
burned past one mark since Tarrek had fled, running out of the hall
and into the night. He had left behind a group of drunken men sitting
in an embarrassed silence, broken only by the crackling of the
dwindling fire.

Tarrek's departure had been like the man himself: loud and
disruptive. His drinking horn had been thrown across the room to
clatter loudly to the floor, the hops ale it contained painting a messy
brown rain cloud on the wall. He had shoved at the table when he
leapt up from his bench, sending the men seated on the other side
reeling onto their backs from the force of it. The main door was a
heavy, oaken affair, banded in black iron. Tarrek had flung it open as
easily as a child might toss a leaf over his shoulder.

And his eyes. Lorres had never seen Tarrek's eyes so full of hurt,
of betrayal.

Lorres now stood in his brother's bedroom, had done so since
Tarrek had run off. The alcohol that had earlier this evening set their
spirits dancing was now simmering behind his eyes as a dull ache. He

stood and watched, never taking his eyes away from the window that overlooked the rose garden.

As he kept his vigil, he replayed the scene in the hall over and over. He studied it all—the men, the table, the ale—dissecting it from every angle, trying to figure out where it had all gone wrong and how he could possibly hope to fix it.

Again and again, he watched his brother storm off into the night.

Again and again, he was pierced by that look of utter betrayal.

The hours marched on toward daybreak. His legs, slender and finely attired, tingled, then cried, then finally went numb. Still, he stood and watched,

Logically was the best way to approach any problem, he found, and logically, he knew he would never be able to track Tarrek through the forest in the dark of night. So he would have to wait for him to return. If Tarrek did not come back to his room, then their mother's rose garden is where he would be.

In a household full of men, Fernig had called it her Lady's Retreat. Though she had yielded all other matters of the estate to her Lord husband with a happy grace, in this, she ruled absolute. Every corner, every petal on every plant within its stone walls bore traces of her spirit; even now, seven years after her death. Though he still paid for its upkeep, Odaran Thain had not set foot within the garden since that day. For his sons, however, it had become a sacred retreat in troubled times.

His sons ...

That was how this whole ugly mess had started. They had all of them—Lorres, Tarrek, a few of their men-at-arms, and the estate seneschal, Dorn—been drinking and gaming in the great hall. The old steward, too deep in his cups, had started ruminating on days gone by, and mentioned to Tarrek, "the day Lord Thain brought you home to your mother."

Lorres had frozen. The rest of the company had taken a minute to understand the implications of Dorn's words. The only person who didn't was the old man himself. He had continued his slurred recollections, oblivious to the growing tension around him, and to the horrified realization spreading across Tarrek's face. He had stopped only when Lorres had snapped at him, with a voice sharp enough to cut. Lorres wished he *could* cut the old man, cut his foolish tongue right out of his dull-witted head.

It was a closely guarded secret among very few of the household that Tarrek had not, in fact, been born of Thain blood. He did not take the news well.

Now Lorres was left to tread the dire after-currents of the devastating incident. The scathing look of betrayal Tarrek had thrown at him upon learning the truth wounded him deeply, and from that wound welled a guilt that threatened to drown him. Yes, he had lied. Their entire lives together he had lied, had even spun a stirring fiction of Tarrek's birth, as if it had really happened under their roof. And even if it had not, did that negate all the experiences they had shared? Playing and squabbling as children, all the adventures and arguments that paved the road to manhood? A lifetime of competing and commiserating together, as all brothers do?

But he knew no amount of rational justification could sooth the memory of that burning, hateful glare. It was no less than he deserved.

I'm sorry, Tarrek. If only you knew what I protected you from.

But he could never know. Lorres had given his word.

The sun had not yet raised its head above the forested horizon, but the beginning notes of birdsong promised its imminent arrival. Soon, he knew, the comforting smell of fresh baking bread would begin to wander up from the kitchens. His stomach clenched in an agonizing pucker, reminding him of how long he had gone without food. He silenced its protestations with a mental slap. He stood and watched.

The glass of the window appeared to be melting, the fading stars beyond it smearing themselves across his vision. Lorres rubbed his burning eyes, blinked, then started.

There Tarrek finally was, standing in the rose garden. Lorres spun around and stumbled to the door on legs that did not want to cooperate after the abuses they had suffered over the past hours. The door handle played dumb, pretending to forget how to work. Lorres cursed it out as he managed to bring it into line, wrenched the door open, and ran down the corridor toward the garden and his brother.

He is my brother. I have to make him understand.

Four cobblestone walls, twelve feet long and taller than Lorres could stretch up, enclosed Lady Fernig's Retreat. Most of the stones were grey, but there were lines of smooth river stones, rusty red in colour, set between them in swirls and curls. Fernig had brought these red stones with her when she had married Odaran. They were from her family's estate, picked by her own hands from the riverbank where she had played as a child.

Ornate iron shepherd's crooks stood in each corner, with glass oil lanterns hanging ready to provide light when the sun went down. The wicks inside were dark now, but Lorres did not need them lit. The shapes and colours of this place were imprinted on his mind and his heart.

Roses flourished everywhere, artfully placed and expertly tended. In red and white, yellow and every shade of pink, they grew on shrubs, on long stems, and graced the crowns of trees.

A wooden trellis, covered over with climbing roses, provided shade on the brightest days. A stone bench underneath that once boasted cushions, now lay bare. Round stepping stones, inlaid with tiny mosaics of coloured glass, wove a gentle path from the bench over to the only entrance, where Lorres stood now.

He did not come here often, but he felt to boycott the place entirely, as his father did, was too great an insult to his mother's memory. It had been months, though, after her death, before he had found the courage to step foot within these walls once more, and every time since then had been like that first.

That warm wonderful scent; he could never decide whether she had smelled of roses, or the roses of her. All he need do was close his eyes and she was there before him in his mind's eye. Her long, dark hair, like a raven's wing unfolding down her back, matched his own. His thin face and acuminate nose were hers as well, though in shape only. The gentle tenderness that had always blossomed from Fernig's delicate features was something Lorres had never been able to match, nor did he want to. He wore his cold aloofness as a shield. Better people think him uncaring, than to think him weak with emotion. He would never admit the pain this place brought down upon him, the vice around his heart that stole the life from his limbs every time he crossed the threshold of his mother's garden.

Tarrek stood facing the east wall. His arms, large with corded muscle, hung loose by his sides, and though he seemed to stand calmly, Lorres recognized the tense lines across his brother's back and shoulders.

He is my brother. He is!

Tarrek did not speak, did not turn around, and Lorres knew he could not be the one to open the difficult discussion that lay before them. Tarrek simply would not speak of it until he was ready. He was built like a brick wall, and was just as stubborn. But neither could Lorres stand there in silence. He had to say something, anything, to drown out the deafening sound of the wordless accusations being bellowed at him by Tarrek's solid back.

"You took your time."

"I was thinking." There was a slight hesitancy to this last word, as if he wasn't finished with his sentence. "And ... I got lost."

Yes, that would make him hesitate. Always hated looking stupid, Tarrek did. At another time, in a different situation, Lorres would have dug in with a thinly veiled insult: lighthearted, but cutting nonetheless. Indeed, he now noticed Tarrek's shoulders hunching slightly after this admission of ineptness, as a child who is expecting a smack for having done something wrong.

Lorres was surprised to find this stung him a little bit.

Am I always that cruel to him?

He took a brief moment then, to put himself in his brother's place, and saw the situation "through his opponent's eyes," as he had been taught.

Odaran had always used his sons' strengths to the family's best advantage, and Lorres was best at talking. Negotiations, arbitrations, trade agreements; he handled all of it. Lorres could talk circles around anyone he met. He had a gift of language, and an eerie ability to sense what his opponents were going to say before they did. It was often bantered about by the household staff that, "Master Lorres could talk you into paying him to take your prize stud bull off your hands, and convince you it was your idea."

He hated thinking of Tarrek as his opponent now, even if only to himself, but there were greater things at stake here, greater truths that must be protected, no matter the cost. Everything depended on him maintaining control of this conversation, and tactically was the best way he knew how, the only thing he was ever good at.

He saw Tarrek now, world turned upside down, heart heaving, mind rebelling against the new truths that had been forced upon him. Saw him running, racing, as fast as his powerful legs could carry him, away from the lies of his existence, and the men who had spun them. Being swallowed by the trees of the forest as they grew denser the farther away from the manor house he ran. Who knows how long, how far he had run before finally stopping? Probably by tripping over a stump and tumbling face first into the dirt. Standing up, staring into the darkness, seeing nothing but the shadows of branches and deeper shadows. How long until he was able to get his bearings?

No wonder it had taken him all night to make his way back. Still, Lorres had just suffered through several hours of sore legs and an empty stomach, not to mention a lost night's sleep, while waiting for Tarrek to wander back home. Feeling more than a little frustrated, he found it impossible to keep at least some of that frustration from leaking into his speech.

"You must have known I'd be waiting for you."

Tarrek's voice chilled, his words dropping from his mouth like broken shards of ice. "Turns out there's a lot I don't know."

Then he turned around, and the angry, wounded confusion that twisted his face momentarily stole the air from Lorres's lungs. One other time only had he seen such a look; when Odaran had told them Fernig had died. Tarrek had been thirteen.

"Who am I, Lorres?" Tarrek's hands lay flat, open, entreating. All he wanted was the truth, and it was the one thing Lorres could not give him. Not the whole of it.

The vigil Lorres had kept in Tarrek's room had been spent in preparation for this conversation, for this very question, and for the ones he knew would follow. He was his father's top negotiator, was trained to protect the family's interests above all else, and he was very good at his job.

It was time to put up his first argument. "You are my brother."

"I am not your blood." A predictable counterargument, for which Lorres also had a counter.

"That doesn't matter."

"Yes, it does." That stubbornness again. "Blood is who we are. Our blood defines us, carries our passions and our history. It tells us where we come from and who we are meant to be. Our blood is our destiny, and it will guide us to that destiny if we listen closely enough to follow where it leads us."

Lorres could not help but raise his brow slightly at this uncharacteristic display of deeper thinking. Tarrek was not usually the philosophical type.

"My, you did have time to think out there."

Tarrek was staring at his hands, as if seeing them for the first time. They were large, rough, accustomed to holding weapons and tankards. Yet he no longer seemed to recognize them.

"If I am not of Thain blood, then who am I?"

A little silence grew between them while Lorres contemplated every response he could possibly give, none of which, he knew, Tarrek would accept. Finally, he simply said, "You tell me."

Tarrek's mouth opened, then closed, devoid of an answer to give. His back shed the tense line of anger it had been carrying, and his solid shoulders dropped in despair.

"I don't know anymore." Such a small voice, coming from such a large man.

That small, despairing voice was almost enough to break Lorres's resolve. How could it not? No matter his origin, Tarrek had been raised as his little brother: his to teach, to tease, to protect. He desperately wanted to set it all right, and all he had to do was tell Tarrek the truth. But he could not. He had given his word.

I need to remind him that family is more than just the blood that runs in our veins.

He straightened his spine, and gathered his hands smartly at the small of it. He shifted the tone of his voice to be calm, direct, certain: a school teacher explaining a simple principle to his class.

"You are Tarrek, lover of pies and composer of bawdy drinking songs. Your preferred weapon is a mace and your favourite colour is orange. If you could sleep until noon every day, you would. You love to cuddle kittens. You hate that I know that, and you're terrified I will tell someone one day." Lorres paused, then took a calculated risk. "Honey mead makes you think you can sing."

"I can sing!"

"Hardly." Lorres allowed a small smile to curl his lips, and felt it grow when the same smile appeared on Tarrek's face. It was an old joke between them, and being able to share it now, in the middle of this argument, gave him hope.

He let his eyes wander over to the pink and white blossoms that surrounded them. Her blossoms. This was not going to be easy. But it was his best chance.

"This garden is your most cherished retreat, because the perfume of the roses makes you think of her, paints her portrait in your mind."

Lorres closed his eyes as a memory came to him. He was six, sitting under those blossoms with Fernig, snuggled in close beside her while she read to him from her favourite book of poetry. Her warm breath drifted over his ear, carrying with it her gentle, joyful voice like a stream happily rolling over the rocks beneath.

The sudden tightness in his throat had to be swallowed, his trembling lips brought back under control, before he could speak again.

"And that pressure on your heart, beautiful and unbearable." He turned back to Tarrek, the savage intensity of that very pain burning in his dark eyes. "That is the love between a mother and her son. That is family."

The roses seemed to wilt, so heavy with heartache was the silence that hung between them in the early morning air. They stared hard at each other, neither willing to concede the true depths of the emotion they were both drowning in.

It was a cold, harsh move, using Fernig's memory like this, and it tore a wound in each of them. But he did what had to be done. If there was nothing else to tie the two of them together as brothers, their love of this woman could. And if his wounded heart was the price of reminding Tarrek that he truly belonged to this family, then that was the price Lorres would pay.

Tarrek was the first to break their heated glare, dropping his gaze to the ground. His green eyes, glistening with his own memories, shut tight.

"You're a cruel bastard." His voice was low, scraping against the conflicting emotions that strangled it.

The words, hard as they were to hear, conceded the victory to Lorres.

"I know." And he did. He knew how ruthless he could be, sometimes had to be, when engaging in a verbal joust. Occasionally, he even reveled in it. This was not one of those times.

When Tarrek spoke again, he was still quiet. But that frozen sharpness had returned, frosting the edges of his words.

"Why didn't you tell me?"

"I promised Father I wouldn't." This truth, at least, Lorres could offer him, pitiful excuse though it was.

Truth, it may have been. But it was not one Tarrek wanted to hear. His head came up as he rounded on Lorres. His fingers curled and clenched. All of him seemed to get bigger. For one tense, horrible heartbeat, Lorres feared Tarrek might just strike at him.

"All these years, Lorres." Tarrek took a step forward, then another, his voice rising with his temper. "All the opportunities you've had to reveal the truth."

Lorres stood his ground. He'd taken a black eye from his brother before. "I gave him my word!"

"How long have you known?"

"I've always known. Since the night Father brought you home. You were just an infant. He brought you home and told me you were my brother and that was that."

"And you never questioned him about it? Not even once?"

Of course, he had. On and off and on again for years. Finally, when Lorres was eighteen, Odaran had called on him late one night. After revealing the real story of his adopted son's origin, he had bound his heir to eternal silence. *Swear it to me, Lorres. You must never allow him to learn the truth.*

And he never would. Tarrek could beat on him until the moon rose again. He would never betray his oath to his father. Of course, that was not the way he preferred things to go. Just because he could take a beating from Tarrek didn't mean he wanted to. He needed to diffuse this anger.

He relaxed his body, laid his arms loosely by his sides, palms open. His voice became gentle and rounded with earnest emotion.

"No, and I don't care to question it now. You are my brother, Tarrek. Nothing will ever change that."

Tarrek turned away. The balled fists of his hands unclenched to grasp at his messy blond hair instead. His breath huffed through his nose. "But that's not how I started my life."

He started pacing, short fast steps over grass that bent under the weight of his frustration. "When I took my first breath I was someone else with a different name, a different future. Who was I supposed to be?"

Though the threat of a fist in his face seemed to have passed, the conversation was now drifting into much more dangerous territory. Lorres fought the seed of panic blossoming in his stomach as Tarrek continued down this treacherous inquisitive path.

"I'm two people. No, I've been two people. But I only know one. I need to know the other."

Lorres drew himself up as straight as he could, and layered his voice with definitive certainty. "The other doesn't exist. It was a possibility that never came to pass and it doesn't matter." He spoke as a general, someone who does not expect questions or arguments. He wasn't sure he could handle either.

"It matters to me." Tarrek paused, then inhaled. His body tensed in the same way it did right before he loosed a bow string or lead a charge into battle. Lorres saw it, recognized it, and he knew the next words his brother would speak.

"Do you know who my real parents are?"

Not a flicker of eyelid, not a trace of flushed skin, not a tremor of the hands; nothing could betray the lie Lorres was about to deliver. He dug into the very bottom of his well of self-discipline, pressing his voice smooth as possible, and looked directly into Tarrek's eyes.

"No."

"Lorres—"

"I swear I don't. If mother knew, she never told me." He feared his desperation was obvious, prayed it was not so.

"And you never thought to ask Father?" Tarrek's eyes were sharp and distrustful, the pitch of his voice peaking in accusation.

"I'm sorry, it didn't occur to me. Where you came from has never concerned me."

Tarrek stared at Lorres, searching for something more, anything that might help him unravel this conspiracy that now twisted his entire life. Lorres held his gaze steady. Inside, he felt his resolve crumbling piece by tiny piece, as he silently screamed at his brother to look away.

After an eternity, Tarrek broke eye contact. His bottom lip disappeared between his teeth, as it always did when he was furiously struggling with some mental enigma.

"When is Father due back?"

Lorres could barely keep from releasing an audible sigh of relief. "Three days. Maybe four." And then, because he simply could not bear the guilty weight pressing on his heart, "I'm sorry."

Tarrek took a deep breath and exhaled, long and loud. "Don't be. I guess I understand why you didn't tell me."

It wasn't until he heard the words that Lorres realized that was not what he was apologizing for. "No. I'm sorry you found out."

Confusion, briefly, drew Tarrek's brow down to hood his eyes. Then he came to the same conclusion. "Me, too. I think I was better off not knowing."

With that, Tarrek turned back to where he had been when he first came to the garden, facing the east wall. He was done with the conversation. Lorres knew better than to press further, and in honesty, he was quite done as well. His legs threatened to refuse working entirely if he did not allow them to rest soon. The dull ache behind his eyes had mutated into a furious throbbing drumbeat. His heart felt wrung out and bruised.

He suddenly, strangely, had the urge to lay a comforting hand on his brother: squeeze his shoulder, rub his arm, pull him into a tight embrace that would somehow bridge this terrible gulf that had stretched between them. But he forced the urge away. Now was not the time. He wasn't even sure if Tarrek would accept such a gesture. And in any case, sentimental overtures were not something he was practiced at.

He turned himself and began the stiff walk back upstairs. His bed was where he was headed, and he imagined he would cry out loud in relief when he finally lay his weary body down on it.

I should probably pen a note to Father first, send it out with a rider right away. He needs to know what has happened.

Lorres could only imagine the reception Odaran would receive from his younger son upon his return home. The anger that Lorres had managed to turn from himself would be thrown directly back at their father. That would be a volatile confrontation, one that would shake the household from the gates to the stables. Lorres was not entirely sure he had the emotional strength to withstand that storm.

He opened the door to his suite, stood a moment on the thickly woven carpets. His bedchamber stood to the right, and it called to him with a yearning he could barely resist. Instead, he turned to sit at the desk he had specially commissioned for his twenty-fifth birthday. Rich, finely carved, and elegantly masculine, it embodied Lorres perfectly.

He chose a pen and quickly scripted the note, keeping it short and simple as Odaran preferred.

You need to come home. Tarrek knows.

Pressing his seal, summoning a page, delivering instructions: all these were performed in a hazy cloud of fatigue. Lorres wasn't even certain his eyes were still open as the young servant left the room. He thought again of his bed, with its sumptuous downy mattress and its soft, soft pillows. He fairly whimpered with the realization that getting to it meant standing up and walking, neither of which he was capable of anymore. And so the desk became a mattress, his arms, pillows, and he couldn't even muster up the energy to care.

Well, Father, it's done. I've kept my oath. I hope it was worth the price.

The thought drifted through his mind, faint and dreamlike, as he surrendered himself swiftly into the darkness of slumber.

***

My Forever Love
by Donna J. W. Munro

U.S.: A family's horrific legacy brings new meaning to "to have and to hold."

Loretta's smile always made my skin hot and my feet cold.

I met her in '08. God, she was beautiful. White blonde hair that tumbled in commas and question marks around her shoulders, down the snowy skin of her back. In English class, I watched her from two rows back. I loved her voice first. Ms. Partridge made us read the romantic poets—Shelly, Keats, Byron, Wordsworth. She'd volunteer to read and the words on the page would spring up like lilies in bloom. "The world is too much with us, late and soon," she read out for us.

She spoke beauty and I was all ears. Back then, my bones stuck out in goofy angles. Full of hormones, peach fuzz, and fear, I just watched. Smiled when she smiled. Bobbed on her wake when she flowed past in the hallways. We started as friends, loving the words left in yellowing pages. We hunted lyric in poetry books. I slipped her small, handwritten poems gleaned from the library's dustiest occupants. Like fortunes without a cookie, they rustled in her fingers. Words won her heart. And why shouldn't they? We had made ourselves from those beautiful pieces of genius.

By the end of college, writing entwined us. Our vows, promises written with fairy dust and gold, fluttered off her lithe tongue. We danced to the poetry that love makes, our families murmuring beyond the gulf that the dance floor created. We were alone and beauty wrapped us in its wings as we spun and laughed. Our wedding day, finally here.

"I don't feel so good," Loretta said to me, wedding dress sparkling like a cream cupcake in a bright light. White on white on white. I draped my jacket around her thin shoulders where it hung dramatically as Dracula's cape. The sound of the party faded, the way the world did for me when she spoke. The music of her voice crackled and her eyelids crinkled, crunched with some vicious pain twisting behind them. Loretta shrieked and from her nose velvety crimson blood gurgled out, dropping like paint upon the canvas of her gown. Red so much more bright against the white on white on white. Then her eyes, beautiful black pupils and irises so dark you couldn't tell them apart, rolled back into her sockets. I held her and sank to the floor, barely aware of our guests crowding in to watch. Hands pulled at her and me, but they wouldn't separate us. I clung.

Sirens, screaming. I only had eyes for Loretta. But Loretta's eyes ...

When they finally rolled back down, out of her brain, they were white. White on white on white.

She shoved me out of her way and lurched toward her father, a gentle, bald man who always told me to call him Dad. She sunk her pretty white teeth into Dad's bicep and even through the tux, a hunk came away in her wide red mouth. I grabbed her, my hands hooking around her shoulders and pulling her back.

Dad collapsed, blood jetting and soaking everyone around them.

"Loretta?" I said. Though my voice had the sort of strange tone a sharp note has in a happy tune. Dissonant. Out of tune.

She struggled to reach her mother, mouth snarling with strips of torn meat hanging from her teeth. Feet thundered on the dance floor as people ran from her. People who had hugged her not thirty minutes before. Now, Loretta smeared with gore, growled, trying to grab the fleeing guests. I kept my arms around her, even as she struggled with so much anger, so much power in her thin arms.

"Bring her!" Loretta's mother, heels clenched in her blood-coated hand, waved me to the back entrance of the reception hall. Loretta's white orbs fixed on me and for a moment, I thought she'd swing her head around and take a chunk out of my forearm. But she didn't. The flesh around her white eyes softened. If there had been a pupil and iris, the expression her eyes created with the soft sweep of downward pointed lashes and the narrowness of her lids opening, I would have said she looked at me with love.

"Loretta?" I said again.

This time, her mouth sagged open and gurgling issued from the maw that I loved so to kiss. Her tongue, stained with her father's blood, wobbled in the cavern of her mouth. She couldn't seem to make it work. Perhaps she forgot how. When we pushed past the heavy double doors, Loretta's little brother pulled up with a squeal. His mother grabbed hold Loretta's arm, deftly dodging her snapping teeth.

"Help me," she barked in my face. She pulled open the side door of the van with a jerk and hopped in. I gathered Loretta up into my arms, white clouds of dress trailing in all directions, then struggled into the back seat. Loretta didn't snap at me like she had her parents. She stared at me with those white-washed eyes, gore-streaked features softening into a question. She still knew me. I reached my hand out to stroke her hair and she growled, teeth grit together like a beaten dog's. I drew my hand back and stared at her as she watched me, head tilting like a curious hound on a scent.

"Where?" Loretta's brother asked.

There were mumbles as they discussed things. The boy pulled to the front of the reception hall parking lot. I won't tell, can't make sense of all I saw there in the parking lot. Terror and screams and Loretta's dad shambling in a game of slow-motion tag. As we turned, the lamps of the van caught him, shining brightly as he bit into the skull of a blue-haired grandmother, pulling away a bloodied wig in his stained mouth.

"Let me out!" Loretta's mom said. The swirling light of police vehicles and ambulances racing toward them split the dark sky with a manic rainbow. I fought the urge to giggle. "Take them to the cabin and come back for me. I'll get your father under control."

The boy, hardly fifteen, nodded and stomped on the gas pedal, fishtailing in the gravel as he eased us out of the madness.

"Jack," I said, "are you old enough to drive?"

The gangly boy I'd known so long tossed his head to the right, shifting the dark hair hanging in his eyes. Still straight and skinny, all wire and muscle. Still pimply and voice creaking with occasional high notes.

"Look," he said back, glancing in the rearview as he drove, "I've been driving and practicing for this for years."

"Huh?" I asked, ever the great conversationalist.

Jack shook his head and swerved onto the highway ramp. "It's about an hour there. Don't nap with Loretta changed as she is, but you can use the seatbelt to strap her in snug until we get there. That way she won't change you when her mind goes."

"Change me?"

The boy muttered something about dumbasses and ignored me, cranking up the oldies station. He started to sing, tunelessly to the tune of some '80s hair band classic wailing about "nothing but a good time." What an odd kid.

I took his advice and wound the seatbelt around Loretta. I trapped her hands and wrapped them close to her neck, then looped part of the belt around her neck, below her chin to keep her safely settled.

"There," I whispered into her lovely ear. "We will get you all fixed up, my love."

Her white eyes turned their gaze back to mine and for a moment I filled up with hope, light as a balloon. Other than the blank eyes and the gore, she was my Loretta. The girl I'd met in high school, the girl whose voice sang whenever she spoke. Her lips worked, slapping together like some old man's mushy mouth, maybe trying to speak. I reached out my hand to stroke her cheek, but she squeezed her eyes shut, clenched her mouth and drew her face away.

"You are such an idiot!" Jack said from the front of the van. "Keep away from her. If she bites you, you'll turn and then I'll have to kill you. She's treatable, you aren't."

I struggled to understand him. I mean, up to this point, Jack had been Loretta's obnoxious kid brother. We played catch and talked about if DC or Marvel comics were better. We went to movies and ate hotdogs. He'd never been difficult to understand. But now, he had the van revved up to ninety miles an hour, driving like he'd done it every day of his life. I sat next to Loretta practically mewling with my fears and he seemed to be so together.

"What does that mean? What happened to her?" The hot frustration welled up out of my belly, putting my teeth against the edge of my words.

Jack turned down the rattling '80s metal blasting through the speakers. He put his hand back on the steering wheel and tapped his fingertips like a nervous drummer. The silence stretched and I thought I'd have to ask again, but he said, "Fine."

Loretta huffed quietly in what looked like a shallow sleep. I crawled forward a row until I was just behind him.

"So after you guys met, I think that's when Dad learned about our family curse. When he told me, I decided I would never, ever get married. But Loretta already loved you by then."

"Curse," I said. "Are you kidding me?"

"No, man," Jack said. "I wouldn't kid. I swear."

I glanced back at Loretta as her head lolled loosely.

"It's in our blood. Something must have hurt her right before she changed. Something big. We die a little and then we hurt others."

He turned off of the highway onto a road that ran parallel to the Piney Creek, through stands of trees so woven with the dark that the leaves seemed to be night sky. The car's tires crunched and rattled in the rock-filled ruts of the narrow country road that led to the cabin. He'd been there before, though always with the whole family, always in happier times.

"It happened to Grandma and we had to put her down. We just couldn't fix her. But Granddad figured some things out after and now there's hope. We just have to get her, and now Dad, away from regular folks. Then we can get it fixed up."

I thought today would be the happiest day of his life, just a few hours ago. Now, looking at my wife and knowing that she was some kind of patient zero contagion, that my love might have started the apocalypse, made my mind spin.

"We can fix her," Jack said. "We'll get her restrained and safe, then I'll go to get Mom and Dad. They know how to bring her back."

I shook my head. "Wasn't your dad dead? I mean, that wound ..."

"Nah. We're hard to kill. No matter how bad it looks, we don't die unless we are put down. Beheaded." Jack's eyes met mine for just a second too long and I realized that information was more than just a fun fact. He wanted me to know how to end her, if it came to that.

The cabin sprouted from a curve in the road, white siding like a reversed shadow against the vault of the woods behind it. We pulled up the drive and through a rolling, automated fence crowned by curling razor wire. The gate rolled open to let in our car, then rolled shut again. Along the last hundred yards of the trip, low lights lit the drive like a runway. The cabin itself was a wonder. Whoever thought to use the word "cabin" to describe the brick mini-mansion surely didn't know a thing about actual spider-infested, brown well-water pumping, running to the outhouse in the middle of the night cabins from my summers back in the day.

Jack parked, opened the side door, and unlocked the cabin. I tugged at Loretta's bindings, releasing her arms and drawing her to me. Drool rolled from her plump, red lips. How could something be so disgusting and beautiful at the same time? I pulled open the side door and drew Loretta out while Jack returned to help me with her. She let me grab her wrist and pull her from the back seat, but when she leaned forward, she snapped at her brother's reaching hand.

"Crap, Loretta!" Jack said. His voice broke with that sopranic squeak he battled with. It would have been funny if my wife's lips weren't smeared with her father's blood.

I slipped my hands under her armpits and around her neck. I dragged her into the house, a beautifully furnished and well-appointed place. Nicer than their regular home. I guess Jack saw me looking around, read the questions in my eyes.

"Eventually, we'd have brought you in on the family secrets. Once you'd been around a while. But damn if she didn't change way ahead of schedule," he muttered, grabbing her limp feet, directing us up the steps to the second floor.

He set her feet down in front of a tall oak door. She swayed next to me, nearly falling into me. She didn't seem weak so much as gravity seemed to pull her harder than the rest of the world. Jack turned the knob and pushed the door open on a room cloaked in deep, velvety black.

Loretta mumbled and crunched her jaws together with a clacking creak, just missing the meat of Jack's forearm. Drool spattered on his sleeve and my skin. She didn't try to bite me as I dragged her slippered feet across the herringbone wood floor into the dark.

Metal clicking together in the dark made me want to grab her, pull her under my chin, and squeeze her against me, but she was bitey and I couldn't be sure how long my good luck with her would hold out.

"Bring her over here," Jack said. His voice sounded suddenly older, like his father's. Way too old to be a happy teen brother on the day of his sister's wedding. He flicked on a light.

"What ... I mean ..." I couldn't finish the question. "No."

He stared at me as I pulled Loretta closer to me, no longer worried about her teeth. I wouldn't be a monster. Not to my girl.

"She needs you to do this, bro."

He used careless words that spilled creaky sarcasm, but the tremor in his tone gave away their gravity. The kid I'd thought up to this very day full of immature judgment and apathetic distraction, stood eye to eye with me like a man, mouth set in grim lines. Before us stood an open cage, not large enough for an adult to stand in, lined with pillows and pads, a small toilet to one side encased in cushion foam. The bars of the cage weren't metal, like in some zoo from the '50s or some horror movie you'd see on late-night television. They were clear and slightly pliable. I could see them stretch a bit under the pressure of his hands.

He noticed me watching. "We designed these to be forgiving. In case one of us turned. We will put her in here until the curse can be reversed. She won't hurt herself or you."

I clutched my bride to me. Surely, if she wasn't after me, I could just care for her myself, outside of the cage. I could just keep an eye on her. Wash her face and clean her up.

Jack shook his head like he could see through my skull and read my thoughts. "Nah, man, you can't leave her out here with you. She's gone ghoul."

"Ghoul?"

He nodded. "It's old. In our blood. We're ghouls way back—some kind of medieval shit. You'll have to ask Mom when she gets here. Not like zombies. Those are dead. I mean, they aren't real, you know."

Loretta looks up at me with damp eyes and saliva still frosting her tongue and bloody teeth. Even behind the animal fever that seemed to swim in the rheumy fluid of them, I still saw recognition. Even love.

"But if she's not dead, then I should be able to bring her back, right? Like, she'll get better after a while, won't she?"

"This isn't a cold." Jack walked over and took Loretta's hand, though she gnashed and growled. "She's not going to drink some soup and sweat it out. It's a taint in our blood and only Mom and Dad know how to fix it. Our family fought against ghoulism in our blood for centuries. Sometimes, it happens. It might take a year to bring her back from this. But she can come back."

He pulled her away from me with a gentle hand, dodging her clashing teeth.

"Come on, sissy. Let's go." He urged her with gentle nudges into the cage. Loretta glanced once at me with eyes made of pain and storm, then crawled in, settling onto the cushions. She leaned back on the bars, pulling her knees up under her body and fussing with the hem of her stained gown.

"My poor Loretta."

"She will get hungry, Richie," he told me. "She will eventually want to bite you. Who she is will go in and out as her body struggles. Without the healing ..."

I waited for him to finish, but his words died away. He closed the cage just as she leapt forward, lunging for Jack's fingers. Her eyes blazed with a hate I'd never seen on her sweet, sweet face. How terrible it was. For the first time since she'd changed, I felt the fear, the desperate loss that wrapped itself around my lovely bride. I reached toward her, to gentle her, hearing her lush voice singing in my mind. Her gaze locked on my hand. The eyes I'd loved turned feral. Inside the hungry glance her hesitation crumpled. She surged forward, grabbing my finger faster than I moved. She had me, crushing my fingers, pulling toward her open mouth.

"Loretta!" I screeched, jerking back on my hand. Jack slid in between us, shielding my fingers with his own skin. Her fingers clamped around mine as bands of iron, but Jack's own fingers had matching strength. He pried her fingers apart, releasing me. I fell onto my ass with a thump. Jack struggled, now his own hand trapped by her grip.

"Lore, let me go. Come on, fight it!" He said, keeping his voice as smooth and musical as I had ever heard from his jagged teenaged mouth. No snark, no attitude. Just a loving song that I knew the two shared when others weren't paying attention.

Her eyes found his and softened a bit. Her mouth opened and a grating squeak sounded. With a quizzical, almost fallen expression, Loretta dropped her hands and shuffled back. Horror flashed around the white of her. The gore smeared, monster face stretched into a rigid mask of shock. She didn't want to hurt him.

Her brother's voice had brought her back.

Jack shut the door of the cage and stepped back. He flipped a switch on the wall, lighting the whole room. The little entry of the cage, what I'd thought was the whole cage, let into a larger cage, set with a cot and a sink.

"We'd never used this before, but now ..."

We stared at her as she pressed herself into the corner of the cage, body jerking in what looked like sobs. No sound came from her. Nothing.

"What is this?" I asked, finally able to breathe again.

"We knew someday we'd need a safe place, so we made one. Far from people and with comforts and safety. There's food and weapons. It's as good as a fortress."

"Or a prison," I said.

We stood, watching her for a while. She seemed to be fighting with herself, vacillating back and forth between a sort of animalistic clashing of her teeth to a softened, slack-jawed stare that looked inward as much as out. What could I do for her?

Jack said, "I don't know what will happen. If we can get back to you, we will. If not, you have to take care of her. She's your wife. This is that whole 'in sickness' thing you promised, right?"

His mouth stretched into a pointy grin we both recognized as fake. We stood there for a moment staring at each other. My fist clenched impotently as I wondered things I didn't dare say. What if he never came back? What would I do if she couldn't be healed? Instead, I asked, "Is it communicable."

He nodded. "We can turn back. But those we bite? They need to be buried upside down with their heads between their knees."

"So, you might ..."

"Don't think about it, okay? I'll do my best. You're safe from her here. We'll be back, latest, by tomorrow. Just keep her quiet. Feed her rare meat."

He stepped forward and crushed me to him in an awkward, manly hug. One that would have happened at our wedding if he'd kept sneaking cups of beer and dancing with bridesmaids. I took the hug, hoping there would be more.

He left me there. Last I saw of him was the winking of the red taillights filtered through the dusty cloud kicked up by his tires. In his absence, even the crickets didn't sing.

That was a month ago.

After a week, the television stopped broadcasting about the devastating virus spreading through blood, saliva, and even mosquito bites. After a month, the HAM radios giving coordinates of survivor camps and places to get test inoculations turned to static.

Loretta never did get her voice back. Some days she keens like a banshee with tears streaming from those white orbs. Others she sits catatonic. The cabin stock of meat is almost gone.

Soon, I'll need to make a choice.

I remember the year I met Loretta, fell in love with her musical voice. She read the famous story "Lady or the Tiger" where a princess is left the choice of whether to send her lover into a door that promised freedom in the arms of another woman or into the deadly jaws of a tiger who would end him. I remember being angry at the choice. Why should she have only those? Why not some alternative where they both could end up happy?

Until now I didn't understand that big choices are like that. I love Loretta. Even now as she sits in the rags of her wedding gown, mouth crusted with the pieces of her last meal, I love her so much it hurts. Without hope of a cure, what's left?

I could step into the cage, give myself to her hunger, and then maybe join her inside—two ghouls in love. Or, since she will never be the Loretta I loved again, perhaps it would be better to walk away. To free her to be what she is in the world and then try to make my own sad way without a ghoul for a wife.

Will it be the lady or the tiger?

***

Unfinished Business

by Jay Seate

U.S.: A haunting supernatural story of familial failure.

The house stood expectantly, a property with a remarkable history of misfortune. It was dilapidated, long unused, dying, if not already dead. Most of its paint had peeled and turned a dingy gray giving the appearance of a scaly skin. Spider webs of cracked glass crawled along its windowpanes. A remaining shutter hung askew from a broken hinge. Some of the gutters around the eaves drooped loosely, bent and rusted, having long since lost their ability to catch water.

To the side, was the shell of an abandoned vehicle and bleached lumber scattered in haphazard piles, all looking as forlorn as the house. Back in the day, Allison's father planted two saplings, now overgrown and untended. Some of their twisted branches hung from the trunks like dismal dislocated arms. Others reached into the darkening sky like fingers of the damned, two of them reaching out toward the house as if a skeletal mother were reaching for her stillborn child. She found little comfort in this creepy place where, within the house, death had once been its occupation.

With its slanting angles and sloped roofs, the two-story structure stood against the horizon like a cardboard cutout in front of the diminishing light. She observed the dark windows, but not for long, fearing the sight of some unpleasant memory looking out. And yet, the house still hypnotized her. There had always been something abnormal about the place. Even before she and her sister were old enough to hear stories about ghosts and goblins, Allison felt things she could not explain. And now, after so many years, she had returned to the old house, brooding and bleak in the wash of twilight, still holding its secrets and looking back at her as if holding its breath to see what she might do.

This was the moment of decision. Could she slip away before she was noticed? She had returned to the place where she had grown up, a place with a mental door left ajar, a door her father and mother had died trying to close. The sight of the house made her shiver. She could never know all the actions that had occurred within its rooms, but the house knew. There had been times when the dusky walls themselves seemed to breathe and were ready to reveal their secrets.

Although the wooden porch drooped in places, it still cloaked the front of the house just as Allison remembered. She envisioned her mother sitting on the porch, her rocking chair creaking back and forth, a book face down in her lap, her hands folded atop it, daydreaming about what her life might have been, while rustling wisps of her hair gently blew to and fro like the lace curtains from an open window.

Most surprising was the faint sound of wind chimes that had been removed from the porch even before Allison left, taken down after Margie's disappearance. Allison remembered sitting next to her sister on freshly painted steps. At ages six and eight, the little girls looked equally fresh and new in brightly colored Easter dresses and shiny patent leather shoes. Margie held a doll that Allison coveted. Allison thought it prettier than any of her own, but that's the way it seemed to be; Margie first and Allison second. When they played the little girl fantasy games, Margie was always the princess and Allison was her lady in waiting. Worse yet, Allison had been convinced her parents only wanted one child, one golden-haired daughter to light up their lives, and that Allison was nothing more than an accident. The recollections flipped past like pages of a storybook. Margie, her laughter tinkling musically like the porch wind chimes, the favored child, the best loved, the most adored, the eldest.

As she approached, Allison observed the old house's leering façade once more. If its silhouette was not intimidating enough, the knowledge that the cavernous dwelling once served as a funeral home was. That was before her family moved in. She used to sense a piteous despair moving through the rooms of a house that just "felt wrong." Then there was the presence of "others" even before she learned about the house's former use.

The basement was where bodies had been transformed into presentable corpses suitable for public viewing in the parlor above, souls not remembered in life, only as ghosts. As a young girl, Allison had never gone down alone to stoke the coal furnace. It was bad enough knowing her mother or father or older sister were down in that dark shadowy place in the company of the ugly leviathan. To her, the cellar door led to where the beast lurked, a monster with a hungry mouth that ravenously swallowed its dinner of coal or split wood. Its frightening metal tentacles crawled up to the heating ducts leading to elevated floors. From her bedroom on cold nights, she could hear it beckoning with its blasts of warm air humming an unpleasant, insistent lullaby capable of swallowing one's soul.

That was not the only vision of the house's interior. There were many, creating understandable apprehension. Why Allison had returned was of no importance. She was here, the final member of the family, returning at long last. It was time to discover if the spirits of the dear departed were still captives within the fiber of this haunted place.

The front door was slightly ajar. The remnants of red paint darkened to the color of dried blood still remained, but none of these portends were a barrier to her. Its hinges squealed as she entered. The interior seemed barren at first. Allison reflected on things that had happened within this house, absorbed the current aura, and listened for ghosts. Was it the scurrying of mice she heard, or voices? Allison wondered if the sounds kept most thrill-seekers away. With the exception of some graffiti and the living room light fixture having been ripped from the ceiling, there were few signs of trespass. Empty candy wrappers were scattered about, but neither vagrants nor horny teenagers would want to tarry here for long.

The rooms, however, *were* filled with ghosts of old furniture. Except for the starkness of its tomblike emptiness, the place had changed little. She began to recognize details in sharp relief. Every deterioration stood out with almost hallucinatory clarity. Varnished tongue-and-groove wainscoting and patterned wallpaper was now dulled to a smoke-smudged, oily tan. None of the latches on cabinets quite closed, a sorrowful sight to be sure. The dank, musty smell of neglect was strong, but Allison adjusted to the sights and smells quickly. Within seconds she found her bearings and the place began to produce a dreamlike calm. She was alone in the house where she was born. Well, not quite alone. Persistent shadows skulked in corners. There was the constant undertone of whispering voices in the corridors and from vacant rooms.

What do ghosts understand? What must they think when people look through them and they lose their fragile illusion of still being alive? Are they looking for resolution to bring forth a final rest?

She went to the stairway that led to the second floor and glided to the room that belonged to her sister. Although empty, Allison could easily imagine the way it had once been. Every edge and corner was sharp and clear, filled with pretty things she herself had admired, a shrine to the dead princess.

*

Growing up, Allison often felt helpless, unable to connect as Margie began blossoming into a young woman. As a teenager, Margie had friends of her own beyond the world of sisters. She remembered pulling the traditional younger sister routine when Margie was asked to a dance. "I don't ever want to go out with a stupid boy," Allison declared at the dinner table over a steaming bowl of tomato soup. She'd wanted to dump it on Margie's head. She wouldn't have looked so prissy then. Still, she wished to be more like Margie. That might have solicited the affection her parents seemed to shower on her sister.

Margie was seventeen and Allison fifteen at the time of the event, a mystery never solved. Margie was the apple of her parents' eye one day and nonexistent the next. The wooded and watery areas in and around the town of Plainsville were searched. Investigators investigated, search parties searched, but all efforts failed to uncover a body. For a few months, calls would occasionally come in from people who claimed to have seen Margie walking through a park or loitering in a nearby town or in the woods bordering railroad tracks. All, of course, were bogus, derivative of urban legend. There was never any closure, a concept that seemed laughable to Allison. At least, no one ever spoke about heaven having a new angel.

On some level, people believe the worst thing their minds can imagine: a young girl in the bloom of life, taken by some loony, they theorized. It happened somewhere all the time. Allison's parents had dreadful fantasies of Margie carried off by a cruel and heartless man who defiled, killed, and buried her in some unknown place never to be found. They were sick with grief and for a while, Allison thought it was exactly what they had coming. She had busied herself in her mother's garden during that terrible time, so as not to dwell on the thick permeating sadness surrounding the house any more than necessary.

The family dynamic became as fragile as spun glass. No more perfect Margie, only Allison, who could hear her mother's heartbroken sobs from behind a closed door. Her father would go days without speaking. They would sometimes wander out of a room like an unfinished sentence and Allison would sit with her mind in knots searching for a way to be the new number one daughter.

When her mother started spending large chunks of time on the porch looking wistfully into space, her father took to crawling into a whiskey bottle, both thinking about how their lives had unraveled. The light had gone out in her parents' eyes and nothing Allison could do would rekindle it. No matter how hard Allison tried, she continued to feel inferior. It was clear she would never be Margie's equal in beauty or charm, forcing her further from normalcy, hearing voices, and seeing things out of the corner of her eye.

The parents had lost something they could never get back, haunted by the black hole of absence and never healing from the shock of Margie's disappearance. They kept vigil the rest of their lives, never recovering from the loss, hoping she would magically return. "The pain of discovery would be more bearable than the pain of uncertainty," her mother said.

Allison was not uncertain. She had been aware of ghosts since she and Margie first sat on either side of the Ouija board. The game's planchette practically flew around when they asked their questions. It had certainly been right about which of *them* would die first.

After Margie was gone, Allison thought she saw her now and then hiding in a corner, or standing like a marble statue near a window gazing with sightless eyes upon a world taken from her. Although startling, Allison never screamed or said anything to anyone about these visions because she wanted to believe it was her mind playing tricks rather than black magic. Still, from the time Margie was gone and ever after, Allison looked at the house's windows differently, as if they were looking inward, keeping an eye on what she might do next. Gusts would flutter into the curtains as if ghosts were seeking entry from the outside. She got nervous whenever the furnace hummed with fire or belched out too much heat, but the worst was when her father burned trash and newspapers that produced bits of ash and char she could see floating above the roof, dancing and fluttering in the air. It was a horrible reminder.

There were times when Allison thought the house might swallow her up with its smells and memories and general morbidity. She remained with her folks until she was out of school, old enough to find a job in another part of the country, and escape this home filled with unhappy memories ensnared with lost souls both living and dead.

So the years wore on. She talked to her parents by phone, but rarely visited. When she did see them, the gray in their hair and their wrinkled features heavy with disappointment, withering away like houseplants deprived of water was too much to bear. The old house with its history and its memories were best left to those without her predilection for seeing and hearing strange things.

*

Allison left her sister's room and went down the hallway to the one that had been hers. She tried to recall the hopes and fears she'd experienced within its confines while the murmurs of others could be heard in the walls, still not free of the house's scrutiny.

Another part of the house called to her like an irresistible pull of the tide—the underground basement where the evil monster lived. She reluctantly made her way downstairs to the room that held her worst fears, a space suitable for both embalming and destroying. It also held the secret that only she and the furnace monster had knowledge of. For Allison, the past and present were beginning to mix together. She halfway expected to find the furnace glowing and groaning as it shoved hot air through its cylinders. For now, however, it was dark and quiet, as neglected as the rest of the old house. But the secret could not be forgotten. Wasn't that the real reason for her return?

The secret.

Yes, the one she shared with this despicable mass of metal. Margie had never run away. She'd been home the whole time, first as charred bones, and later, as separated parts, buried around the property, bone by bone.

Allison had killed her sister and stuffed her body in the furnace. Scenes from the fatal day flickered across her consciousness like an old silent movie. At fifteen years of age, she was tired of getting only the leftovers of affection. For the rest of her life, she would have had to live up to the standard of her parents' sweet Margie, who could seemingly do no wrong. Allison had gone into the basement with her sister and knocked her out with iron tongs. It had been like clubbing a baby seal.

She covered Margie's mouth in case she should come to while Allison stuffed her into the large mouth of the giant beast. She worked quickly at stoking the furnace with more coal and leaving her sister to melt away in the conflagration. She shut off the flue in hopes the odor would not escape through the pipes and fill the house with the smell of cooking flesh. The intensity of the heat made quick work of Margie.

Allison turned from the beast, but did not leave the basement right away. She thought about all the cadavers that had occupied the spacious room way back when. She almost expected to see them lying about and wondered if any of them had been burn victims. When someone was dead, it didn't matter how they had met their end, did it?

In the aftermath, it was a good thing Allison had shown an interest in gardening. It gave her a reason to spend so much time there disposing of bones. Initially, she escaped the torment of her actions. She never feared Margie's dead spirit or any of the others that whispered to her because she didn't really believe the dead could harm the living. But her act had taken its toll. After leaving home, the years to follow were marked by an inscrutable depression and the bitter knowledge that loneliness would forever be her lot. She chose a path without the comforts and pitfalls of a husband or children. This led to a rather aimless, unfocused life lacking the ability to find contentment, joy, or warmth, shuffling from one noncommittal relationship to another. Generosity and selflessness were never in her character. Others told her she sometimes looked haunted. Maybe those people were able to see beyond her exterior into her soul.

Thanks, in part to *her* actions, death still hovered about the old place. And now, Allison felt sure Margie was back along with the rest. She would have to face what she had done, the act which had prevented her from the chance of a happy existence. Moreover, she felt the house itself had come alive with her reentry, and it needed to be fed.

It was a new kind of reunion, here at the crime scene. And not unexpectedly, the iron monster in the basement suddenly belched and began to spring to life, a functioning entity complete unto itself. After Margie, had it developed a taste for something besides wood and coal? Would Allison be forced to relive the day she disposed of her sister, her body leaving by way of the smoke stack and the heating ducts? Or would Allison be thrown into the fiery furnace and enter hell's kingdom herself?

She turned away from the monster and floated back up the stairs to the main floor where the windows still watched. The moaning sounds in the walls continued, but now they sounded almost gleeful. What powers did this old house hold? How many ghosts haunted its hallways?

With a shock, Allison recognized the irony of it all now, how her return had come about. She too, had passed from a physical existence in a conflagration. The tether binding her to life had not been severed peacefully, for she had been trapped in a burning house somewhere dying in the most horrible of ways. How apropos for the final curtain of her life. If only all of it was just a terrible nightmare, but she knew the time for dreaming was past. No, this was all too real, too vivid. These were no hallucinations. On this plane of existence, what she could see and hear was real. *This was happening.*

Voices in the house and around its corners became more distinct—chanting, troubled voices, a chorus of the damned. Allison saw the first of them, gauzy figures with disembodied voices seem to surround her. None were Margie as she might have expected. The hair of one of the wraiths stood on end and a long, white burial garment trailed to the floor. Her expression was one of betrayal. Who knew how many spirits dwelled within the passages of time while the old house had stood witness? How many had been offended by what the new one now amongst them had done, all drawn to this place where they had died or been prepared for the hereafter. How spiteful might the waiting dead be? If alive, Allison would have screamed, knowing she might have to answer to them all, one by one.

Never had she thought much about what she'd deprived her sister of. But what about now, when Allison was no longer anyone, as dead as the rest of the spirits she sensed around her? This was a new playing field where the phantoms were equal to whatever she herself had become. Once again, the unexpected sound of the wind chimes. Once more, the voices became louder accompanied with moans, layered and overlapping.

And finally, rising up from the cellar was another figure. The cacophony of voices raging through the old house faded into insignificance as a more dominant presence took over. Allison felt fear certainly, but extreme sadness washed over her as well, her guilt at long last surfacing. All the birthdays Margie never saw. The rivers of hot tears Margie never shed over triumphs and tragedies. Allison remembered the little eight-year-old Margie in a yellow pinafore and the seventeen-year-old Margie in a felt skirt. Ghosts that outlast all others are the ones that never got the chance to fully live, she suddenly understood.

It was Margie. Above the blouse and felt skirt, her death ensemble, a translucent face levitated as shiny as candle wax. It possessed layer upon layer of emotions—truth and falsehood, youth and age—all going back to that moment when Margie was betrayed by her sister. Slowly and relentlessly she floated toward Allison.

"I've been waiting ... waiting ... waiting." Those brief words disintegrated as the revenant began to hum highly shrill notes Allison recognized from a children's song they used to sing. It brought a message of missed opportunities, suffering, and madness. It was time for the younger sister's fate to be fulfilled.

"I'm sorry for what I did, Margie," Allison's essence tried to articulate.

Too late to be sorry, sister. Much too late was the unspoken response that floated along the aching joints of the old house.

Dead for thirty years and still the queen bee, Allison thought. Margie's clothes began to change. They turned from an array of colors to an ashy gray. Her face deteriorated into a lurid scowl, her eyes swimming black pupils. A miserable history from deep within the house began to rise up through the floor like the smell of rot. A heavy moan of dread escaped Allison, for that was the only sound she had the ability to make. Something horrifying was pulling her toward darkness. The sooty remnants of Margie's scorched hair flowed around her head like a nest of long worms. Her arms extended out like soiled beckoning scarves, stretched forward, soon to wrap her sister in an embrace with hands, face, and body now as charred as the clothes that had burned off of her, binding two spirits together for eternity.

The dead are patient, but the time had come—that moment when a being turns a light on their soul and inspects it. Allison knew she had arrived at this place for a reckoning, as had many others, even though they had been physically gone for years. They were *all* here now ... finally ... including bereaved parents who suffered knowledge of the truth when they died. The house was complete. *Her* death had brought her back where so many dark spirits remained, especially the one of the girl she had betrayed. The structure felt like a great maw that had swallowed her whole as Margie had, at last, found her. Allison made no further attempts at contrition. She knew peace would never be part of her existence. Never, never, never, never. An eternal shriek escaped her, audible only to the dead.

She was in a place where souls wandered and waited. And now she was one of them. The sound of the reawakened furnace mixed with the rusty laugh from Margie's ghost. Every element that should be there was present now. No further reason to exist. If anyone had been within a hundred yards of the old house that day, they would have smelled the electric stench of ozone and burning wood. It was a place where anything horrible was possible. Absolutely anything.

***

Portals

by J. Michael Major

U.S.: *This modern fantasy depicts how a picture can be worth more than a thousand memories.*

The old man sat alone in the nursing home lobby, in an overstuffed chair that faced away from the television and the residents lost inside it, staring down at his frayed-edged photo album and traveling deep into the memories of the faded snapshots within, waiting for his portal to open.

On this day, Clarence Hughes wore charcoal slacks from his only remaining good suit, black socks, and scuffed Florsheims, and red suspenders over a white shirt turned gray by the institution's laundry service. He wore no tie, and his collar was open and ringed with sweat from the July heat and humidity that oozed past the laboring window air-conditioning unit through the cracks in the siding and the screen door that was somehow always left ajar. Not quite his Sunday best, he knew, but nice enough to show respect. He had long since given up hope of knowing when the exact moment would arrive.

The imitation red leather creaked when he settled the album in his lap. Most of the thin black cardboard pages were nearly torn away from the spiral binder from all the time he perused it. A single photograph was adhered to each side of a page by double-stick tape on the back.

His hands caressed the album as he painfully turned another page. Mahogany hands once straight and strong, now twisted with arthritis, the knuckles swollen and blue. His fingers bled easily from cracks in his skin and the occasional paper cut that wouldn't heal, and he took great care to prevent any blood from staining his pictures and obscuring the memories they contained.

Clarence understood the importance of keeping his portals clear.

A crash of dishes broke his concentration, dragging him back into the world he so desperately tried to forget. Or at least ignore. But the sights and sounds and smells of the nursing home continuously pierced his consciousness like a burglar with a crowbar invading his home. At all hours of the day and night, screams echoed down the chalky green-tiled corridors. Residents shuffled by with their walkers or whirred past him in their squeaky wheelchairs. The smells of urine and decay masked with Lysol had soaked into everything, making it unpleasant to breathe. Souls trapped within the television static taunted and teased him, and the inept and often mean-spirited attendants shook him awake to take his medicines or because they mistakenly believed he was better off in the present. He spent as much of his remaining energies blocking out the external distractions as he did on focusing on his memories.

The photographs helped. The album contained the selected highlights of his life. His wedding. Holidays. Special events. Relatives and friends. The earliest were black and white, a few from the '40s and '50s were studio-colorized, and the rest, color prints. His fingers traced the worn snapshot edges that curled away from the pages, and even with his eyes closed, he could feel the magic within. Treasured images, each one centered on a page like a window to the memory, or a doorway into other times.

But the photos that held the most power for him were the ones he'd taken himself. While the group shots in which he'd partaken, held a special magic of their own—his wedding, most especially—it was disconcerting to immerse himself in an image that he was already a part of, and it always felt as if he were looking at someone else instead.

No, the purest magic emanated from the photos he remembered taking. Like the one now open on the page. An eight-by-ten shot that his buddy, Rick, had painstakingly colorized under Clarence's watchful eye and directions. He smiled. Though the pigments had faded, he could still recall the true colors and smells around him when he squinted through the viewfinder and captured the moment for eternity so long ago.

It was a hot summer afternoon, he remembered, cooled by a breeze off the lake that rustled the leaves on the trees. The sky was empty of clouds and so blue it hurt his eyes to look at it. While most of the adults prepared the barbecue and shucked corn in back, the five teenagers played in the shade under the watchful eyes of his uncle who carefully pretended not to pay attention to them as he played his battered old acoustic guitar on the front porch swing. A worn railroader's cap perched on his head as his fingers slid up and down the frets, somehow finding all the notes he needed even though the A-string was broken. A beach ball hung suspended in the air between his brother, Larry, and cousin Steve. His sister, Maddy, rested on her forearms and stuck her tongue out at him, while Maddy's friend Flo—sweet Florence, wearing a white dress with red polka dots and no shoes—leaned against the porch railing and smiled shyly as Clarence took the picture.

All gone now, but not forgotten.

Clarence squeezed his eyes shut and breathed deeply. Footsteps approached, but he pushed the sound away. He opened his eyes slowly, focusing solely on the photograph. His vision narrowed, moving beyond the borders of the page and into the snapshot itself. He imagined peering through the viewfinder as the branches swayed, the breeze carrying the lake smell of dead fish and burning charcoal, the ball dropping closer into his brother's hands, and Flo smiling, as a finger stabbed him in the shoulder and roughly pulled him back from the brink.

*

"And this here's Clarence," Dwayne said, poking the old man. "He don't like being disturbed."

Tammy wondered briefly, then, why Dwayne seemed to enjoy doing just that. During the course of the hour as introductions were made on rounds, Tammy noticed how he had managed to purposely insult or irritate every patient in some way. Was he showing off? Or was it bitterness at having to care for others less fortunate than himself? She couldn't imagine why the patients put up with his behavior unless they were afraid of him, and she intended to broach the subject carefully with the director as soon as she was more secure in her position here. Tammy bent at the waist to lower herself to Clarence's eye level as Dwayne shook his shoulder, hard this time.

"Say Clarence, buddy. C'mon, I need you to meet our new helper." The man finally responded by lifting his eyes from the page. "There you go. This is Tammy. She's gonna be giving you your medicines from now on."

Tammy waited until Clarence turned his attention toward her. "It's nice to meet you, Mr. Hughes," she said.

Clarence blinked slowly, as if waking from a dream. Like most of the other residents, he needed to do things at his own pace, and she gave him all the time he needed. His chart informed her that he was eighty-two years old. He'd been a resident here for the last seven years, first arriving when his wife had begun her cancer treatments. He was completely bald, though his eyebrows were gray and bushy and his earlobes furry. His breath smelled of ill-fitting dentures caked with tartar. His gnarled hands were painful even to look at, and the knots on his forearms hinted at the man's once great strength that had wasted away. Yellow in the corners, his rheumy brown eyes were milky with cataracts, and when they met her own, his eyes spoke of loneliness and neglect.

"Hands," he said. His voice was like sandpaper on dried parchment.

Tammy leaned closer. "I'm sorry?"

Clarence swallowed hard. He pointed to the tube of lotion that weighed down the pocket of her white clinic jacket. "I gots to have my hands rubbed ever' day."

"Oh, my goodness. Of course." She unscrewed the cap and was just about to squeeze out some of the lotion when Dwayne's beefy hand knocked the tube from her grasp. It clattered to the floor. Tammy recoiled as if he'd slapped her in the face.

"What you thinkin', girl?" Dwayne said. He indicated the open, bleeding cracks on Clarence's hands. "You don't know what he's got or where he's been. Put some gloves on before you touch these people."

*

Clarence wanted to slap him. What a piece of work, he thought. Treating the residents no better than animals in a zoo and acting like he knew everything. Who was he to suggest they might have diseases the way *he* catted around? And so stupid he never realized everyone called him Duh Wayne behind his back.

No, it was a sad reminder of how far things had fallen. For any of them. Clarence remembered when his hands were strong enough to squeeze the juice from a cantaloupe, and he would have beaten a man who dared saying anything like that about him. Especially in front of a lady. But now everyone tolerated him, because they didn't have the strength to fight back. They needed him to help them get up or to lie down, and sometimes even to wipe them on the toilet, with Duh Wayne complaining about it the entire time. Day after day, little by little, he stole their dignity away by not having the decency to show them respect.

Duh Wayne stood there, smirking, enjoying the obvious discomfort he'd inflicted on Tammy. He was a big man, over six-foot five, and pudgy, like a football player gone to fat, and his eyes held the emptiness of someone whose mental capacity never extended beyond the physical. His hairstyle was called dreadlocks, as if its very name should instill fear, and he wore his resentment and hostility for not having a better life like a tailored suit. He grudgingly did his chores, all the while blaming anyone he helped for his misfortunes, never comprehending that in order to receive respect, you had to give it first.

Clarence watched Tammy struggle to keep her emotions in check, doing her best to stand up to Duh Wayne without making a scene. He was glad to see her nametag spelled TAMMY the old-fashioned way, not the pretentious TAMI so many of the younger generation

preferred. A kindness warmed her hazel green eyes when she looked
at him. Her skin was pallid and her mousy brown hair was tied back
in a bun. She wore no ring on her finger, and she had the resigned
appearance of someone who cared for others because no one cared
for her.

He liked her immediately. He wanted to smile at her, to reassure
her that everything would be all right, but he was afraid his denture
would slip and he'd look like an old fool.

A howling arose inside the TV, its ghosts tempting the residents
with their sweet, vacant siren song. Naturally, the attendants didn't
hear. Clarence knew he'd have to warn Tammy about Duh Wayne
later when he could talk to her alone. Duh Wayne was the director's
brother-in-law and anyone who complained about him was
automatically fired. He'd hate to see that happen to her. But the
ghosts acted up whenever a portal was about to open, trying to lure
another unsuspecting soul into their void of chaos and confusion,
and the thought of being trapped in their world forever scared him
more than anything.

He dropped his gaze and concentrated on the picture.

*

Tammy picked the tube off the floor. Snatching the proffered
gloves from Dwayne, her face masked the seething emotions
beneath. How could he embarrass her like that on her very first day?
And how could he be so openly rude to Clarence? She simply
couldn't understand how he was able to keep his job when he treated
people that way.

She slipped the gloves on, squeezed lotion onto her fingers and
rubbed Clarence's hands gently until the cream moistened his skin.
He kept his head down the whole time. She wondered, at first, if he
was too embarrassed to look at her because of Dwayne's actions, but
then she realized he was staring at the photograph on the page.
Curious, she stole a glance. The faded snapshot was of a family
outing, but she could tell his attention was focused on the pretty
young woman in a polka dot dress with a sweet smile and the biggest
brown eyes she'd ever seen.

"Is that your wife?" Tammy asked. When he nodded, she said, "She's beautiful."

*

Clarence appreciated how Tammy didn't touch the photo with her lotion-smeared gloves. Duh Wayne wouldn't have thought twice about it and had, in fact, soiled many of his snapshots by putting his grubby hands on them. But this photograph, more than any other, was special to him, and he protected it with a vengeance.

"What's so important about this picture anyway?" his friend Rick had asked him. Clarence had given Rick the photo to colorize about three weeks after he'd taken it, when the memory of that day was still sharp and clear. He wanted to preserve it as much as he could, and so they sat, the two of them, late into the night in the back of the portrait studio Rick would later own and operate for fifty years until his death, fussing over the proper colors and shadings.

A gooseneck lamp illuminated the eight-by-ten black-and-white print they'd pinned at the corners to a drafting board. Dabbing his paintbrush into the various glass jars on a metal cart beside him, Rick had carefully applied the watercolors directly onto the picture. Following Clarence's directions, Rick's deft touch enhanced the image, bringing out the natural hues without turning the snapshot into a painted portrait—as was the then-current fashion—or worse, a garish cartoon.

Why was the photo so important? Even now, more than sixty-five years later, Clarence wasn't sure he could answer the question any better than he did that night. How could he describe the feelings it evoked, remembering the moment in his life when everything changed? When all his hopes and promises and opportunities opened before him?

He remembered sitting on the porch with Flo after dinner later that same day. His relatives had stayed inside, so they could be alone, and his cheeks flushed with embarrassment whenever someone peeked at them through the window or he heard giggles from behind the screen.

The sun was setting over the tops of the trees. Flo stretched her legs out in front of her, crossed them at the ankles, and rocked them back and forth on her heel. Dirt had crept up in the spaces between her toes. She asked him if he liked her dress, and when he said he did, she whispered, as if she were sharing her deepest secret, that red was her favorite color. From that day on, he wore something red every day to keep her near him. He could feel her heat and hear her breathing, and his heart raced. And when the sun broke through the lower branches and bathed them in golden light, her eyes looked up into his, and he kissed her for the very first time. He tasted barbecue sauce and buttered sweet corn before she turned away, smiling, trying to hide her pleasure and blushing in a way he would not see again until their wedding night.

Why was the photo so important? How could a man ever describe the magic of falling in love?

*

"She died five or six years ago," Dwayne said. "And all he's done since is stare at that book. Like it could make her come back to him or something. Shit, dead is dead. Ain't nothing gonna bring her back."

Tammy just stood there, appalled. How anyone could be so callous right in front of the poor man was beyond her. Didn't this idiot have any feelings? Any compassion? She inched her way between them as if her body could shield Clarence from Dwayne's hurtful ramblings.

"Be nice," was all her anger allowed her to say.

Dwayne raspberried. "Don't mind Clarence none. I doubt he even knew I was talking about him." He gestured toward the other residents sitting in the lobby, their eyes glued to the TV screen. "Any of them, really. The way they all sit around like toadstools, I don't think many of them have it together anymore." He tapped the side of his head. "Up here. But, at least the ones watching TV are trying to do something with their minds. Clarence just sits there all day with that damn book.

"Why, do you know, the other day he spent an entire afternoon sitting in another resident's room and neither one of them said a word the whole time?"

*

Leave it to Duh Wayne to get it all wrong.

Clarence was always amazed by how little the younger generations understood. It was as if, lost in their worlds of petty gripes and constant material gratification, they somehow missed all the simple rules that had been passed down for centuries. There were times Clarence worried what might happen to them, to the future generations; but not having had any children of his own, he was less burdened by the sense of loss they seemed intent to bring down upon themselves and the others around them. That was their choice, he realized. It was hard enough for him to worry about his own problems.

And just because the residents' thoughts were turned inward didn't mean they didn't understand what was being said around them. Duh Wayne was in for a rude awakening someday. Clarence and his friend, Roland Greenfield, did have a little conversation that day, but Duh Wayne had missed it because he'd been busy putting the moves on the Hispanic girl that did the laundry.

"Think he's looking for love?" Clarence had asked.

"Love? Shit. All that boy knows about love is grunt and release." Roland wiggled his shoulders and tried to scoot further up in the bed. "Say, how 'bout giving me a hand with this?"

Clarence leaned him forward, fluffed the pillows and positioned his friend so he could sit up better. Roland thanked him with a grateful sigh. His skin was as thin and pale as a sheet, and covered with liver spots and crusty bruises from daily injections. Clarence knew Roland didn't have much time left and was surprised at how quickly he was deteriorating. Even without his glasses, his blue gray eyes seemed too large for his shrunken face.

"I've been trying to get that idiot's attention all day," Roland said. "I'm not sure if Duh Wayne's ignoring me or he just can't hear right."

Clarence pulled his chair closer to the bed and rested the photo album in his lap. "With the volume he plays his iPod at, I wouldn't be surprised if he's going deaf."

"You ever hear the stuff he plays? If that's all they have to listen to nowadays, I'd wanna go deaf myself."

Roland shook his head. "I tell you, the present doesn't hold a damn thing for me. At least you've got your photos. Look what my son brought me." He indicated the school portraits of his grandchildren taped to the wall. "He thinks that's what I need. Like some kind of reminder to stay in his world. The other day I asked him if he remembered the time we went fishing and caught the baby shark, and he says, 'Sure, Dad, but that was a long time ago.' And then he starts telling me what his kids did in school that day."

He shrugged. "I love them and all, but it's not what I *need* right now, you know?"

Clarence knew. No one wanted to be focused on the present when his portal opened. The present was a time filled with sickness and pain, a reminder of lost hopes and broken promises and missed opportunities that haunted sleepless nights. Who wanted to be stuck in a world you no longer had any connection to?

No, that's what memories were for. It was one of those simple truths, passed down from generation to generation, that the modern world had somehow managed to forget. The mind knew when the body was going, and memories were how the soul prepared for the transition. It took a lot of energy to stay focused, and with the body saddled with sickness and aging, the mind turned inward, making the person appear slow and inattentive. It was the reason Alzheimer's patients lost all but their earliest memories, and the elderly wanted to talk about the past.

Memories provided the portal of your own choosing.

Some people imagined their portal as a white light. But what lay beyond that? If it was winged cherubs and harp players, Clarence preferred to deal with the pain of his arthritis, thank you very much. No, Clarence found comfort in the familiar. That's why he had his pictures. The photographs weren't portals—the memories they contained were. The details they provided made it easier to focus and took a lot less energy than the others around him had to use.

Clarence worried whenever someone died suddenly. A car crash, a drive-by shooting, something that didn't allow the person to prepare. He hoped they all had those few seconds for their bodies to understand what was happening when their lives passed before them, the mind spinning memories like a slot machine in front of their eyes as the soul desperately prayed for a winning combination. Even the suicides understood the importance of visiting the past before forcing their portals open. He knew some arrived lost and confused, but once they got where they were going and adjusted, they could switch to any scene they wanted.

The portal was just a transition. It wasn't the final destination.

But the television was dangerous. It interfered with the natural transition by sucking the viewer's memories dry and replacing them with vacuous images. So when their portals opened, that was where they went. Clarence heard their tormented souls screaming inside the static at all hours of the day and night, lost and confused and so desperate for company they tried to lure others in with them. Clarence warned his fellow residents, but to no avail, and that was the reason Clarence never faced it. He was afraid of what might happen if his portal opened then.

Yes, Clarence and Roland understood the importance of their memories. And so they sat the rest of the afternoon, friends giving each other the comfort they needed by just being there, Roland visiting his memories as he slipped in and out of sleep while Clarence studied his photographs, until Roland's family arrived hours later and shooed Clarence away.

*

Tammy peeled her gloves off and angrily stuffed them in her pocket. Outraged by Dwayne's insensitive comments—right there in front of the poor man!—she wondered if he even had a compassionate bone in his body. Someone like him shouldn't be working here, and she was more determined now than ever to talk to the director at her first opportunity. No matter what happened.

She ignored Dwayne's glare when she knelt beside Clarence and took his bare hands in her own. "You let me know when you need your hands rubbed," Tammy said. "Anytime."

His eyes moistened. "Thank you."

*

Clarence hoped she understood how much he appreciated her act
of kindness. She restored a sense of dignity to him that Duh Wayne
had always denied. Probably because the punk didn't have any
respect for himself.

He rubbed his watery eyes. Clarence was so tired. Tired of Duh
Wayne's rude behavior. Tired of taking his medications. Tired of a
life in the nursing home that had robbed him of everything he ever
knew. Tired of resisting the lure of the television's siren song. He was
tired of struggling day after day to stay focused on his memories, and
tired of waiting for his portal to open.

The room swayed, and the photo swam before him. He blinked
to clear his eyes. The borders seemed to slip away then, and the true
colors emerged and brightened. The branches swayed in the breeze,
and he heard his parents' laughter. The air smelled of barbecue sauce
and boiling sweet corn. The ball dropped into his brother's hands
and he turned to look at Clarence, smiling. His uncle tipped his cap
and rested his forearms on the guitar, and Flo was off the porch,
running, and jumping into his arms. He squeezed her to him. His
hands were long and straight, and strong enough to hold onto the
woman he loved. Forever.

"I've missed you so much," she sobbed joyfully into his ear.

"I'm here, baby," he said. "I'm home. At last."

And all his opportunities lay ahead of him once again.

*

"Ah, for chrissakes! I hate when they do that," said Dwayne.
"When they go in their rooms, I can just flip the mattress over. But
this ..." He waved his hands in disgust. "Now I gotta steam the
cushions."

Clarence slumped in the chair. The photo album had slipped
from his fingers, and the pages, remnants of a lifetime no longer
wanted or needed, spilled onto the floor. A large dark stain colored
his trousers and puddled the chair beneath him. The smell of urine
filled the air.

Tammy tenderly closed his eyes for the final time as the other attendants rushed forward to help. Lost in their own worlds full of wants and needs and inconveniences, they prepared his body to be taken away, never hearing the howls of the ghosts trapped within the television set, or noticing the faint smile on the dead man's face.

***

Death's Day Off

by Donna J. W. Munro

U.S.: Death is the cocoon. The job has rewards.

Being a pan-dimensional, everlasting, powerless, multiplistic creature is sometimes hard.

Death's burden, being everywhere, but nowhere, connecting with none but the dead and only in the moment between lives means a solitary, busy existence. Many avatars of Death exist at once, serving and carrying human souls from here to there, but all are one. Death is a they and gender neutral besides. Who has time for sex and who wants to be tied to one biological destiny anyway? Not them. Besides, people see what they want to see.

It bothered them that they showed up in the moment of transition as the reaper. Such a grim countenance! When humanity was younger, they'd have been silver gossamer and misty light with a rainbow path for the souls to cross. Now, most see them as dark-robed and death-headed. The grinning bone mask weighed them down even as they knew the souls craved it, recognized it as some masochistic destiny to be frightened in the transition.

Take Lisl, for example. She'd suffered from cancer. Painful infusions of chemicals left her weak-kneed and hurling up her food in acrid streams. The disease erupted in growths that spread like blooming wildflowers on her organs. She died in a convulsive rictus, black blood pooling in her mouth and dribbling out of her nose.

Her soul rose above the doctor and nurses pulling the probes and wires from her blue skin. She turned to Death's open arms and shrieked.

"It's true! Oh, God!" She wept. Death's visage, only frightening because she willed it, threw her into a babbling frenzy of confession. None of it mattered. Death cares nothing for the befores or the afters. The ferrymen's burden is to collect and deliver. To soothe in those moments. Not to judge those they carried.

"Hush now." The skeletal visage softened in the sweet musicality of Death's words. "No more pain, Lisl. No more suffering"

Death reached out to her and she let go of that life. Shed all the fears. Caterpillar to butterfly. Death is the cocoon.

The job has rewards.

Death doesn't sleep. Doesn't answer to the other everlastings serving as gods. Death isn't bound to region or time. Death is powerless, so Death doesn't get asked for anything.

But Death gets tired.

They find no rest.

This piece of Death slips from room to room, moving like a leaf in a gust across the boughs, clutching dead souls in the billows of their cape. This other piece of Death trails fingers along foreheads of villagers suffering the last gasp of a diseased mosquito swarm's bite.

Every day. Every second. So many dead.

Death stops for a moment, raising tired hands to the sun.

Long retired from moving for humankind's pleasure, the sun lets heat spill out for all. The sun just is. Death wonders if they might do the same. So, they sit there, everywhere, in the sun's light or the glow of the moon on the other side of the planet, just for a bit.

"A bit" to a pan-dimensional, everlasting, powerless, multiplistic creature is quite different from "a bit" to humans. The moment stretches into weeks.

News channels proclaim, "No One Dies!" and "Judgement Day is Upon Us!" People bleed out but don't die. Hearts stop, but the people keep screaming.

Death pulls back their hood and lets the sun warm their cheeks. They feel peace.

Souls trapped in rot seek Death for release. They rear up failing muscles and walk out of morgues in shambling clusters. The living scramble, seeing zombies from nightmares and B-movies. But the dead only want deliverance.

"What if I stay here?" Death asks the sun and the moon. "Retire from moving, like you. They would find me."

Death notices the crowds of dead ringing around in a moaning, pain-filled canticle.

The sun stays silent. The moon turns its face away, leaving Death in the dark.

The living sees the dead gathering, but can't see Death. Only the dead and dying see Death's face. The living plot to bomb the massed dead to ash. They fear what they don't understand. Perhaps that would be the beginning of the end. One bomb, misplaced. More dead. Another. A cascade. Massive retaliation and mutually assured destruction. Who knows?

Finally, a diseased child, close to passing, sees Death resting. She asks her father to take her into Central Park for one last walk. Her father knows the dead flock there, but can't deny his sweet daughter's last request. He carries her, following her whispered directions leading them to the center of the winding circle of the dead, where he only sees a grassy eye in the hurricane of zombies.

The girl kisses her father goodbye, then she crawls to the center. Death's face turns as she whispers, "I see you."

Her name comes to them. Chloe, only six, dying of a disease that ate her odd genes. Her heart spasms and grunts with each beat.

"Help me?" she asks.

Death looks down at their hands, no longer bony frightening hands. No black robe or scythe. They are beautiful, golden, and lit from within like the sun. They lift her, clutching her and flying with the wings she imagined.

Death returns to work, releasing the shuddering dead from their torments. A sigh of relief rises as a great wind across the world.

The living don't know what to make of it, but they are glad. They welcome Death in a way they hadn't before.

Being a pan-dimensional, everlasting, powerless, multiplistic creature is hard, but from then on, the dying humans see Death for what they are—a kindness. And Death spreads golden wings and carries them away.

***

ABOUT THE AUTHORS

Trece Angulo

Trece Angulo is a Gen-X writer living in Seattle ... and also a contractor, architect, and landlord, the skills of which help significantly in the construction of science fiction and fantasy, her chosen genres. She spent her formative years on the East Coast in a decaying industrial city and the combination of early urban blight and the later beauty of the Pacific Northwest has influenced her strongly. Another influence is an uncle who was involved in science fiction First Fandom from the 1950s to the 1970s, from whom she gained an appreciation of Jack Vance, Philip Jose Farmer, Ray Bradbury, Ursula K. LeGuin, and Tanith Lee. One of her favorite themes is the gulf between fantasy and reality and the toll it takes on the human heart. She is has written two unpublished fantasy novels and is currently working on a science fiction one about a spacefaring descendants of Homo Sapiens Denisova who have invaded present-day Earth.

Trece writes erotica and horror under the pen name Cobalt Jade and has independently published a novella, the Arabian Nights romantic adventure *The Tale of Lassok and Zairbhreena*. Another recent story, "Arabica" has been published in the *MASHED* anthology by Grivante Press. Her writing blog is at cobaltjade.com. She may be contacted on Facebook, Twitter, and Tumblr under that name also.

Nathan Batchelor

When Nathan isn't writing or reading, you can find him running, hiking, or lifting weights in the gym. He spent his first two decades of life in a secluded Alabama forest town with one red light, before landing in Columbus, Ohio, where he lives with his cat and significant other. He graduated with honors from (The) Ohio State University with a degree in biology. He has fought wild fires on the Florida plains, been lost in the Allegheny mountains, and pressed in the clutch on a tractor going downhill.

He has been obsessed with horror since reading Clive Barker's *Books of Blood* and fantasy since he was old enough to imagine swinging a sword, and now reads a wide variety of fantasy, horror, poetry, and philosophy. He enjoys struggling through fiction in French, Spanish, German, and Chinese, listening to synthwave, playing Hearthstone, and watching anime when the weather gets cold. His favorite works include *His Dark Materials* by Phillip Pullman and *Dark Gods* by T.E.D. Klein.

"Alabama Shaman" is Nathan's first published work. He is currently working on other short stories involving a man afraid of roses, a paranoid entomologist, and robotic polar bears. You can reach him at nathanrbatchelor@gmail.com

Michael D. Burnside

Michael is the creator of the role playing games Space Conspiracy and World War Two Role Play. His fiction writing includes steampunk, science fiction, fantasy, and horror. His stories have been featured in several anthologies including *Fossil Lake: An Anthology of the Aberrant*, *Fossil Lake II: The Refossiling*, and *Life after Ashes*. His short stories have also been featured in magazines such as *Devolution Z*, *Outposts of Beyond*, and *Gathering Storm Magazine*. Michael lives in Dayton, Ohio with lots and lots of cats. Read more nice things about him, as well as some free stories, at www.michaelburnside.com.

Tara Curnow

Tara Curnow was blessed with an overactive imagination, but cursed with a hand that can't keep up with it. She has been writing stories ever since she learned how to put pen to paper, scribbling down everything she can, yet still there is always more boiling away in her head.

"Of Thain Blood" is the first of her work she has ever submitted for publication. She is currently working on a full-length novel telling the story of the Thain brothers.

Tara and her husband live with their children in beautiful British Columbia, Canada. She fills her free time with acting, singing, painting, and reading fantasy novels. Oh yes, and writing.

Photo Credit: Captured by Jo Photography

Kevin Henry

Kevin Henry lives in a small town in Ohio, USA, where he rebuilds diesel engines for a living. He is the author of horror, fantasy, and science fiction short stories as well as the as-yet unpublished *Soul Forge Saga* epic, dark fantasy series. His writing has been influenced as much by Steven King and Dean Koontz as by Robert E. Howard and H.P. Lovecraft and lies in a strange sweet spot somewhere in between.

Find him at: www.facebook.com/authorkevinhenry/

Learn about the Soul Forge Saga at: kevinhenry68.wixsite.com/soulforge

Kevin's publishing history:

1. "Engines of Destruction" (short story)
2. "Last Stand in Rosehill" (short story)
3. "Innocence and Blood" (short story)
4. "Charred Walls of the Damned" (short story)
5. "The Floating Island of Tauret Mok" (short story)
6. "The Oath" (short story)
7. "Primordial Madness" (poem)
8. "Fall of the Men of New Innsmoore" (poem)
9. "No Other Loss" (short story)
10. "Webs of Love" (flash fiction)
11. "Parasites" (flash fiction)
12. "Shadow of the Moon" (flash fiction)
13. "House of One Thousand Screams" (flash fiction)
14. "Self Portrait" (flash fiction)
15. "Drowning In Sorrow" (poem)
16. "Revenge of the Phantom Stranger" (short story)
17. "The Antithesis Project" (short story)
18. "The Sinner" (short story)...Ariel Chart Fiction (arielchart.blogspot.com)

Kathryn Hore

Kathryn Hore is an Australian writer of dark, speculative, and crime fiction, as well as business and corporate non-fiction, which is not as unrelated as you might think. Her work appears in several anthologies and magazines, including *Midnight Echo* magazine, the *Crime Factory* journal, anthologies such as *Dead Red Heart* and *Hear Me Roar*, the Australasian Horror Writers Association showcase *In Sunshine Bright and Darkness Deep*, and the AHWA best of anthology *Dead of Night*, among others.

When not writing, she works in information governance, records, archives and libraries, because along the way to becoming a writer she had bills to pay and she fell in love with the intricacies of managing information in all its forms. Well, someone has to. She takes photos of weddings and spiders, if not at the same time, and lives with a real photographer and their two small children among the gumtrees on the urban-rural fringe of Melbourne. She haunts all the usual social media outlets, just look for @kahmelb and shoot her a friend/add/follow on any of them, or you can find out more about her and her writing on her website: www.letmedigress.com

Twitter www.twitter.com/kahmelb

Facebook www.facebook.com/kahmelb

Goodreads www.goodreads.com/Kathryn_Hore

Blog www.letmedigress.com

Daniel M. Kimmel

Daniel M. Kimmel's movie reviews appeared in the *Worcester Telegram and Gazette* for 25 years and can now be found at Northshoremovies.net. For seven years he was the "Movie Maven" for *The Jewish Advocate* and later served as its editor.

His book on the history of FOX TV, *The Fourth Network*, received the Cable Center Book Award. His other books include a history of DreamWorks, *The Dream Team, I'll Have What She's Having: Behind the Scenes of the Great Romantic Comedies*, and *Jar Jar Binks Must Die ...* and other observations about science fiction movies which was shortlisted for the Hugo Award for "Best Related Work."

His first novel, *Shh! It's a Secret: a novel about Aliens, Hollywood, and the Bartender's Guide*, was a finalist for the Compton Crook Award. His latest book is *Time on My Hands: My Misadventures in Time Travel*. His short stories have appeared in a number of anthologies include *After the Happily Ever After*, *Alternate Truths*, *An Atlas to Time, Space,and Bonfires*, *Science Fiction for the Throne*, and *Tales from the Boiler Room*, as well as the website hollywooddementia.com. He lives in Somerville, Massachusetts, and is currently working on his next novel.
https://danielmkimmel.wixsite.com/author

Paul Lubaczewski

Paul is a bit of a jack of all trades, or as he likes to put it "keep it interesting." Caver, photographer, Scadian, brewmaster, musician with the late '80s, early '90s punk band, The Repressed, music critic for *Sparkplug* magazine and New Wave Chicken, DJ, as long as it's interesting. Originally from Philadelphia, Pennsylvania, he's lived all over the United States, finally settling in the mountains of Appalachia for the peace, and adventure they provide. He loves his wife, Leslie, and his three children, two adult girls and a teenage boy, and with the boy about, it's a wonder he gets any writing done at all.

Selected Bibliography Fiction

Devolution Z #13 "What Is A Paddywack?"
Schlock! 5th Anniversary Edition "On The Track Of An Answer"
Weirdbook magazine #35 "Revolution a la Orange"
Hellfirecrossroads #6 "The Fire That Remembers"
Under The Bed Vol. 5 #2 "From The Dust Of The Earth"
Hammer Of The Gods: Viking Sagas of Sword and Sorcery (anthology)-"The Lost Saga"
Bewildering Stories #707 "The Organic Act Of 2916"
Aphelion Issue #208 Vol. 20 "All The Time In The World To Read Them"
Riding the Dark Frontier Volume 2 (anthology) "Jangling Spurs and Tumbleweeds"
Not Taking A Fence (anthology) "Country Road"
Dark Dossier #9 "The Masks We Wear"
https://www.facebook.com/lubaczewskiearlsonrevpaul/

J. Michael Major

J. Michael Major is a member of the Mystery Writers of America and the Horror Writers Association. His debut crime novel, *One Man's Castle*, won the Lovey Readers' Choice Award for Best First Novel. His three dozen short stories have been published in such anthologies as *Splatterlands, DeathGrip 3: It Came From The Cinema, New Traditions in Terror*, and *Tales of Masks & Mayhem, Vol. III*, and such magazines as *Weirdbook, Mystery Weekly Magazine, Bare Bone, Pirate Writings, Into The Darkness, Hardboiled, Crossroads, Outer Darkness*, and many more. He has several other stories submitted to various anthologies and magazines, and has just started work on a three-novel series.

Though he wrote many stories while growing up, especially in high school, a college English teacher "sucked the joy out of writing," and he gave it up for several years, until he discovered the Science Fiction Book Club while attending dental school. Inspired by what he read, he started writing again and submitting the stories for publication. He sold his first story a couple of years after graduation, and hasn't stopped since.

Michael balances his time between his family, his dental practice, and his writing. He has been married to his wife, Eileen, a pharmacist, for more than twenty-five years. His son recently graduated with a dual degree in accounting and finance, and is currently working on his MBA, and his daughter is studying to be an elementary school teacher. He lives in the Chicago suburbs.

Learn more about Michael on his website at www.jmichaelmajor.com, Like him on Facebook at www.facebook.com/MajorWriter, and follow him on Twitter at www.twitter.com/MajorWriter.

Lauren Marrero

Lauren Marrero is an author of historical romance and fantasy. An avid traveler, she is always willing to go off the beaten path, through crumbing ruins and rainforests, in search of a good story. This has led her into some pretty hairy situations, but it's all fuel for the writing fire. She considers herself an action junkie and is a firm believer that almost any story can be improved by blowing something up. You can follow her adventures at www.lauren-marrero.com

LJ McLeod

LJ McLeod lives in Queensland, Australia. She currently works as a medical laboratory scientist in pathology, and writes in her spare time. She has been published in *Specul8*, *The Twilight Madhouse*, and *Cosmic Roots and Eldritch Shores*. She has been nominated twice for the Aurealis Award. In her spare time she enjoys diving, reading, and traveling.

Paul K. Metheney

Paul was the featured author for dozens of sports magazine articles, has five stories this year published in various anthologies, is contracted for a collection of his own short stories, and is working on a much-delayed novel or two.

Paul has nearly three decades working in advertising design, print, and graphic design. For the last twenty-five years or so, he has been working in the web design, SEO, PPC, social media, and marketing fields, including writing marketing copy for his clients' blogs and social media. He teaches those subjects as well at the local community college.

Paul can be reached at his blog on writing, teaching, poker, travel, reviews, and all things politically incorrect at paulmetheney.com, on Twitter at @PaulMetheney, and on Facebook at http://facebook.com/Paul.Metheney.

In full disclosure, Left Hand Publishers, besides publishing some of his work, has contracted Paul's company, Metheney Consulting, as one of their book cover design artists and marketing consultants to help assist with author's branding and marketing.

Paul is happily married to his one-time high school sweetheart, loves riding his Can-Am Spyder motorcycle, occasionally smokes a good cigar, and is an avid poker enthusiast.

Donna J. W. Munro

Donna J. W. Munro has spent the last seventeen years teaching high school social studies. Her students inspire her every day. An alumni of the Seton Hill Writing Popular Fiction program, she published pieces in *Every Day Fiction, Syntax and Salt, Dark Matter Journal,* the Seton Hill Kindle anthology *Hazard Yet Forward* (2012), the new anthology *Enter the Apocalypse* (2017), and the upcoming anthologies *Buried, Blood, and Sacrifice.* Contact her at https://www.donnajwmunro.com or @Donna_J_W_Munro

Jay Seate

After Jay read a few stories to his parents, they booted him out of the house. Undaunted, he continues to write everything from humor to the erotic to the macabre, and is especially keen on transcending genre pigeonholing. His tales span the gulf from Horror Novel Review's Best Short Fiction Award to *Chicken Soup for the Soul.* They may be told with hardcore realism or fantasy, bringing to life the most quirky of characters. Novels include *Valley of Tears, Tears for the Departed, And the Heavens Wept,* and *Paranormal Liaisons.* His story collections are *Carnival of Nightmares, Midway of Fear, Sex in Bloom,* and *A Baker's Dozen.* Links: www.troyseateauthor.webs.com and on amazon.com. Blog: www.supernaturalsnackbar.wordpress.com Facebook author page: J. T. Seate.

Book Publishing credits:
Carnival of Nightmares - Horror Collection - September - 2010
Midway of Fear - Horror Collection - November 2011
Valley of Tears - Novel - February - 2012
Tears for the Departed - Novel - March - 2012
And the Heavens Wept - Novel - April - 2012
Paranormal Liaisons - Novel - March - 2016
30 Multi-Author Anthologies - including *Chicken Soup for the Soul,* Adams Media, Pill Hill Press, *Library of the Living Dead,* Xcite Books, Ravenous Romance, Library of Horror Press, Grand Mal Press, Burning Bulb

Publishing, Sam's Dot Publishing, SQ Magazine, Constable & Robinson Ltd. UK, Gumshoe Review, Gothic City Press, Jupiter Gardens Press, Sirens Call Press, Torque Press, Prairie Times

Contests:

Another Realm Editor's Choice Award – "Dancing with a Blind Girl" - 2006

Whisper's Pack a Punch Award – "Tough Love" - 2009

SQ Magazine's Best Short-story Award – "Faye's Diner" - 2012

Horror Novel Review's Best Flash Fiction Award – "Cactus Berries" - 2013

Lakewood Historic Society Annual Award – "A City in Transition" - 2014

Lakewood Hist. Soc. Annual Award – "Molly Brown's Summer Retreat" - 2015

V. Franklin

V. Franklin enjoys sleeping in, beekeeping, cold-war era B-movies, gin, Halloween decorations, gluttony, coffee, and what has been described by some as "old people music."

Please look for "Mr. Brown" in *Simple Things* edited by Franklin Wales, no relation; and please look for *The Apple* on Amazon E-Books.

OTHER LEFT HAND PUBLISHERS' ANTHOLOGIES

REALITIES PERCEIVED

Nothing's more dangerous, or delightful, than invoking a cadre of talented authors to create short stories that defy our perceptions of reality. Do we create our own truth? Or does our view of it shape our world? Neither heroes nor heavens, victims nor villains, may grasp the true nature of our being.

From science fiction, to horror and the supernatural, to dramas about the fabric of our existence, this international fusion of artists will thrill you with an eclectic selection of tales that cross all genres.

Sit back and be prepared to have your perception of reality both challenged and distorted.

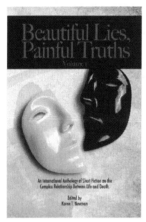

BEAUTIFUL LIES, PAINFUL TRUTHS VOL.I

There's an ironic beauty between humanity's love of Life and fear of Death. Life seemingly brings joy, happiness, hope, and love. Death can end sadness, illness, suffering, and pain. We asked writers to "Let the title and quote take your imagination, your story, wherever it wants to go." Join them now as an international blend of authors, both fresh and seasoned, bring you an exceptional menu of speculative fiction, mystery, realism, horror, and the supernatural. If your palate varies from the macabre to the dramatic, *Beautiful Lies, Painful Truths* provides an assortment of tasty treasures that will chill, delight, and give you food for thought.

THE DEMON'S ANGEL

Neha was excited to enter her sophomore year in high school. That was until the boy she went out with sprouted wings, and Lucas, the man who raised her since she was a baby, turned into a demon.

Neha is far from human. She is an angel, the natural enemy of demons. An angel raised by a demon has never been heard of before, which makes some angels see her as a threat. Neha not only has to prove that she does not know anything about demons, she has to prove that she is on the side of the angels.

And she is. So she thinks.

This Young Adult supernatural thriller follows the tribulations of the teenaged Neha as she learns both the truth about her past and herself.

Reviews

"Intensely unique.

The character Neha is something very remarkable, she has depth and grows as a character, especially when she feels she has to prove herself. She thinks she's proving herself a good angel to the other angels, when in fact she's also proving it to herself. Neha is not your typical teenager, nor typical angel."

Amy Shannon, Author. Writer. Poet. Storyteller. Blogger. Book Reviewer.
Review Blog: http://bit.ly/2iPVV4x

***

"This flight of fancy with engrossing plot twists tempts anyone ever dumbfounded by a parental deception."

Wendy Landers, Book Reviewer
Author of Just Let Time Pass
www.wendylanders.com

Made in the USA
Middletown, DE
30 August 2018